NEON DRAGON

HARDSCRABBLE BOOKS—FICTION OF NEW ENGLAND

For a complete list of titles in the series, please see www.upne.com

NEON DRAGON

JOHN F. DOBBYN

UNIVERSITY PRESS OF NEW ENGLAND *Hanover and London*

Published by University Press of New England,
One Court Street, Lebanon, NH 03766
www.upne.com
© 2007 by John F. Dobbyn
Printed in the United States of America
5 4 3 2 1

Library of Congress Cataloging-in-Publication Data
Dobbyn, John F.
Neon dragon / John F. Dobbyn.
     p.   cm.—(Hardscrabble Books : fiction of New England)
ISBN-13: 978–1–58465–614–2 (cloth : alk. paper)
ISBN-10: 1–58465–614–X (cloth : alk. paper)
    1.   Lawyers—Massachusetts—Boston—Fiction.   2. Boston (Mass.)
—Fiction. I. Title.
PS3604.O227N46 2007
813'.6—dc22   2006031249

 University Press of New England is a member of the Green
Press Initiative. The paper used in this book meets their
minimum requirement for recycled paper.

The happiest part of having this first novel published is being able to dedicate it to the one whose faith and love and inspiration are its life's blood and the reason it is seeing the light of day—my beautiful bride, my partner in everything, and my very best friend, Lois. God bless you. I love you.

1

SUPPOSE YOU WERE TO WAKE UP one Monday morning to a promising, amber sun rising out of Boston Harbor. You walk through the Public Garden past the sleeping swan boats under a symphony of chiming crystal icicles on every perfect branch. The first thing that touches your tongue is a golden sip of Hector Brolio's ambrosiac coffee on Washington Street. At that point, would you be inclined to look up and say, "This is going to be the worst day of my life"?

Neither would I—at least not until Judge Amos Bradley's clerk gave me a determined "get in here" sign outside of the courtroom, followed by his South Boston–accented stage whisper.

"Hey, Michael. Hustle it up. The judge is about to hear your motions."

The little pit of acid that bubbled up in my stomach was by no means uncalled-for. I was a third-year associate with a Boston law firm that read like the passenger manifest of the Mayflower—towit, Bilson, Dawes, Lefbridge & Sykes.

My four years as a federal prosecutor with the United States Attorney's office plus three years as an associate with Bilson, Dawes had finally elevated me to the bottom rung of the litigation section of the firm. "Litigation," not to be confused with "trial work," is the buzzword for upscale court representation of properly moneyed clients in the pristine arena of civil law.

I had just recently become entrusted by the firm to solo on pretrial motions, in spite of the fact that I had been handling the defense of major criminal cases on court appointments for the previous three years.

This particular Monday morning, I had a motion hearing before the Honorable Amos Bradley, rumored in every bar frequented by Boston trial attorneys to be destined to be the next African American justice on the Massachusetts Supreme Judicial Court. I had the rare pleasure of trying to convince him that one of our prestigious clients, Martin Lothrop III, should not be required to answer interrogatories disclosing the innermost financial secrets of his empire of rat-ridden apartments from the South End of Boston through Roxbury to the edge of Jamaica Plain.

Our client ran a profitable roach kingdom because he followed the rules. Rule One in the guidebook for successful slumlording was known to Caesar—divide and conquer. As long as the opposition is an individual impoverished African American or Puerto Rican, no sweat. In the case at hand, rule one had been badly neutralized when a public-interest group brought a class action on behalf of the army of our client's tenants.

In that case, fall back on rule two—never let them see the enemy; i.e., never hold a square inch of property in your own name. Let each apartment house be owned by a corporation, which is in turn owned by a corporation, which is controlled by a joint venture, etc., until the spider at the center of the web is all but invisible, and even the web itself can be traced only by a skillful investigator with time and determination. "Time and determination" are synonymous with "outrageous expense."

My motion was to quash interrogatories filed by the plaintiffs that would have forced the spider, our client, to disclose how the monthly rent checks from little Mrs. Morales in Roxbury and Joseph Brown in the South End and others around the city worked their way through the maze and into his corporate bank account. If the plaintiffs were successful, they might get the court to order our client to pull funds from his other hidden enterprises to lift his squalid apartments from grotesque to merely intolerable.

My simple task was to convince Judge Bradley, who had climbed to the bench on a courageous civil rights record, that the esteemed Martin Lothrop III's finance-play was none of Mrs. Jimenez's business, and therefore, he should not have to answer her interrogatories. Does the genesis of the bubble of stomach acid become apparent?

The motion session began at ten sharp. Judge Bradley barely sat before focusing a look in my direction that seemed to have behind it the wrath of the just God.

"I'll hear your arguments, Mr. Knight. Let me tell you first that I've read this."

He was holding my written brief on the motion between two fingers, much as one would handle a used diaper.

"Do you wish to argue each of these points, Mr. Knight?"

"I do, Your Honor." Said I, the sacrificial lamb.

Point by point, I made whatever arguments I could dredge out of a slightly slanted reading of the Constitution, the Declaration of Independence, the Gettysburg Address. I'd have cited Dr. Seuss if I could have gotten any yardage out of it.

I made a separate argument on each of the interrogatories individually. Every time I'd finish an argument and take a breath, I could see His Honor bend to scribble "DENIED" on that clause of my motion. He all but added an exclamation point. What took a fresh bite out of my withering self-confidence with each "denied" was the fact that Judge Bradley never even looked at my opposing counsel for a bit of counterargument.

After nine or ten of these little forays and retreats, I took a glance over at my esteemed opposing counsel, Ms. Deborah Dane. The contented smile on her face turned to a grin when I gave her a look that must have clearly said, "How's about we change sides for a few minutes?"

At eleven o'clock on the nose, the judge rose and called for the morning recess. By the time the bailiff cried, "All rise," I had one lucid thought left—downstairs for a gasp of sweet, clean air, and a chocolate blitz at Bailey's.

The thought died in the birthing, however. The last communication Judge Bradley sent in my direction was a "come in here" gesture as he disappeared into chambers. I looked over at plaintiff's counsel for illumination, or better yet, accompaniment. She smiled, shrugged, and passed quickly out into the free world.

The bailiff gave me a noncommittal smile as I passed into the walnut-paneled chamber. Four round-back oak chairs sat in reverent audience before a massive desk. Judge Bradley stood something over six feet tall. In his late fifties, he still had the well-proportioned frame that had scored a number of touchdowns for Harvard some thirty years ago. He had a reputation for good humor off the bench. At this particular moment, as he sat sideways to the desk, drumming his fingers together in front of him, I'd have preferred a chat with Torquemada.

He waved me into one of the chairs and started before I fully landed.

"Mr. Knight, I won't mince words. I want to retain your services. I'd like you to defend my son in a criminal matter."

For some turns in the conversation you're prepared. Others leave you wondering if you'll ever get your jaw in an upright position. I managed the next question on instinct.

"On what charge, Judge?"

"Murder." There was a pause before and after the word. I let the silence hang until he picked up the thread.

"You might have heard about the elderly gentleman in Chinatown. The shooting yesterday. The police have arrested my son, Anthony. He's being held for trial in the Suffolk County jail. Martin Muller handled the arraignment this morning. He pleaded not guilty."

I was still fighting my way back through shock. I could see that it was no easier on him. My mind raced back to my morning reading of Mike Loftus's column on the front page of the *Boston Globe*.

Mr. Chen An-Yong watched the ritual as he had for seventy-two years. He sat in the window of his second-level apartment over the grocery store that had been his world since he came to

Boston's Chinatown fifty-two years ago. His eyes were riveted on the twenty-foot red, green, and gold cloth lion snaking its way to the door of his shop. The percussion of firecrackers, as deafening as machine-gun fire, filled the teeming streets of Chinatown and lay down a pall of gray smoke. Drums and rasping cymbals followed the gyrating oversized head and whipping tail of the lion, as the black-clad men beneath it manipulated their way through the mass of people to each restaurant and shop along Tyler Street. Shopkeepers ignited five-foot chains of firecrackers as the lion approached. A string from above each doorway dangled lettuce to feed and cash to appease the symbolic beast for the coming year.

Mr. Chen was not alone. He was never alone. If his own grand children were not surrounding him, he was sought out by other children and adults of the Chinese community who had felt his warmth or received the favors of his wisdom or material goods. That was nearly everyone.

Four of his grandchildren crowded into the tiny window. The slight figure of Mr. Chen could be seen behind them by people in the street waving greetings. According to witnesses, something caught his attention that caused him to lean over the children to look below. In an instant, he straightened and fell backward.

He was rushed to Boston Medical Center, where he was pronounced dead on arrival.

This was a passing of great import. A thirty-eight-caliber bullet sent the entire Chinese community into a mourning that is reserved for the truly beloved. In the gentle frame of this man, who would scarcely be noticed by those of us who pass through Chinatown's streets to its restaurants and shops, dwelt a major piece of the soul of the people to whom Chinatown is home.

I pulled it together quickly enough to ask Judge Bradley the next logical question.

"If Marty Muller handled the arraignment, why . . . ?"

"Martin was available at the time. I'm asking you to take up the representation."

The tone had a finality to it that discouraged my questioning his choice.

"What evidence . . . ?"

"Apparently two witnesses have identified Anthony. I believe they're obviously mistaken. That's not a judge, that's a father speaking. I know this is totally beyond anything my son could possibly even consider. The judge, on the other hand, knows that mistaken eyewitness testimony could lead to conviction."

By now I was back in the game enough to wonder at the greatest irony of the situation.

"Judge, I'm honored, but why would you pick me? You didn't seem overly impressed this morning."

He looked directly at me for the first time.

"You were arguing law. I was dealing in justice. That wasn't your fault. You had no say in the client or the issue. I've heard about how you represent criminal clients when you have a choice. My offer speaks for itself."

The room took on a definite spin. Fears, qualms, concerns crowded into my stream of consciousness faster than I could factor them into a decision. I'd handled everything else, but never a murder case. I felt like a Little Leaguer being called up to pitch for the Red Sox in the World Series.

On the other hand, I'd been chosen on confidence by the boy's knowledgeable father. On the third hand, if I blew this because I was too young, too inexperienced, whatever, it could be the end of that boy's life outside of prison, and, as an afterthought, my life as a lawyer.

There were at least five more hands, but they were cut off when Judge Bradley stood up.

"I know it's a difficult decision. You understand why I need an answer now. The investigation has to begin immediately, while the evidence is fresh."

He looked at me with an expression I'm still analyzing. He had faced one of the most trying decisions of his life in selecting one person to save his son, and he had made it. There was that kind of mature manhood in his look, and he was calling on me to show the same. There was also the helplessness of a man who could only hire a defender and then sit on the sidelines while two combatants jousted for the rest of his son's life.

"Will you do it?"

Like it or not, that question allowed only one answer.

2

JUDGE BRADLEY REASSEMBLED the court long enough for me to move to suspend the hearing. That brought a quizzical look from my esteemed opposing counsel, who had come back to the arena with a distinct taste of blood from the morning's minivictories. Her visions of finally nailing my lacerated corpse to the courthouse door vanished when Judge Bradley granted my motion without so much as a glance in the direction of the plaintiff's table. The last thing His Honor wanted was a full discussion in open court of the reasons for the adjournment. Plaintiff's counsel may have been steamed, but it was the first motion I'd won since that interminable morning had begun. I was happy to delude myself with a false sense of being on a roll.

Since I was in the courthouse anyway, I thought I'd touch base with the prosecuting attorney. I managed to be buzzed through to the office of the District Attorney herself, Ms. Lamb, by name, if not by disposition.

I knew that there was no point in dealing with any of the assistants. There was not a snowball's chance in Birmingham that Her Eminence would deign to share one vote-catching headline from this case with an underling. You didn't have to be in the inner circle to know that from the day she rode into office on pledges of career commitment to the prosecution of the scourges of society, she had her antenna tuned for the case that could move her into the statehouse. This one smacked of the governorship.

I had met the First Lady of Prosecution at several bar functions. We had also had a brief meeting four years previously to work out the federal and state prosecutors' interests in a drug case, so introductions were not necessary. If she was surprised by my announcement that I represented young Bradley, she hid it well.

"The hell you say!"

I smiled, rather pleasantly considering the inference.

"One of life's little surprises, Angela. Has an indictment been returned?"

"You haven't talked to him yet?"

She wore that half grin of someone who knew they'd made it to the NCAA Final Four, and who'd just heard that the next opponent would be the Perkins School for the Blind. I suppressed my Latino instincts and followed the cool demeanor of my Anglo half.

"I'll see him this afternoon. What about the indictment?"

"Of course. I just got the presentment from the grand jury. Murder one."

It sounded more like a verdict than a basis for negotiation.

I nodded.

"I know it's early in the case. You have a better feel for it than I do at this point. Just for discussion, what do you think you might be looking for in negotiation before the press goes off the deep end?"

She sat back in her swivel chair and spun it around to look me

dead-on in a gesture that went beyond confidence and spilled into arrogance. If there was ever anything cuddly or cute about Ms. Lamb in her playpen days, she had accomplished its complete eradication in twelve years as a lawyer. At five feet five inches, she was one hundred and twenty pounds of pure prosecutor.

She was adorned in a severely tailored suit, capped on one end by sensible shoes and on the other by darkish hair drawn in a bun tight enough to induce claustrophobia. The horn-rimmed glasses focused laser beams from the depths of two humorless pools of ambition.

"Sure we can deal. I don't want to be unreasonable. I'll settle for a plea to premeditated murder with a recommendation for life without parole."

I smiled, still the soul of restraint. "Do I sense that we're being a little inflexible here?"

"You haven't begun to see inflexibility. I'm going to personally throw the key to his cell into Boston Harbor, and then . . ."

"Don't tell me. You're going to Disney World."

Humor was not her consuming passion, especially when it interrupted a flow. Personally, I had little else going for me.

Before accepting her invitation, in effect, to get-the-hell-out-of-her-office, I asked for a copy of the coroner's report on the deceased and a copy of the indictment. She agreed to send a copy of the coroner's report to my office as soon as one was prepared. The indictment she was delighted to hand over on the spot. No major concession. As defense counsel, I was entitled to both.

SUFFOLK COUNTY JAIL is the holding pen for the not-yet-convicted. There was little hope that young Bradley would have any other address pending the trial since bail is almost never granted on a murder-one charge.

I sat in the interviewing room in one of the two chairs that flanked a well-worn wooden table that had listened to the intimate sharing of truths and lies between counsel and every conceivable variety of felon since long before I'd joined the battle on the side of defendants. I'd been there before, and every time, I thanked God for the particular twists and crossroads of life that put me in the chair to the left instead of the right of the door. When the interview ended, I was out of there. The person in the other chair was going back to hell. It could easily have been otherwise.

I knew more about young Bradley than most of the people I'd met in that room. Without much thought over the years, I'd read the articles about the young halfback at Arlington High School running in his father's footsteps. My interest was more in football than in Bradley, but he did well enough to be a recognizable name, which is an accomplishment for a high-school player.

He played freshman ball for Harvard, but like many high-school hotshots, he could never quite make the jump to the college level. He was given the option to ride the bench as a sophomore, probably out of deference to his father's record with the Harvard team, but young Bradley chose to opt out. He left the team and all the bonuses that went with it. His life from that point in time to this early February of his junior year was a blank to me, since he was out of my most constant source of information—the *Globe* sports section.

Most of the prisoners I'd seen come through that door blended with the society-gone-wrong surroundings. I've seen sullenness, anger, craftiness, and, worst of all, resignation. But every inch of the six-foot-four-inch body that stood holding out a strong right hand seemed to say, "I don't belong here!" He was clean looking, with enough sincere humility to counterbalance the self-confidence that goes with an attractive appearance. But there was more to it than that. Something smacked of quality. Maybe I was seeing a reflection of his father, but there was a bright look in his eyes and a gentleness that made me want to win this one for the right reasons.

Introductions were briefly made, and we both sat down.

"Your dad asked me to represent you, Anthony."

"I know, sir. Thank you."

It certainly beat "the hell you say!" as a reaction. This kid was beginning to grow on me.

"What happened yesterday, Anthony?"

He gave a slight palms-up gesture. "I wish I knew myself, Mr. Knight."

"Just tell me what you did."

"Church in the morning. Back to the house. I live in Dunster House down by the river. I did some reading for a paper. I guess it was about two in the afternoon, a friend of mine came by and suggested we go into Chinatown for dinner and see the Chinese New Year's."

"Who's idea was it, yours or—what's his name?"

"Terry Blocher. It was his idea, but I was ready to go."

"OK. Leave in all the details."

"Well, that's what we did. We had dinner at the Ming Tree restaurant on Tyler Street. Things were really getting revved up outside. By the time we came out at three thirty, there were fireworks going off everywhere. The street was about an inch deep in firecracker paper. Some people were throwing cherry bombs. It was deafening. Terry had decided when we came in that it was too loud. He said he was going to walk back to Park Street and get the train back to Harvard Square.

"I saw the big cloth lion with people under it coming up to the little Chinese grocery shop across the street. The noise got even louder because the people at the shop lit off big chains of firecrackers in front of the lion. There were drums, cymbals, you couldn't hear yourself think."

"Where were you standing in regard to the shop?"

"I guess right in front of it. It's a narrow street. I was probably ten yards from the shop."

I figured the estimate was good. Who could judge ten yards better than a former running back?

"Did you see anyone in the window above the front door of the shop?"

He thought for a second.

"There were people at every window on the street. I'm sure there were people there, but nothing stands out."

"So how long were you there?"

"It's hard to say. Maybe three or four minutes. The noise was getting to me, too, so I moved down the street toward Beach Street. I just got around the corner, when two policemen stopped me. They told me I was under arrest for murder. The whole thing was unreal. They gave me warnings about the right to remain silent and brought me to the station house."

I leaned back and looked at him. He was sitting up straight and looking me right in the eye. I liked that. In fact, the more I grew to like about him, the larger the knot grew in the pit of my stomach.

"When you went into Chinatown, did you have a gun with you?"

He looked at me like I'd asked if he'd been dressed in drag. Then he realized that the circumstances made the question seem less ridiculous.

"No. I don't have a gun."

I leaned back to keep eye contact.

"They're charging that an old man in the window above the grocery shop was shot to death just at the time the cloth lion was at the door. Did you see anyone with a gun?"

He shook his head.

"Did you hear anything like a gunshot?"

"Everything sounded like a gunshot."

"I know. Someone had a great sense of timing. Can you think of any reason why two witnesses might have picked you out of the crowd?"

He leaned forward with his head on his hands. "Almost everyone there was Chinese or maybe Vietnamese. I was about a head taller than anyone and the only one I could see with black skin. I'd be pretty hard to miss."

"What I meant was did you make any moves that could have been mistaken for firing a gun?"

He shrugged and just shook his head.

I flipped the notebook closed and stood up. He was on his feet too, looking perplexed and making me wish I could walk him right out the door with me.

"Where are they keeping you, Anthony?"

He caught my meaning. He was the son of a judge who had dealt with some of the people with whom he was presently sharing quarters. Jailhouse murders are far too common and easy to cover up in a silent society.

"I'm OK so far. They keep me in a single cell and bring in my meals."

I jotted my cell-phone number on my card and gave it to him with instructions to call night or day if things changed, even a little bit.

3

BY TWO O'CLOCK I was back at the office. Bilson, Dawes had the tenth and eleventh floors of a triangular building on Franklin Street. They had grown from the ten partners and five associates I had joined as an associate three years previously to twenty partners and seven associates, piggybacking on the financial success of their corporate clients. Since success breeds success, the partners kept a sharp eye on the gate to let in as new clients only corporate personae on the rise. When Willie Sutton spun off his famous answer to the question of why he robbed banks, he was also laying down a game plan for Bilson, Dawes's selection of clients: "That's where the money is."

On the walk down the hall to my office, I had the feeling that I'd brought a blast of the winter chill in with me. While the joy of human camaraderie was not exactly the hallmark of the firm on its best day, I noticed as I'd pass their offices the partners giving me fleeting glances that were even more drained of warmth than usual.

I was something of an anomaly at Bilson, Dawes. The firm, and therefore the partners, thrived—in fact, more than thrived—on fees from clean, unsullied *civil* litigation. By contrast, my earlier days at the U.S. Attorney's office had given me a familiarity with most of the judges at the federal district court, which meant that a fairly steady stream of criminal court appointments to represent indigent defendants followed me to the firm. For all of their pious and publicized pro bono posturing, the partners suffered this acne on the pristine skin of the firm not gladly. And the frequently scruffy, scratching, whiskey-breathing criminal clients who decorated the firm waiting room as a result of my court appointments did nothing to liberalize their sentiments.

I never made it to my office. Julie Benson, my secretary of three years and one of the human elements that made life tolerable at the firm, nearly had tears in her eyes when she intercepted me with a note.

"SEE ME IMMEDIATELY! A.D."

To the outside world, "A.D." stood for Alexis Devlin. To any associate and most of the junior partners, it meant "Angel of Death."

I had had no direct dealings with Mr. Devlin—"Lex" to those who dared—since he joined the firm two years previously. Word around the courthouse had it that in his day, which was some ten years past, he was the best there was at the criminal bar. For some reason, as he was rising from star to legend, he suddenly dropped out. You heard conflicting rumors among those with their three-piece suits pressed to the bars of the city's watering holes, but no one really seemed to know why. Word had it that he had a taste for the grape, but you could lay that one at the door of a fair percentage of the trial bar. Given the pressures of the trade, it's endemic.

Then about a year after I came to the firm, he dropped back in. To almost universal surprise, he accepted the offer of Bilson, Dawes to bring his still-legendary skill with a jury to the civil side of the court.

I had not had the pleasure of working with or for him, but the associates who did bore mental lacerations that they would only bare to each other in the copy room.

As I walked back down the corridor to the gates of hell, it was clear that word of the summons had gotten around. Every associate I passed seemed to take one last look at me in life. I winked and smiled the smile of the incredibly brave. I whispered to myself for confidence, "Latinos rush in where Anglos fear to tread."

His secretary never looked up. She just waved a pencil in the direction of the door behind her. There was apparently no question that I was the next item on the menu.

I opened the door. He was standing with his back to me at the window behind his desk. Maybe it was the expectations raised by the associates' stories, but I could actually feel the weight of his presence in the room. When he turned around, I was struck almost breathless by the power of that presence. But it was far more than that.

He was on the phone. I doubt that my presence meant more to him than the cigarette butts in his ashtray, but I could not take my eyes off of him.

At about seventy years, he was block built, with a jaw that could cut granite and a nose that changed direction like the Boston streets. His double-breasted pin-striped suit coat lay open to expose burgundy suspenders and a blending tie that suggested that he took his style from an era I'd only heard about. On the other hand, I thought that there was more character in that face than in any I'd seen since the death of another man who'd done more than pass through my life, and who, by coincidence, somehow resembled him.

I stood there swimming in recollections that were churning my insides. While Mr. Devlin ignored me, I was back in the then Puerto Rican ghetto of Jamaica Plain on the southwest side of Boston. My dad had died when I was fourteen. My mother moved us to the Plain to be near some of our Puerto Rican relatives and for the comfort of a familiar culture after the loss of my dad. It was a reasonable move at the time, but by the time I was sixteen, our street had become the territorial border between two constantly warring gangs.

My mother was somewhat oblivious to it, as adults could be, but I had a choice to make. It was join the Diablos or join the Coyotes or lose everything from my lunch money to my life to members of both gangs every time I walked to school. For reasons that seem inadequate now, I joined the Coyotes.

The initiation was not exactly a fraternity hazing. For the first part I was sent out to hot-wire a particular vintage Cadillac parked outside of the Vasquez Funeral Home during a wake. Thank God, as fate would have it, I never got to the second part of the initiation. I would have belonged to them for life.

In those days before keys with electronic chips, you could punch out a car's ignition slot, cross a couple of wires, and be on the road in a matter of seconds. And so I was. And so were the police. I was busted within eight blocks of the funeral home by a cop to whom I did not look like your average Cadillac owner.

I was tried as an adult because of the "seriousness of the crime." It was actually because the then DA was targeting gang-related crime. My timing was impeccably bad.

The day of my trial, I found out that the car belonged to a big-ticket criminal-trial attorney by the name of Miles O'Connor. He came as a witness, but he stayed in the courtroom while my public-defender lawyer, who had graduated from law school a few hours before taking on my defense, fumbled his way through to my conviction. To be fair to my baby lawyer, he had a guilty client with no extenuating circumstances.

When the judge gave the prosecution two weeks to assemble a presentence report, Mr. O'Connor stood up in the back of the courtroom.

"Your Honor, may I speak?"

The judge recognized Mr. O'Connor, as would anyone who had ever read a Boston newspaper or watched the eleven o'clock news. The judge invited him to approach the bench. When Mr. O'Connor walked his ramrod-straight six-foot-two frame, impeccably draped in an eight-hundred-dollar suit, past me on the way to the bench, he glanced down at the little cockroach who had disrupted his routine. I was certain at that moment that between him and the judge, car theft was about to become a capital offense.

Mr. O'Connor's back was to me, but I could hear every word.

"Are you considering jail time, Judge?"

"I am, Mr. O'Connor. Unless there's something very convincing in the presentence report, this boy is going to do some serious time. I can promise you that."

I went into shock. They were planning my life in the worst possible terms. My mind went into neutral and my ears jammed. For some reason that I couldn't understand, the conversation went on and on. My mind and my hearing unblocked toward the end of it in time to hear the words that turned the course of my life in the least expected direction. Mr. O'Connor never looked back at me when he said it to the judge.

"Give him to me, Your Honor."

I think the judge went into shock, and I came somewhat out of it. I was able to follow the details they discussed, which roughly came down to probation with the appointment of Mr. O'Connor as my guardian. The judge issued the order and I followed Mr. O'Connor out of the courtroom that day in complete awe. I've never gotten over it.

Mr. O'Connor gave me room and board at the thoroughbred-horse farm he owned north of Boston. He set me to a daily routine of mucking out three barns of stalls every morning. If the job was not completed to his satisfaction by six in the morning, it was as if the job had not been done at all. I came to believe in my bones that Ulysses had it soft with the Augean stables.

There was a daily inspection by Himself, and perfection was the barely passing standard. That left time to shower and don the uniform of a student at Chambers Academy, also his idea. After school, there was the washing and grooming of every horse in the stable before dinner and several hours of homework. I didn't sleep so much as lapse into unconsciousness by nine to hit the stables by four the next morning.

Mr. O'Connor threw me into the mix of private-school students who had lived the polished life since they came out of the womb. When my self-confidence took the occasional, or rather frequent, nosedive, he was at my back to drill it into me that I could compete with anyone even-up.

And compete I did, for him. I spent three years at Chambers, and at the end of each of the three, Mr. O'Connor was in the audience for the awards ceremony. I was not the brightest bulb in the chandelier there, so I worked my skinny ass down to the nub to see to it that he heard my name every year among the prizewinners.

I made it past the cut into Harvard College, but it was Mr. O'Connor who paid the freight. There was no doubt about whose shoes I wanted to fill. I knew the jump to Harvard Law School would be anything but automatic. That meant passing on the "mixers" and "smokers" and "gentleman's Cs" and most other social byplay that could have endangered the goal. It was a small price to pay for the smile I saw on Mr. O'Connor's face in the audience at the Harvard College graduation—and then again when I saw him rereading my letter of acceptance to Harvard Law School.

I asked him one time why he did it, everything from that day in court on. He said it was an impulse, and the impulse got stronger every year.

There is not a softer or more heartfelt way to put it. Mr. Miles John O'Connor, God rest his worthy soul, was the toughest son of a bitch that ever lived. And I came to love him more than I thought anyone could love or admire another human being.

What brought all of this flooding through my memory bank while I stood there being ignored by Mr. Alexis Devlin, was that he was, in some ways, the spitting image of Mr. O'Connor. The Lord knows it wasn't their appearance. Mr. O'Connor had been trim and athletic and perfectly clad from the crest of his wavy white hair and handsome

Irish features and complexion to the Armani shoes six feet and two inches below. Mr. Devlin was roughly carved out of granite like a character on Mount Rushmore. The suit he was wearing was expensive, but I think he sent his larger brother in for the fitting.

The similarity that struck me deeply was in the way their bearing left no doubt of the immensity of their character. Other men, taller men, had seemed like pygmies in the company of Mr. O'Connor. I was getting waves of a similar sensation in the presence of Mr. Devlin.

THE MAN WAS NOT GIVEN to social preliminaries. I restrained a slight jump when that voice that reverberated off of courtroom walls caught me dead on.

"You've accepted the defense of young Bradley. Why?"

That was a question I still hadn't answered for myself.

"Judge Bradley put the request in a way that was hard to turn down, Mr. Devlin. I don't honestly know why he picked me."

"He didn't pick you." He spun the heavy leather desk chair around and dropped into it. "He was after me. Now he's got me."

"Mr. Devlin, there was no mention . . ."

"You're three jumps behind, Sonny. You wear the firm name. This case is going to get more space in the *Boston Herald* than the Kennedys. Amos Bradley is no fool. He knew I'd be drawn into it."

It had the ring of logic, and it answered the question I'd had since I left Judge Bradley's chambers—why pick a rookie when there are a handful of seasoned all-stars ready to take the bat? Still . . .

"If he wanted you for defense counsel, Mr. Devlin, and I don't doubt that he did, couldn't he have just asked you?"

"No. He knows I'm out of criminal work. I wouldn't touch it, even for him." I saw his shoulders drop a bit, and I saw something in his eyes that I still can't fathom. "I guess I'm back in it. Let's get to work."

He grabbed a yellow pad and pen with an energy that made me

wonder if it was totally against his will. I wondered if something had flowed through the old fighter when he'd heard one more bell.

"Let me have the indictment and the coroner's report. I assume you got them immediately."

My right fist clenched behind the chair at the accuracy of my first instincts. The celebration was short-lived. I handed over the copy of the indictment that was still in my suit-coat pocket.

"The DA said she'll send the coroner's report as soon as it's ready."

His eyes were back on me like a microscope.

"That's twice you let yourself be taken advantage of today, sonny. Don't keep up that average if you're going to work around me."

He grabbed the phone and punched numbers into it. I came around and sat in the chair I'd been gripping. If he hadn't invited me to sit down, at least he hadn't forbidden it.

"This is Lex Devlin. Let me speak to Mrs. Lamb."

There was a pause, but not a long one. Even the queen DA responded when the king summoned.

"Angela, this is Lex Devlin. I'm entering the defense of young Bradley."

I'd have traded tickets to Fenway Park for the final game of the World Series to see that grin drop from her lips when she realized that the Perkins School for the Blind was being augmented by the Boston Celtics. There was no audible comeback.

"I'd like you to fax the coroner's report and a full set of pictures. I'll need them immediately."

She apparently saw no advantage in playing snooker with the master, because whatever she said equaled "yes."

I noticed that Mr. Devlin cut the good-byes to a minimum and rang off without broaching the subject of a plea bargain before he had enough evidence to deal from a position of strength. I absorbed the lesson without necessarily mentioning that the count of my day's miscalculations was up to three.

"How did you know she had it already?"

Mr. Devlin looked up over the half-glasses that were still focused on the indictment.

"Learn fast, sonny. This graduate course is going to be brief. This case is going to set all of Chinatown on end. That means City Hall's interested. You've got the son of a black judge not everyone wants on the Supreme Judicial Court for a defendant. That'll get the bar on edge. Believe me, sonny, that coroner's report was on her desk by midnight."

He pulled off the glasses and gave me the full look. He held up the indictment.

"How'd you ask for this? I bet you walked right into her office like a piece of raw steak."

He won the bet.

"Don't. She's too powerful on her own turf. Catch her on neutral ground, like outside of a courtroom."

"Yes, sir. I notice you called her in her office. That's not the same thing?"

He put the glasses back on, but not before I caught something in his eyes. Associates generally stop at "Yes, sir."

"I can. You can't. Not for a lot of years, sonny."

He read the indictment while I absorbed one of life's realities. He threw it back to me.

"Start a file. This is straight premeditated murder. She's going for the full penalty. What have they got?"

"Judge Bradley says they have two witnesses from the Chinese community that can identify him. They say they saw him shoot the victim."

"And what does he say?"

"He says he had dinner across the street at the Ming Tree restaurant on Tyler Street. He walked over to see the lion. They have a cloth lion with three or four men under it . . ."

"I know. I've seen it. What'd he do?"

"He says he watched the lion approach the Chinese grocery store across from the restaurant. He was about ten yards from the building.

Firecrackers going off all over the place. It got too loud, so he left. He was arrested a few blocks away. He didn't even know there was a shooting."

He leaned back in the squeaking chair. I saw the *Globe* on a table to the side open to the conclusion of Mike Loftus's article. I assumed he knew as much as I did about the second-story location of the old man when he was shot.

"We need to talk to those witnesses. The DA doesn't have to tell us who they are. She can claim she's protecting their lives. That means we have to find them on our own. I don't want to see them for the first time at the trial. Why don't you go down to Chinatown? See what you can find out. Make it fast. The DA'll be pushing for an early trial date before we get our feet too firmly on the ground."

I was up and heading for the door when that voice spun me around again.

"Sonny, I want you on this full time till this trial ends. Whatever else you've got on your calendar goes to another associate."

He was back at the window, and it was my turn to turn him around.

"Mr. Devlin." He looked back. "My name is Michael Knight."

He turned back to the window.

"I know *who* you are, sonny. I want to know *what* you are."

ON THE WAY BACK DOWN the corridor to my office I had to pass the office of Whitney Caster, junior partner. Whitney was around my age, but had come directly to the firm from law school. That gave him enough of a head start to put him in a position to give the orders.

Old Whitney suffered from that two-edged phobia that infects the brains of a number of middle-level lawyers. He was petrified of criticism from any member of the firm above him, and equally petrified of competition from those below him.

It was, in fact, old Whitney who was responsible for the pretrial motions on the Lothrop case that I had spent the morning arguing. I had the dubious pleasure of telling him that (a) the morning's motion session before Judge Bradley had been a total disaster, and (b) he could find another lackey to do his dirty work, since I was off the case.

"The hell you are, Knight! You'll go back and reargue that motion. If you think I'm going to get my ass reamed by Mr. Dawes for this, you can guess again. Who the hell gave you the authority to get off this case?"

He was already hyperventilating from being up against a rock. In a quiet, respectful tone, I boxed him in with a hard place.

"I'm working for Mr. Devlin full time. You might take it up with him."

One could gag on the silence that followed. I knew he'd rather open a vein than even meet Mr. Devlin in the corridor. I bade him a happy afternoon and took my leave.

4

I FIGURED THE WORD of our embroilment in the case and my usurpation by Mr. Devlin would spread like an oil slick through the three networks of the firm—secretaries, associates, and partners. The partners would be clued in by nightfall, the associates by mid-afternoon, and the secretaries by simultaneous broadcast. All to the good. It would save explanations to every partner who needed a gnome to answer the call of the list at court or a sacrificial lamb to argue un-winnable motions.

I was out of the office by three and into a stand-up hot dog on Washington Street by three ten. I tried to focus on the case as I chewed, for two reasons. First, I occasionally make the mistake of pondering the contents of those eight-inch oral suppositories, which is even more detrimental than eating them. Secondly, there was a decision to be made.

The immediate problem was finding the two witnesses. Chinatown was about five blocks to the left on Washington Street. On the other hand, that haystack might not even contain the needle. We had no way of knowing if the witnesses were locals or visitors.

Another possibility occurred about four inches into the hot dog. There had to be a police report of the killing and of the arrest. The report would contain names and addresses of the witnesses. Simple. All I had to do was get my hot little hands on the police report. Not so simple. Ms. Lamb had undoubtedly given the word that the report was not to be disclosed to defense counsel—for the protection of the witnesses, of course.

I headed in the direction of the new precinct building for Area A, which covers all of downtown Boston and north to Chelsea. As I passed the two rounded buildings on Cambridge Street that look like a broken comma and are known as One and Two Center Plaza, a notion was incubating. The Area A precinct building is a state-of-the-art Bastille. Twenty feet inside of the front door is a five-foot desk that looks like a parapet, presided over by the officer on duty. Beyond that point, outsiders goeth not. I needed an entrée.

I ran up the Center Plaza steps to slip out of the wind. I made a cell-phone call to city hall and worked my way through information to reach an acquaintance who worked in payroll. He was on a work break, so I got him at his desk. It had been four years since I had sweat blood to get his son probation for unarmed theft from a candy store that turned out to be a postal substation, making the crime a federal offense. He was still grateful enough to pull some information out of his computer without asking embarrassing questions.

The police precinct had converted the system of recording police reports from stone and chisel to computers a while ago. A number of civilian data-entry people were still hired to enter police reports and other information into the system.

My city hall friend read to me the list of names of data-entry people employed at the Area A building; I marked time through the Joneses and O'Briens and Kosciuskos until he came to Manuel Morales. Home address—Center Street, Jamaica Plain. At that time and in that particular section of the Plain, it meant a 99 percent chance that he or his forebears were from the sunny isle of Puerto Rico. It was not because of the climate that they used to call it "Jamaica Spain."

It might seem that with my having a name like "Michael Knight," my forebears ran on both sides to the decks of the Mayflower itself. Not quite the truth. In acquiring ancestry, I was farsighted enough to choose a Puerto Rican mother and a WASP father—both of them gems in any hue of skin tone. The bonus in fate's choice is that I can play in both sandboxes. With the twin tickets of Harvard and Harvard Law School and a six-foot-two-inch frame under skin pale enough to see through, I can walk into the Boston Conservative Club and get a table center court. Thank you, Dad.

On the other hand, I have my mother's legacy of jet-black hair and a slender build that never seemed to hold an extra pound. Since my mother spoke Spanish to me from my cradle days, I can slip in and out of a Latino accent like a loose sweater. I can drop my hundred and sixty fat-free pounds down a little, walk with a bit more grace and rhythm, and blend into any Latino section of the city. Bilson, Dawes knew that in making me an offer they were getting a pregnant pony—a twofer. They got an up-and-coming pin-striper who can mix with the State Streeters, and double points for hiring a minority.

I JOTTED DOWN THE NAME, Manuel Morales, and walked to the brick precinct building surrounded by blue-and-whites on Sudbury Street.

BUSINESS COMES IN WAVES to the center desk inside the station-house door. The officer on duty was blond, buxom, and beleaguered. I waited until she was going in three directions—to check on the release of a prisoner for a mother and father, scan the sheet of located stolen cars for a teenager, and take information on a missing person from a barely prehysterical wife.

I flashed a business card from a computer retailer who had recently tried to sell me a laptop computer. That got her attention. I didn't say it was my name on the card. If she wanted to assume it, that was her business.

I asked her to call Manny Morales in data entry. She took me out of order because mine was probably the easiest and least emotional demand she had had to deal with all shift.

She grabbed one of the three phones in front of her and tapped in four digits. She asked for Morales. In about three seconds, she handed the phone over the counter to me. With me on the shelf, she was back in the maelstrom that had now grown by a young couple who were reaching high C over a car theft. In the confusion around me, I could have been talking in an isolation booth.

I cupped my hand over the phone and said, "Officer Morales?"

"Not 'officer,' just 'mister.' What can I do for you?"

The words were not much, but the rolled r's and Latino cadence of the syllables were like Mozart to my ears. I followed suit by coloring the vowels and pointing the consonants until Manny and I sounded like a couple of muchachos from San Juan. I explained that the software company had sent me to check the computer system for viruses. Since Manny's job involved the keyboard and not the internals of the computer system, I was hoping that his training gave him a notion of what a virus was, but no clue as to how you diagnose or medicate it. I had taken a computer course at Harvard, which at least let me bandy about a few words of computer literacy.

I caught the desk officer's attention long enough to put her back on the line. At Manny's request, the officer gave me a clip-on pass that got me into the bowels of the station house. I followed directions back to the computer room, where I spotted a long, lean, white-shirt-and-tie type, about three inches taller and ten pounds lighter than me, sitting at a computer console. He had the dark hair and well-structured cheekbones to go with the accent.

There were five other men and two women at other consoles in the room. Only one of the women came unglued from the screen long enough to take note of my presence as I crossed to the one I assumed was Manuel Morales.

Manny shook hands and pulled up a second roller chair with a sweep of one long leg. I took it and mumbled "*Com-esta?*" on the way down.

He grinned and came back with, "OK, man. What's up?"

I took the hint that we were perhaps not in a haven of racial impartiality and switched to English.

"How long since they checked for viruses?"

He slouched his long frame back in an easy posture, which told me that no alarms had gone off yet. I carefully avoided the serious crime of impersonating a police officer. I had absolutely no idea of the degree of criminality attached to breaking *into* a police station.

"I don't know, man. I just got in here last week."

Alleluia.

"Then I guess you're not aware of our company policy. We give follow-up service to check for viruses in the programming every two weeks for the first three months. They'll be giving you training. Let's run through it."

I swiveled up to the side of the computer to let him follow my lead and slide in.

"We can do it with any sample report. Let's call up the list of police reports for—let's see, let's take yesterday afternoon and evening. Why don't you go ahead and call those up while I start my report?"

I fiddled with a notebook while Manny's lean fingers played the keyboard like a piano. The screen responded with a list of police reports by time of day. At that point, I slipped in and took the keyboard. I knew enough to scroll down the list until I found the report of the murder of Mr. Chen filed at 4:30 PM the previous day. I centered the cursor on that report while Manny slipped back in the chair, obviously at ease with the break from the boredom of entering data written in stilted police-ese. I hit 'enter,' and there before my eyes was the forbidden fruit.

I scrolled through it to the section on witnesses. True enough, there were two. I feigned nonchalance while playing with the cursor and any function key that would not change the screen. I jotted the two Chinese names and addresses on a notepad in script only I could fathom and closed the book on my virus report.

Manny displayed precious little interest in my little charade, which made the close-out easy enough.

"OK, Manny. No problem. If anything ever looks unusual on the screen, just call the company. We've had all kinds of virus problems out in Springfield. *Buena suerte,* man."

If nothing else, Manny was the master of nonchalance. Before I could bounce out of the chair, mentally giving myself a high five for brilliance in espionage, Manny swiveled himself clockwise, which put his mouth close to my ear.

"*Buena suerte* yourself, man. You may need the luck. You know what you're messin' with?"

He had me close to paralysis.

"I don't get you, man."

He said it low, and casual, and in Spanish. "That's a crock about the virus, brother. They have automatic virus protection built into the program. I know you're a defense lawyer. I saw you in court once. You did a good job for one of the brothers."

I looked him in the dark, emotionless eyes. I got no reading, so I still didn't know whether or not I was an ex-lawyer.

"Does that mean no whistle?"

"It means you just came through here to check for virus."

The relief squeezed out in a major exhale.

"I don't want to push it, but why?"

"I noticed you checked the Bradley case. We got orders not to give a copy of that report to defense counsel—which, of course, I didn't do. I think the DA's tying your hands with this Bradley kid. I'm not going to buck the DA. I just choose to believe your cover. I'm not a cop. I just punch keys here."

I whispered, "*Gracias,* man." His elbow stopped my rise out of the chair.

"You didn't answer my question."

I looked back at him with a question mark.

"You know what you're messin' with?"

"Like what?"

His eyes scanned the room without the slightest movement of his head. He was apparently satisfied, but he stuck to Spanish.

"You know the dudes around Center Street in the Plain? The Cavallos?"

"I know they can get dicey. Why?"

"You know nothing, man. They could take out your kidneys while you're reaching for your wallet. What I'm saying is that they're choirboys compared to what you're going to find in Chinatown."

"You talking about gangs? If they're so bad in C'town, how come I never heard of them?"

He sprang up and gave me a head-beckon. I followed him out to the corridor that led back to the front desk. He stopped halfway down the corridor.

"You better get out of here."

He was right. I started to move, and he moved with me.

"You never heard because they keep it in-house. Chinese preying on Chinese. The cops don't interfere much for reasons we don't need to go into. You maybe break the circle. You move into their game without knowing the rules . . ."

He shook his head in a way that made me glad he didn't put it into words that could generate nightmares. I shook his hand with a "*gracias*" that came from deep down.

IN THIRTY SECONDS, I was back on the street taking stock. I had two names and addresses in Chinatown, my bar membership intact, and a lump the size of a wonton in my chest.

5

IT WAS ABOUT SIX in the evening when I blended into the rush-hour flow that was swimming aggressively up Tremont Street like spawning salmon. I was with the tide as far as the Park Street station, and against it from there to Boylston Street. I had built up a bit of aggression of my own, since the only thing I had had to eat since my ritual Dunkin' Donut in the morning was that homicidal hot dog. A left on Boylston Street led through the bottom chamber of what's left of the pornographic cesspool, known euphemistically as the "Combat Zone," and emerged on Essex Street at the outer boundary of Chinatown.

One of the two witnesses mentioned in the police report was a Mrs. Lee. She was listed as the owner of a restaurant on Tyler Street called the Ming Tree. The name of the restaurant rang a bell from my conversation with young Bradley. I thought it might be an enticing place to refuel. On the other hand, in my condition a falafel from a lunch wagon in the South End would have been enticing.

Tyler Street is a short one-way passage, flanked on either side by orange and red neon that proclaims the predominant Golden Palace Restaurant on one side, and the China Pearl on the other. Sandwiched between a sunken Chinese-medicine and book shop and a street-level travel agency next to the Golden Palace is an unprepossessing stairway leading to the second-floor Ming Tree. A blowup of an article from the *Globe* tells those who pass beneath it that the food surpasses the decor. No great feat.

By the time I turned off Beach Street to Tyler, the northeast wind was whipping snow sideways. I found it difficult to separate in my mind the gnawing bite of the cold from the bite of the hunger, and both of them from the intimidating sense that I was cruising in totally unknown shoals.

As I started up the steps to the second-story restaurant, my eyes were drawn to the black draping around the grocery shop across the street. Now that I was tuned to it, I could see black signs of mourning on each shop on the street. A picture of an elderly Asian gentleman was in the window of the grocery shop, surrounded by flowers. Many of the other windows in the second-story homes had a similar display. The kindness and gentleness in his face were saddening. The community had truly suffered a loss to the soul.

The ancient stairs talked to me as I climbed to the red door on the second level. An etched shrub in the opaque glass in the door resembled my conception of a Ming tree. It flickered with shadows that indicated a waiting line inside.

I opened the door into a railroad-style room, long from the street back, but narrow enough so that only two tables and an aisle between them could fit crosswise.

To my left, just before the two tables by the window that faced onto Tyler Street, the cashier's counter wrapped around a silk-suited Asian man in his thirties with a more professional haircut than you generally see in Chinatown. He had an easy smile, and spoke comfortably in barely accented English with the non-Asian business suits who were eating at a table near the counter. It was light patter that bounced from the Celtics to the construction of the "Big Dig" on the southeast artery. It was so innocuous that I couldn't understand the discomfort he was setting off in my mind. I promised myself an honest-to-goodness lunch the next day as an antidote to paranoia.

All of the eighteen tables were occupied, and a young Asian couple stood waiting in the aisle ahead of me. The room was warm, clean, and well lit, which met the first of two checks I like to give to a first-time restaurant. The second was also met. At least half of the customers were Chinese, and happily, a third of those were middle-aged to elderly. A Chinese client once told me that the best Chinese food is served in any restaurant where you hear Mandarin spoken. Second-best is where you hear Cantonese. I asked him, "What if you hear nothing but English?" He said, "Go to an Italian restaurant."

The couple ahead of me were taken to a table in the back. When the fiftyish woman in the Chinese-cut aqua dress waved a menu at me from halfway back, I sign-languaged my desire to wait for the tea sippers at a table in front by the window overlooking the street. She picked up on it and seated the two men who came in behind me.

It was just a few minutes before I was sliding into the far seat at the window table. I wanted a full view of the entire cast in the restaurant. By turning around to the window, I noticed that I could look straight across the street to the grocery store to the left of the China Pearl Restaurant. There was a large window on the second floor just above the grocery shop. I could visualize the old man and his grandchildren crowded into the window to get a view of the pandemonium below before a bullet took his life—and maybe that of our client. The clink of a glass of water being placed onto the table brought me around. I felt a tiny jolt from an instant of eye contact with the silk suit at the cashier's desk, which I dismissed as meaningless, since so far there was nothing to distinguish me from any other drop-in customer.

I took the menu from a slight girl, about five feet tall, with a face that could have lit up the room if it could smile. She was somewhere between fourteen and twenty. Her beautiful, soft almond eyes never looked higher than the top of the table, which made her seem even smaller.

After losing her completely with intricate banter like, "Nice night," and "Thanks for the water," I realized that she was limited to menu-English. We finally made contact when I ordered the hot and sour soup and almond chicken ding with fried rice.

She took notes in Chinese, scooped up the menu, and padded back to the kitchen in Asian red cloth shoes that were the only bit of color in her outfit or personality.

The hot and sour soup spread its tiny fingers of fire to the outer reaches of my abdomen and made life seem good again. By the time of the almond chicken ding, my sense of values had returned, and I could give it an honest B minus—not overwhelming, but nevertheless dean's list.

I was down to the last few grains of fried rice, when the silk suit was beside the table. If the waitress was personality-challenged, he was gifted. The smile was a fixture on the pleasant features, and seemed to come from the heart. He was warm, friendly without being intrusive, easy to talk to, amiable; sort of an Asian Dick Clark. The one respect in which they differed is that I have always liked, admired, and had a warm spot in my heart for Dick Clark. For some reason I couldn't put into words, I had an instant distrust of the dude standing beside me. Go figure.

We covered the weather, inflation, and the quality of the meal. The first bumpy ground we hit was when I asked to speak with the owner, Mrs. Lee.

He asked if he might inquire why.

I said it had to do with the shooting of the previous day. A speck of stiffness crept in when he asked if I was defending the boy who shot Mr. Chen.

"I'm defending the accused. How did you know I wasn't from the police?"

"The police have been over this many times."

"I could have been from the DA's office."

He shook his head. "Too well dressed."

We both laughed and were buddies again. He asked me to wait while he found her. I finished the tea before he came back and invited me to follow him to the rear of the restaurant. We went to the last table before the kitchen. Customers had vacated that section.

The fiftyish woman who had seated me was at the table, sitting erect with her hands folded on the table. The body language told me that this could be like prying open a clam. To add to the challenge, Dick Clark told me that she spoke very little English. He, however, would be delighted to interpret. It would have been hard to change the ground rules without a fluency in Chinese. I can barely fathom fortune cookies in translation.

"Mrs. Lee, my name is Michael Knight. I'm a lawyer. I represent Anthony Bradley."

The name sharpened her rigidity. Dick Clark mumbled some Chinese, and she remained mute.

"Could you tell me what you saw yesterday?"

Again the translation. She looked at Dick Clark while she squeezed out a few sentences. There was obvious pain in what she was saying, and I wondered what her relationship to Mr. Chen might have been.

The translation from Dick Clark seemed a bit full for the number of words she had used. Either Chinese is a very cryptic language, or he was doing some embroidery.

"Mrs. Lee says that Mr. Bradley sat at the table you were at. She served him, since there were not enough waitresses. He watched through the window. When he left, she saw him go into the street. He had a gun. When the lion approached Mr. Chen's store, he fired at Mr. Chen in the window above."

I watched her during the translation. Those stoic eyes seemed to moisten when Mr. Chen's name was mentioned. I asked him directly.

"Was she related to Mr. Chen?"

He leaned back in his chair and took a moment.

"I'll tell you something, Mr. Knight. You may not understand, but I'll tell you. We're an alien people in this country. Even those of us who are citizens. We cling to our customs, our language. Our whole culture gives us a place where we're accepted. Unlike your culture, we revere our elderly. They are our rock. Sometimes that reverence is indistinguishable from love. That was particularly true of Mr. Chen. He was like the root of our soul. When your Mr. Bradley killed Mr. Chen, he sent us into the very deepest mourning. Not just relatives, all of us."

The half of me that was Puerto Rican understood, particularly the emotion of loss. Fortunately, my other half was dispassionate enough to press on.

"Would you ask her this? If the restaurant was busy, why did she take the time to watch Bradley after he left?"

He spoke the Chinese in a low tone of voice, being very gentle with this woman whose locked hands were beginning to tremble. I looked away to avoid embarrassing her. As I looked back toward the kitchen, I caught sight of the red shoes in the small gap between the door and the floor. They didn't move.

There were several exchanges in Chinese between Mrs. Lee and my interpreter before he turned back to me.

"Mrs. Lee says she became alarmed when she saw the handle of a gun in his belt under his jacket when he got up to leave. She was afraid of what he might do with the gun, so she watched through the window. When he got to the street, he took the gun out and . . ." He finished the sentence with a clear gesture.

I was beginning to feel my nose bleed from running into a brick wall. I thought I'd take one more run at it to see if there was an inch of flexibility.

"Would you ask her if it could possibly have been someone besides Bradley who fired the shot? The street was pretty crowded yesterday."

He sang a few Chinese syllables that sent her head into a motion that told me I had just dug Bradley's grave a foot deeper. She went ramrod stiff. Her head shook out "no," while her little staccato voice rose half an octave. She held her hand above her head as if she were holding a gun. So much for flexibility.

Dick Clark stood up for this one.

"Mrs. Lee says that she saw the black hand of Mr. Bradley aiming the gun." He demonstrated. "No mistake. And now I think we should let Mrs. Lee compose herself."

I looked at the tiny, clenched hands of that frail woman, and my heart tightened. I wanted to tell her in soft terms that I wouldn't hurt her. Just two problems—she wouldn't have understood the words if I tried, and worse, I might not be able to deliver on the promise. If it came to saving our client, we might have to do whatever was necessary to destroy her as a witness.

I just stood in agreement. As I turned back to Dick Clark, I caught another glimpse of the red shoes under the door.

"Thanks for your help. Please tell her I'm sorry for her grief."

He nodded.

"If I have any more questions, I'll be back."

"I don't think so."

The engineer was smiling, but the train had just run over my legs. My expression must have registered the jolt.

"I don't mean to be discourteous, Mr. Knight. Mrs. Lee has been badly shaken by Mr. Chen's death. It was an imposition to speak to her tonight, but I allowed it. No more."

I stood beside him and matched him smile for smile.

"I believe my client is innocent. That doesn't mean he won't be convicted on the basis of mistaken testimony. That's my idea of an imposition. If I have any more questions, I'll be back."

I walked back to the table. The waitress in the red shoes padded over with the check and a fortune cookie. I dropped enough money to cover the check and a tip on the tray. I had no desire to prolong it, but I couldn't resist cracking open the fortune cookie. They're always upbeat, and I needed some good news.

When I peeled it open, a second slip fell on the floor. I bent down to pick it up and caught a look of abject terror in the frozen face of Red Shoes. It softened when I slipped the paper into my pocket. I couldn't tell who else noticed. I busied myself with pulling on my topcoat while I read the fortune-cookie missive:

"Success cannot long exceed your grasp."

God bless the chef.

6

TYLER STREET WAS TAKING on a new face when I left the Ming
Tree. The black frozen slush was freshly coated with a new white dust-
ing of the kind of snow you get when the bottom has dropped out of
the thermometer—dry and squeaky to the walk. The wind had fallen
off, though, and a full stomach was better insulation against the cold
than another layer of clothing.

I turned right and walked the half block to Beach Street. A left and
one more block brought me to a well-lit coffee shop with no name on
the right-hand corner of Beach and Harrison. It was smoky and heavy
with the drone of mumbled Chinese coming from the clutches of both
young and old sitting around the bare wooden tables.

I found a corner under a fluorescent light and took out the slip of
paper that had fallen out of the fortune cookie. The way my day had
been running, it was no surprise that the writing was Chinese.

I was surrounded by people who could probably translate, assuming, of course, that they could speak English. Somehow it did not seem
like a good idea to ask. I tucked the note away in an inside pocket and
braced for the walk outside.

I stayed in the nook of the entranceway to be out of earshot and out
of the wind at the same time. I tapped a familiar array of numbers into
my cell phone, and my mind ran back ten years or so.

Harry Wong was one of the best memories I had from my days at
Harvard College. He was the grandson of a woman who left China to
start a string of the first Chinese restaurants seen in the suburbs of
Boston in the early twenties. She was a maverick with nerve and a keen
sense of demography. Harry told me that she noticed that most of the

non-Chinese customers of the Chinatown restaurants were Jewish. She picked her locations by cruising the neighborhoods and checking the names on the mailboxes. Whenever she found a cluster of middle-class Cohens or Goldsteins, or better yet, a synagogue, she'd plant a restaurant. In ten years she went back to China with enough money to rule a southern province.

Harry's family migrated back to Boston around the time that Mao Tse-tung's army made capitalistic wealth a scourge to be cleansed. The family transferred its prominence from a southern province of China to the province of Brookline, west of Boston.

Harry and I met as freshmen at the tryouts for an intermural wrestling team at Holworthy House. He was tall for a seventeen-year-old Chinese American, but somehow he came equipped with more speed and strength than you'd expect from his beanpole build. He not only made the team, he managed to embarrass most of the beefy Caucasians at practice—and one particular half Puerto Rican—by pinning us like butterflies while we were still counting his ribs.

One of his victims once asked him what kind of trick he was using. He had a gentle smile and a soft voice with just enough of a trace of his parents' accent to be eligible for racial prejudice from the preppy blue bloods who made up 90 percent of the team. It was a smart-aleck question, but he gave it a courteous answer. Unfortunately, when he said that everything he did stemmed from an ancient Chinese discipline called tai chi, which he had practiced since he was three years old, he was permanently branded as some kind of mystic freak by those who finally had a means of satisfying their need to feel superior to him.

I saw a door shut in his eyes when he heard the half-hidden whispers and laughs. I didn't think I could open it again, but I caught him after practice. I asked if he'd help me. I could feel the defensive refusal in his hesitation. I told him I meant it. I needed help. He was somewhere between anger at all of us and rejection of what he took to be my pity when he snapped out, "I'll be here at five tomorrow morning. Do what you wish."

It was painful, but I had my body at the gym at five the next morning, and every day for a year. Harry brought me into the discipline of peace through controlled patterns of body movement that was his version of tai chi. We were matched to wrestle each other at every practice, since nobody else wanted much of either one of us. I worked harder than I had ever worked at anything in my life, and by the end of the spring term, I could pin anyone in Holworthy House—except one.

THREE TELEPHONE RINGS, and I was beginning to wonder if I could catch him at home. I hadn't seen him since Thanksgiving. But then I could say that three hundred and sixty-four days a year. After college, I went to play in the law, and Harry started devouring the alphabet. He got an MS degree in biochemistry from MIT, and hung on for a PhD in record time. He picked up a few more initials in London before becoming a resident brainchild back at MIT.

Our lives took us in different directions most of the time, but we met religiously for Thanksgiving dinner at my mother's house in Newton. She always cooked what I thought from childhood was a traditional American Thanksgiving dinner—*pollo con arroz* and cornbread.

Six rings, and I decided to try his office. That reached him. He still put an Asian twang on "Hello" and I was mighty glad to hear it.

"Harry, it's Mike. What're you up to?"

"Mike, good to hear from you. What's up?"

"I was hoping we could get together."

"Is it Thanksgiving already?"

"Not for a little while. It's February. Actually I need your help. Could we meet?"

"Sure, Mike. How about lunch tomorrow?"

"How about coffee in an hour?"

I think he caught my urgency. If there was a pause, it was a fraction of a second to reorder his schedule.

"You name the place, Mike."

I looked around. "I'm in Chinatown, corner of Beach and Harrison. There's some kind of a coffee shop behind me. I don't see a name. Can you meet me here?"

His voice picked up tension. "No, I can't, Mike. Listen to me. Don't hang around there. Hang up the phone and just get the hell out of there."

"Why? What is this place?"

"Let's not discuss it at the moment. Walk to the right up Harrison. I'll meet you in the bar at the China Sea."

I wanted to tell him he sounded like a character out of an old Fu Manchu movie, but he was gone.

I was the only one at the China Sea bar, sipping Tsing Tao beer until Harry slid onto the next bar stool.

"Happy Thanksgiving, Michael."

"Happy New Year, Harry."

I reached in my pocket and handed him the slip of paper that had fallen out of the fortune cookie. He lit a cigarette lighter and held it up to scan the symbols.

"You want a beer, Harry?"

He waved off the suggestion. "Where'd you get this?"

"In a fortune cookie."

He gave me a look. "Fortune cookies are to make you Caucasians feel good about leaving a tip. Is this note serious?"

"I suspect it is. Could we share the contents?"

He relit the lighter for another look.

"It's a girl's name. Ku Mei-Li. And an address on Beach Street. You know her?"

I shook my head.

"There's more. It says literally, 'You help her, I help you.'"

Harry looked at me in the mirror over the bar. "Help you what?"

I took another sip of beer to sort out my own questions before answering Harry's. It was an attractive quid pro quo. The *quid* was whatever in the world I could do for someone named Ku Mei-Li. The *quo* was particularly inviting if it meant that my little Red Shoes would give us a counter to Mrs. Lee's damning identification.

I took Harry by the arm and escorted him out the door and down Harrison. I'd given him a brief replay of the day's events by the time we reached the corner of Beach Street.

"So it comes down to this, Harry old pal. We find the address on Beach Street, and either I go in by myself with nothing but hand signals to communicate with heaven-knows-who, or you come with me, and we make sense of this little game."

We stopped. He pulled me into a doorway. I thought at the time he was taking us out of the cold, but he could have been avoiding the eyes of those who were standing in the window of the coffee shop across the street.

"Michael, you have no conception of what goes on in Chinatown. You're like everyone else who comes down here. You have dinner, buy some noodles, whatever, and breeze right back out to Caucasianville. You can't see it, because you don't know what to look for."

"See what, Harry? I'm willing to look. Tell me."

He looked at me and just shook his head.

"It's too much to tell, and too cold to do it here. What can I say, Mike? You want me to wade into a net of organized crime so effective that it has this community almost paralyzed with fear. It's so effective that you don't even know it exists."

I pulled the collar of my coat up around the back of my neck.

"Suppose it exists, Harry . . ."

"It exists."

"Like I said. Suppose it exists. I don't have a lot of choice. I got a name, I got an address. That's a hell of lot more than I had going for me before I came down here. I've got to follow it up. I don't think time is on my side. The question is, do you go with me?"

"This place you're going is a brothel, Mike. For Chinese. Not outsiders. It's protected by a youth gang that could write the book on violence. You could at least pick a better time than the middle of the night. Alone."

"I didn't pick the time, Harry. And maybe I'm not alone."

I forced a goofy smile and stepped out into the street. I was walking, but I was listening hard. My heart came down out of my throat when I heard Harry's footsteps catching up.

7

HARRY SAID NOTHING. I could tell by the set of his chin that the wrong word from me could break the momentum, and any word was the wrong word.

He took the lead as we passed five doorways. The sixth was chipped and grimy and hung at an angle that only time and neglect could effect. The glass was caked with decades of pollution. There was not a clue as to what was on the other side. That would not ordinarily raise the hair on the back of my neck, but that combined with Harry's gripping the doorknob for the duration of an interminable deep breath gave me the galloping creeps.

When he was mentally set, Harry stiffened his posture, gave me a nod, and pushed open the door. I could see that it led to a hallway the width of the door and just as decrepit. Straight ahead about ten feet the rutted floor bent upward in a flight of well-worn wooden stairs. The light inside was dimmer than the neon glare in the street. Harry held the door open for a second and looked back.

We caught sight of them at almost the same moment. Three of the young stone faces I had seen in the window of the coffee shop on the corner were moving down the sidewalk in our direction. Harry gave me a "you couldn't listen" look. There are times, however, when the only way to retreat is to go forward. We moved inside and closed the door.

About the time we hit the first step, I looked up to see the top landing consumed with the bulk of the first Chinese I'd ever seen who topped six feet four and a conservative two hundred fifty pounds. Whatever notion I had of making it past the top of the stairs died in a lump that I couldn't swallow.

Harry never lost a beat. He trudged up the stairs as if he were coming home from a day's work. I felt a cold draft from behind and turned around. The three faces glared up at us from the bottom of the steps behind us. They were well under twenty, and closer to the Chinese proportions I expected, but the bulges under their coats in the neighborhood of their right arm sockets kept me close to Harry's heels where the odds were better.

I stuck, in fact, close enough to Harry to be able to whisper.

"You were always a friend, Harry, but right now you're my life insurance."

Harry's eyes never left the top of the stairs, but I could hear the whisper.

"It's the other way, Michael. You're *my* life insurance."

I neither understood that nor found it comforting.

Harry kept climbing. I took it that the ploy was bluff, rather than fight or even cut and run. Considering that they had us boxed in like a runner between first and second base, it was the only option that might possibly not involve suffering.

I think I jumped when a burst of guttural Chinese came out of the hulk at the top of the stairs. Harry took three more steps without acknowledging the temper tantrum. He was two steps from the top, and close enough to make it possible for one swipe of the side of beef our host used for a right arm to send us both to the bottom of the stairs. Fortunately, he chose to listen instead.

Harry's nose came up to about his navel. To his credit, Harry never succumbed to the indignity of looking up. His voice was calm, deliberate, and pure business.

I couldn't imagine what he was saying in his native tongue. The three of us seemed to hang in suspended animation. I saw those lethal arms poised for a strike that would have decapitated Harry and sent me halfway to Chelsea. I said a few words to the Lord and braced for whatever came in my direction.

When Harry finished, there was a pause for a few electric seconds that seemed longer than the bar examination while King Kong looked at me like something he could put in an egg roll. I had no idea what Harry was saying with astounding composure, but it had a most desired defusing influence. When Kong spoke again, it was with deference, and it sounded like a question. Harry gave him a few clipped words, and he backed out of our way. I heard the door behind us open, and when I looked back, the gang of three had vacated.

With Kong receding into the passageway, I could see a short, plump Chinese woman of what I guessed to be something over fifty years standing by the first door to the right. She was decked out in a green silk-brocade sheath that did not need a lengthy slit to reach her hips. Fifty pounds and thirty years previously it might have been becoming. At this point, her wearing of the uniform of the profession seemed as pointless as a baseball manager wearing cleats.

I assume she had followed the exchange, because she was all grins and welcome in English, more or less.

"You most welcome. Come in. Come in."

Harry and I finished the last few stairs and followed her into a room that would have worked as a sumptuously decorated living room in any home in Brookline. Chinese red was the predominant color in fabrics that could have adorned a silkworm's museum. The lighting was dim, the music was lush, and the aroma would make a water buffalo amorous.

She spoke in a tinny voice, strained through a grin that suggested that she was at our service.

"How we please you, gentlemen?"

Introductions seemed out of place. Since Harry had accomplished the impossible in getting us this far, I took it from there. The object of the moment seemed to be to get alone in a room with Mei-Li with as little explanation as possible. I came directly to the point.

"Mei-Li."

That did it. The toothy grin opened as her head went back.

"Ah. Excellent choice. Very beautiful. And you, sir?"

For the first time that night, Harry was stuck for an answer. The best he could do was, "I'm with him."

I have no idea what that suggested to the honorable madam. Whatever it was, it did not upset her sensibilities. The grin was a fixture, but nothing even registered in her eyes.

"So. Please follow."

She opened a second door and welcomed us to a room that made the first room look like a freshman dorm. She closed the door behind us. I assumed that she went to hustle up Mei-Li.

I looked at Harry, but not before taking in the essence of our surroundings.

"I take it the clientele here is not off-the-street."

He exhaled as if it were his first breath since we came out of the cold. He was smiling, but shaking his head. The message he was sending was something between conflict and frustration.

"You can't understand. There's just no way."

I came close enough for a whisper to work below the level of the music.

"I'm willing to learn, Harry."

Something caught in his throat that made his voice sound like gravel.

"You still don't get it. The people they serve here have more wealth and power in their own world than you could dream of."

"Drugs?"

Harry edged closer and dropped his voice below the level of the music. His hands went up in a gesture.

"Tip of the iceberg. Drugs are big, but this empire runs on everything illegal. Extortion big time. Illegal alien smuggling. Slavery, prostitution, those two go hand in hand. Police corruption. That's a commodity they can sell to other organizations in other states. You beginning to get it?"

"What I don't get is how you know about it. You're not into this."

For a fraction of a second I was tempted to end that last sentence with a question mark. I decided to go on faith. It probably saved our friendship.

"You don't have to be a part of it to know about it if you're Chinese. There isn't any Chinese I know, no matter how far out of Chinatown, who doesn't have family or friends who are being victimized."

Questions were running wild in my mind, but there was one I had to get in before that door opened. I whispered this one.

"What in the world did you say to that ape on the stairs?"

"I used the two words they fear more than death."

"Which are?" He was dragging it out. I didn't blame him.

"Immigration Service."

"The hell you did! You told him you're an immigration officer?"

"No. I told him you are."

I took a deep breath while I counted the number of years following disbarment I could get for impersonating a federal officer. Then I considered what could happen if any of these bozos compared notes with the crowd at the Ming Tree restaurant where I was known as Bradley's defense lawyer. I figured disbarment and jail time would be the good news.

"One question. If this place is populated with illegal aliens, how come they let us in?"

"I told them you're a good INS agent."

"Meaning?"

The knob turned on the door as Harry whispered the last few words.

"Meaning I told them you're on the take. They may not love you, but they sure as hell want to please you."

The ramifications of that were beyond computing. I had about two full seconds to dwell on it before my senses were sent into overload.

There's striking. There's astoundingly beautiful. And then somewhere beyond that there's Mei-Li. The woman that came through that door carried poise, radiance, and charm to a level I'd never experienced off of a movie screen.

You could say it was the cascade of midnight hair flowing to the waist of a lithe body that moved with an almost choreographed grace. Or it could have been the exquisite facial features that expressed elegance without intimidating the male ego. It could even have been the packaging of form-fitting turquoise silk from alabaster neck to floor.

Whatever it was, it was stunning, in the literal sense of that word—until I realized that it was empty. It was a picture carefully assembled for one purpose. She was a prostitute. The whole fragile image was created to carry off a relationship no deeper than a one-sided sex drive. I couldn't help thinking that somewhere beneath that perfection there must be a human being as carefully hidden as any blemish that lay beneath the makeup. If she was in there, she was the one I had to reach to keep my end of the fortune-cookie bargain with Red Shoes.

She closed the door and bowed, respectfully, from the waist. The smile she carried across the room was beautiful, but prerecorded. I don't suppose that mattered to most of the men she found waiting in that room.

If she was surprised to find my round eyes meeting her almond disks, there was no clue in her features. I met her halfway across the room. The problem was an opening move. There was no way to tell whose headset or video monitor was playing the Mei-Li and Michael Show, so a little misdirection seemed in order.

I took her hand while we locked smiles. The bed area consumed the third of the room to the left, and the "getting acquainted" area took up most of the rest. There was a dark corner of dead space off to my right. It seemed the least likely to spawn any action that would be worth recording, and probably the least likely to be the focus of any hidden camera.

I led her slowly to what I hoped would be off-camera. She followed in step. I think as long as I played the John, she'd have dutifully followed me to Taiwan. The question was how to reach the girl inside who made her own choices. I decided, *When in doubt, fly direct.*

I kept my voice so low that it could only have been picked up if she were wearing a microphone.

"Mei-Li, do you read Chinese?"

Her voice was higher than I expected.

"Of course."

I handed her the note that Red Shoes had delivered with the fortune cookie. She scanned it while I read her eyes. The best I could hope for was a flash of gratitude for the rescue she'd prayed for. The worst was what I saw. Nothing. The shell was intact.

She handed back the note without a quiver.

"What does this mean?" The little high-pitched voice gave up nothing but mild curiosity.

"I was hoping you might tell me. Do you have any idea where I got it?"

"No." It peeped out like half a syllable, as if I'd asked if she knew the capital of Montana. I was leery about tipping too much information, and I was getting precious little in exchange.

"Mei-Li, no one can hear us. I can help you if you need it. Are you in any kind of trouble?"

She seemed perplexed by the question, but peeped out, "No."

"Are they keeping you here against your will?"

"No."

"Are you ill?"

"No."

"Are you in any kind of danger?"

"No."

Each little peep carried more of the implication, "and how stupid of you to ask."

Considering what it cost Harry and me in lost heartbeats to get there, plus the need to keep the only hope of help for young Bradley alive, I was beginning to swim in frustration.

Then it occurred to me that she might have tensed up because of listeners. I took her hand and mouthed the words, "If you need help, squeeze my hand."

I could have been holding a dead mackerel.

I could feel trip-hammers pounding on the nerves behind my eyes. An overwhelming sense of defeat flooded over my mind. For some reason, it welled up into anger. I dropped her hand and got a grip on her arm. I moved her back to the far wall. I knew it was the anger driving me, but I let it. I was spitting the whispered words between my teeth.

"Listen to me, girl. If you're not telling the truth, you're playing with people's lives. The girl who wrote that note could have been killed for it. She did it for you. That man over there came through three punks and a sumo wrestler to get here. So did I. You probably won't understand this, but there's an innocent boy who could be convicted of murder if I don't get some answers. Now what's the game?"

I stopped when I heard Harry spit out "Mike!" from across the room. I realize my voice could be heard beyond our little corner. I waited for an answer.

Nothing. She was still the porcelain doll. There was no expression whatever in her eyes. She just shook her head. Her voice was dead calm.

"I'm sorry. There is no trouble. You were kind to try to help me."

That did it. The steam was gone. I knew I was running on empty. I apologized for what had probably been an absurd scene from her point of view and motioned Harry to the door. I put a twenty in her hands for the inconvenience, although at that moment, I felt more inconvenienced than she was. Someone was playing ping-pong with me, and whether it was Red Shoes, Mei-Li, or both, I was fresh out of clues.

The corridors were empty when we made our way down the stairs. It was a relief. I wasn't up to the kind of gauntlet we ran coming in. The door creaked open to a gust of fresh snowflakes that had camouflaged the grit of one of Boston's oldest sections.

I felt ridiculous thanking Harry for risking his life on a chase for a nonexistent goose, but he understood. We wished each other a happy Thanksgiving, and he headed up toward Harrison. I offered him a cab ride, but he wanted to walk. The streets were deserted, and the snowflakes actually felt good on the skin.

It was only a couple of minutes before a cab answered my wave. I gave the driver the address of my apartment on Beacon Street at Berkeley and then remembered that it was Monday, just before midnight. It felt like at least Thursday. I gave the driver a different address higher up on Beacon Street just above Charles. The driver acknowledged, and I started nodding off in the backseat as we headed down Beach Street.

I was drifting into neutral as I watched Harry's fresh footprints in the snow. My last impression was of the steamed-up windows of the coffee shop on the corner and the three sets of equally fresh footprints that came from the door.

8

IT WAS JUST PAST MIDNIGHT when the cab pulled up outside of Daddy's Club. The cabbie gave me a gentle nudge, and the brisk bite of the snow-carrying wind brought me the rest of the way back to the outskirts of the land of the living. I was fighting the temptation to jump back in the cab and call it a night, but Monday night is Monday night, and there are some things that feed the soul more than rest.

I passed a couple of departing, slightly lubricated college kids on my way down the narrow cut-back staircase to the below-ground haunt of one of Boston's great assets. The club draws a spate of yuppies and college types earlier in the evening, but around midnight they begin to dwindle. After the other clubs and restaurants have closed, Daddy's pulls in jazz musicians from in and out of town, as well as devoted listeners who can handle the late hours. It undoubtedly violates the city's code of closing times, but the police give it their best benign neglect.

The whole room is about forty feet by twenty, with a miniscule bandstand at the front and a bar that runs the length of the left sidewall. It is either meticulously clean or filthy enough to drive cockroaches to cleaner surroundings. I have no idea which, because the lighting, or lack of it, would make a mole feel at home.

I slid up onto a bar stool at the near end of the bar, and every muscle in my body rose up in rebellion for not taking it home. But then, this was Oz, Valhalla, Never-Never Land. When I came through that door, the world out there dried up and blew away.

One of the most serious elements of my education at Harvard came from a luck-of-the-draw roommate. My first two months with Harry Ortlieb were, if not hell itself, at least a lower ring of purgatory. Harry was a music major with an addictive penchant for modern jazz. In particular, Harry idolized that rebellious cluster of jazz musicians who took the idiom out of the bounds of comfortable, decent harmony and pushed it into the sometimes discordant world of newfound chords. He personally stocked every recording made in the fifties and sixties by the principal emissaries of that assault on the ear and central nervous system called "bebop."

For the first two months of our freshman year, I spent every torturous moment in our dorm room at Holworthy House fighting the urge to rip whatever CD by Charlie Parker, Dizzy Gillespie, Charlie Mingus, whoever was fouling the air at the moment, out of his state-of-the-art player and tuck it as far up Harry Ortlieb's ass as the length of my arm would permit. My only regret in my fantasy was that CDs have no sharp corners.

Then the third month came, and to my own shock and surprise, if not Harry's, I started to like it. I started asking for particular pieces and actually listening to Harry's explanation of what they were doing. Life became not only livable, but I started looking forward to our late nightly CD concerts with Harry playing DJ.

The effect went further than that. My father/guardian, Miles O'Connor, was, among his many other talents, an accomplished piano player. He drew me to the instrument out of sheer admiration for him. It stuck, and I found that at every stage of my life, whatever demons were haunting me could be tamed, or at least sedated, by an hour or two alone at a piano.

Enter Harry Ortlieb, and every moment I spent at the keys from freshman year on was turned to working out the intricacies such giants as Thelonius Monk had woven around the old standards. And every Monday late night in recent times was spent in that preview of heaven called Daddy's Club.

I GAVE A THREE-FINGER SIGN to Marty behind the bar. He understandingly poured three fingers of Famous Grouse Scotch over four ice cubes. He had the maturity and gentility not to adulterate it with water or some twisted snip from a citrus object.

That first sip of the Grouse awakened taste buds that went right down to my toes. The second sip a minute or two later soothed the wrinkles off the brow and put this wandering soul deep in the proper attitude to hear and appreciate what "Daddy" Hightower on bass and his trio were doing on the bandstand. Sips three, four, and five carried me through the last chorus of a tune written by the great jazz bassist, Charlie Mingus, that had not been done so tastefully since Charlie did it himself.

When they finished, I moved across to one of the small, empty tables and settled into serious relaxation between sets. I was halfway to the Land of Nod when I felt a hand the size of a boxing glove on my shoulder.

"Well, ain't you the picture of piss and hot sauce?"

Daddy slipped into, or rather consumed, the chair beside me.

I nodded toward the bandstand. "That was nice."

He knew what I meant. He just smiled. Daddy was a piece of work. He stood six feet four in a crouch and weighed something less than the *QEII*. He actually dwarfed the stand-up acoustic bass. When he hovered over it, it became like an added appendage of his body.

Daddy had been in the New York scene in Harlem in the late fifties, early sixties, when Thelonius Monk and Dizzy Gillespie and Charlie Parker, and, of course, Charlie Mingus were showing people that there was more to music than Lawrence Welk. When Daddy got into it on the bass, he played with such power and imagination that he could drive another musician to play six levels above himself. Some of the big ones used Daddy as a sideman on recording sessions. He was truly in his element.

Then the late sixties and seventies descended. Rock came along like a tidal wave and pushed some real talent into the backwashes. Jazz clubs withered and died, and the recording industry followed the rock thumpers after the money.

Daddy actually became a bouncer in a club where a group of giftless whambangers packed in an equally tasteless audience of everything from college rowdies to bikers. One night, Daddy waded in to break up a broken-bottle brawl, and they turned on him. It took surgery and six years before he could move his fingers enough to grip a bass.

Eventually it came back. Mostly. Some of the musicians from the old days backed him enough to open the cellar club on Beacon Street, and no serious jazz musician ever came to town without dropping by Daddy's, usually with an instrument.

I looked across the table at that big old smile and the beads of perspiration on that wide ebony forehead.

"No, I mean it was *really* nice."

The smile broadened, and he just nodded.

"She here tonight, Daddy?"

He leaned back in the chair, which must have held together by sheer willpower.

"I thought you might get around to that. Earlier. She asked about you."

"And?"

"She said she might be back. She has a gig over the Hilton. All gown and tux for the snappy set."

"Uh-huh?"

"Uh-huh."

He nodded toward the piano on the bandstand. "So meantime, you comin' up, Mickey?"

Daddy is the only one who ever made "Mickey" sound like a suitable substitute for "Michael."

"I'd only slow you down tonight, Daddy."

His eyebrows rode halfway up to his bald crest. "You think you can slow Daddy down?"

It was my turn to grin. "A herd of elephants couldn't do that."

"C'mon. Let's give that box a *mass*age."

Daddy waved Clyde Williams out of the audience. He'd been sitting ringside with his sax assembled, like a rookie hockey player choking his hockey stick waiting for a nod from the coach.

We followed Daddy onto the stand. I settled into the piano and Clyde loosened up his fingers, while Daddy got comfortable around his bass. It was at moments like this that I said an extra prayer for Miles O'Connor for putting the dimension of music into my life.

I caught a little grin on Daddy's sly face when he yelled over to Clyde and me, "Cherokee." It's an old Charlie Barnett tune that's played at about a hundred beats to the bar. I groaned and my head hit the music rest.

Daddy held up the three-flats sign and launched an avalanche of notes on the bass that I could feel in the pit of my stomach. By the time I waded in, I had adrenalin coming out my ears, and we did it at a full gallop.

We went through eight choruses of improvisation on the fly, when Daddy finally held up the closed-fist sign for the last chorus. I said a sincere prayer of thanks.

There was a nice ripple of applause before Daddy laid down a bass introduction to a mercifully slow and sleepy "I Didn't Know What Time It Was." It was like hot-walking a horse after a race.

Two choruses had me cruising with my eyes shut, when I heard those beautiful lyrics in the clear, sweet voice of one of God's angels. The voice was right behind me, and I could feel the satin touch of long, tapered fingers on my neck.

I didn't want to turn around, or speak, or breathe to break the spell until that last gorgeous line.

I turned around and saw that face with the auburn hair and the smile that makes everything else in the room background. I couldn't remember a time when it didn't, although we'd only met at Daddy's a few weeks before.

Lanny Wells did something in Filene's executive offices during the daytime, but at night her pumpkin turned into a microphone, and she turned into the finest jazz vocalist I've heard since Harry Ortlieb's recordings by Sarah Vaughn.

When Lanny spoke, it sounded like she was still singing.

"Daddy said you'd be here tonight."

"Hey, it's Monday night. How was the gig?" I checked out the evening gown. "Must've been way uptown."

She smiled. "*This* is way uptown. You look like you had a day."

"And a half. I'll tell you sometime."

Daddy leaned over the piano. "Let's give 'em 'Route Sixty-Six.'"

I swung back into position, and after a driving pacesetter from Daddy, Lanny took us on a tour of my favorite road to California.

IT WAS JUST AFTER FOUR in the morning when Lanny and I climbed the steps to street level and hailed the last cab in Boston. We were the only car on the snow-dusted street when we pulled up to her apartment house on Commonwealth Avenue.

I walked Lanny up the six steps to the door.

"Would you like to come up for coffee? I grind it fresh."

"Would the Bruins like to beat the Rangers for the Stanley Cup?"

I love to throw sports analogies at her because she looks so cute while she's grasping for a clue as to what I'm talking about.

"Does that mean 'yes'?"

"It means 'yes,' but no. I have to be awake enough to play in the big league in about four hours. If I sleep fast, I'll get three hours."

I gave it a second or two before asking a question to which I really did not want to hear a negative answer.

"How about a real date? Dinner, North Shore?"

"When?"

That sounded promising. "Wednesday? I'll give you a call. Would you like to?"

"Would Versace like to see Chanel in the red?"

It was my turn. "Does that mean 'yes'?"

She kissed me. "Call and see."

9

IT WAS ABOUT 8:30 AM Tuesday when I stepped off the elevator at Bilson, Dawes. I never made it down the corridor to my office. I was cruising past the cluster of secretaries' desks with a paper cup of black caffeine, when Julie waved to me from behind a telephone. Her right hand pointed south, and her expression said, "Poor baby."

I got the message. Mr. Devlin wanted to see me.

I parked the coffee on her desk and caught her attention. She held a hand over the mouthpiece and looked up. I reached over and pushed her "hold" button. She looked indignant.

"Hey, you just cut off a client."

"No, I didn't. That was your lunch date."

"You listened!"

"Of course. Do me a favor. I may not get serious time in my office till Groundhog Day the way this thing is going with Lex."

Her eyebrows went up. "Oh, 'Lex,' is it?"

"Only out of his hearing. Otherwise it's 'Your Excellency.'"

"You better not get those two confused. You'll be seeking employment."

"Naw, he wouldn't fire me. That would be small and vindictive. He'd just eat me alive. To finish the thought, I'll never get to my mail or messages. Go through it all, will you? If anything looks like an emergency, leave a note on my desk. I may get to it by Friday."

I headed for the lion's den. I heard from behind, "What's an emergency?"

"Death threats, malpractice actions, my subscription to *DownBeat* is expiring. I don't know. I trust your judgment."

THE KING WAS IN his throne room, skimming the *Globe* and inhaling something black and steaming out of a paper cup. I thought of my own, cooling on Julie's desk, and wished that I had known that it was the breakfast hour.

He waved me into the chair in front of his desk. I accepted the invitation, beginning to feel like a golden retriever responding to hand signals.

As he swung around to face me, his blackish blue suitcoat winged open over his barrel chest to a pair of red suspenders. I couldn't help thinking that on another man they could be an affectation. Not Mr. Devlin. I sized him up as a man who measured himself by his own standards and to hell with anyone else's. He was reminding me more of Miles O'Connor every time I saw him. I realized that if I didn't catch myself, I could slip into something akin to hero worship.

"What have you got for me, sonny?"

I wasn't proud of the catch. There was no way to make it look good.

"I've got a witness, elderly Chinese woman, who kills our client with a positive ID. She says she saw him pull the trigger. Why, I don't know. It's hard to read her. She's wound pretty tight, but what really makes it difficult is that she only admits to speaking Chinese."

"Could it be she's telling the truth? I mean about Bradley."

My gaze had wandered to the window, but that last question brought me back to eye contact with a snap. I felt caught like a bug under a microscope.

"I know I should never believe a client in a criminal case. I know they lie to get the best defense out of you. I know that."

"Good. Live by that, sonny. Because if you turn this into a crusade to free a poor innocent defendant, you'll be worse than useless to me and the client. You'll be dangerous. You'll be looking for evidence to back up your theory instead of the truth. That's the best way to get blindsided."

I gave him the agreement-in-principle nod he was looking for, but he knew there was more.

"So? Give it to me."

"I know that. But I talked to him."

"That's why I'm asking. I want to know what I'm working with here."

I sucked in an inch of stomach and looked back into those laser beams.

"It won't change the way I work, but you might as well know this, Mr. Devlin. If they accused my grandmother of doing the Brink's job, I'd be more likely to believe it than that this kid's guilty. It's not because of his background, the judge and all. It's just something about the way he says he didn't do it."

I knew what I meant, but it sounded lame. He took a deep breath before swinging back in his chair. I was ready to be told that he could survive without my help. I had taken the case for Judge Bradley, but heaven knew the judge would be delighted to have the great Lex Devlin in substitution.

There were times the previous night when being back working on pretrial motions for Whitney Caster seemed almost attractive. But this was morning. I'd had a few hours' sleep, and I realized that I'd grown fond of the big league. I watched him rub his eyes while I waited for the shoe to drop.

"How'd you find that witness? I thought the police weren't giving out the names."

I spun out the story of my newfound Puerto Rican contact in the police computer section. I might have been grasping at straws, but I thought I caught the slightest trace of a smile softening those Mount Rushmore features. I was cool on the surface, but inside I was sipping champagne.

The phone buzzed, and he took it. Whatever his secretary said seemed to surprise him. He punched the speaker-phone button and set it back down.

"You never know what a new day'll bring, sonny. I want you to hear this. Put her on, Carol."

There was something reaching for warmth and charm in the female voice that came through the speaker, but it still sounded like a barracuda in drag.

"Good morning, Lex. How are you this morning? This is Angela Lamb."

That was never in doubt. Mr. Devlin matched her warmth. It was like watching two pit bulls sniffing each other.

"Is the sun shining on the district attorney's office this morning, Angela?"

"It's a beautiful day, Lex. I think I have good news for your client."

"That's generous. Let me guess. You caught the killer, and you're dismissing all charges."

I could almost hear her teeth grinding.

"Oh, we caught the killer. He's sitting in the Suffolk County jail. As your little errand boy knows."

This time Rushmore cracked into a slight grin. The gloves were off, and he felt more comfortable.

"You're out of line, Angela. Michael Knight is cocounsel on this case. Matter of fact, since I haven't entered an appearance yet, he's the only counsel on this case. Would you like to speak to him? He's listening to the conversation."

Mr. Devlin threw himself back in his chair. I knew he was eating up the uncomfortable pause on the other end of the line. I also knew that the "cocounsel" speech was to stuff Angela's patronizing remark down her throat. It still felt good.

I threw in a pleasant, "Good morning, Angela."

It seemed a nice complement to Mr. Devlin's salvo to put her on a first-name basis with the errand boy. She handled it by ignoring it.

"I have an offer. Do you want to hear it?"

She was back in character, and somehow it actually reduced the tension. Mr. Devlin stretched back, but his receiver was fine-tuned.

"What have you got for us, Angela?"

"Voluntary manslaughter. He takes the maximum, twenty years with the possibility of parole. Right now he's looking at life."

Mr. Devlin didn't stir. He sat there with his eyes closed. I couldn't believe he was considering it. Not this early in the case. I expected him to explode any second with a bit of well-phrased bravado that would put Angela in orbit and convey the message "no deal"—at least not yet.

The seconds ticked, and I could see storm clouds gathering over Rushmore. A plea bargain is something you accept, reject, or bargain against. This time there was a fourth option.

The fun of toying with the opposition was gone. Something heavy had settled in. I had an outside clue of what it was, and it jarred me more than anything that had happened the previous night.

Mr. Devlin leaned forward and lifted the phone out of its cradle. There was anger and something I didn't want to recognize in his voice.

"I'll be in touch with you, Angela."

The phone dropped into the cradle. He leaned back, and his eyes were closed again. Lex Devlin was an old warrior who bore the scars and the years on the inside. I had come to think of him as invincible. As I looked at him now, the age and the scars showed. The lines in that cragged face opened a glimpse of something I didn't want to see.

We both knew he could take on any prosecutor in the country and do it with a hopeless case and two hours' sleep and take most of the rounds. We also both sensed that this one had slipped into a different plane, a different kind of fight. Ten years ago it wouldn't have mattered. But it had been an expensive ten years on his resources, and I was embarrassed to be watching the old warrior taking a measure of what he had left.

"We have to tell Bradley about the offer, Mr. Devlin. Judge Bradley, too."

I knew I wasn't telling him anything he didn't know.

"Yeah. We'll tell 'em. I won't let him take it, though. Not till I know a hell of a lot more about this case."

He shook his head. "I don't like it."

"I don't either."

He looked over at me with a testing look. "Why not?"

"It doesn't fit with the characters. When I talked to the DA, she was practically salivating for Bradley's blood. The only thing she wanted more than his head on a platter was the governor's seat. This case could give it to her if she doesn't blow it. If she drops it to manslaughter on the deliberate shooting of Chinatown's favorite son, she's blown it. She'll have the Chinese community, the *Globe,* and all the law-and-order boys in her party ready to drop her. That offer didn't come from her. This isn't her call."

Mr. Devlin was out of his seat.

"Which means we'd better damn well find out whose call it is. The first rule in a fight, sonny, is to know who stands behind the man you're trying to knock down."

He grabbed the phone and punched the buttons with the old authority. He was back in the fight. I don't know what drove them out, but the doubts were gone. I could feel a rush of adrenalin in my own veins.

I heard a voice crackle on the other end of the line. Mr. Devlin seemed to be enjoying himself again.

"Conrad. You old Yankee. What are you doing to stay out of trouble these days?"

Mr. Devlin leaned back and laughed out loud at something that sounded like a crack about the Irish.

"If I said what I'm thinking, I'd be in confession tomorrow."

Whatever was said brought another laugh before the tone became serious.

"I want to chat with you, Conrad. I have a feeling the Indians have us surrounded. I want to know what tribe before I make a battle plan. Could you meet me for lunch?"

He smiled, so I gathered the date was set.

"No, not the Union League this time. I need neutral ground. Let's meet at the Marliave. I'll ask Tony for something upstairs. Noon? . . . Done."

He hung up and turned back to me.

"I want you there, sonny. This could be your head on the block, too. Conrad Munsey is chief clerk of the Mass. Supreme Judicial Court. He knows where every body's buried in this town and who put 'em there. We've swapped some favors over the years."

I nodded.

"So tell me what you found yesterday."

I filled him in on my bilingual chat with the woman in the restaurant. He wanted the details of everything said and every tone of voice. I told him about the fortune cookie from Red Shoes and the promise of help if I helped the prostitute who seemed to be doing very nicely without my help. When I finished, Mr. Devlin was wearing a scowl that seemed out of proportion, even given the bleakness of my report. I found it slightly unnerving.

"I'm willing to learn. Did I blow it?"

"I don't know."

He flipped the *Globe* to my side of the desk, opened to a story on page two, right opposite the men's suits ad for Filene's Basement. I read the headline over a Mike Eagan byline.

"BODY OF WOMAN DISCOVERED IN CHINATOWN."

I scanned it quickly, picking out words like "Asian" and "discovered before dawn" and "not yet identified."

I could feel a rock growing in the pit of my stomach. I was out of the chair and standing beside the desk while I asked Mr. Devlin if I could use his phone. He nodded, and I dialed police headquarters. It took a few seconds for the duty officer to transfer me to Manny Morales in the computer section.

"Manny, this is Michael Knight. I was in yesterday about the . . . virus in the . . ."

He cut me off before I got too far into it on a phone line that could have other ears.

"Right, Manny. You didn't tell me anything. You're a good cop. Or whatever. Listen, I need you not to tell me something else. This is a big favor. I owe you twice, *hermano*."

By this time I was full-pitch into a Puerto Rican accent, which raised Mr. Devlin's eyebrows halfway to his hairline. Meanwhile Manny was telling me to cut the PR crap and get to the point.

"I need you to play that computer and tell me about the dead girl they found in Chinatown early this morning. Anything you can tell me from the police report. Like who was she?"

All I heard was the click of the keys in the distance. The vision of the rigid, scared old lady in the restaurant stabbed at my conscience until it was replaced by the beautiful features of the prostitute, Mei-Li. Maybe she needed help more than she thought.

"There's not much here. She was beaten to death. Officer found her back in an alley off Beach Street by Harrison."

Mei-Li's territory.

"What did she look like, Manny? Young? Pretty?"

"Can't tell. She was beaten too badly to recognize. It was done by pros. They mutilated everything that could give an identification."

The rock in my stomach felt as if it was coming up.

"Where's the body now? I might be able to help with the identification."

"Not likely. She's at the morgue on South Street."

"Manny, can you get someone to get word down there that I'm on my way? Get me permission to see her. I mean it. Maybe I can help. This could be good for you."

"The best thing you could do for me is stop trying to lose my job for me."

"Manny, this is the last. I might have seen her last night. You don't have to mention that around the precinct. Just get me clearance to see her."

I HUNG UP BEFORE he could destroy my assumption that he would make the contact for me. I was running by the time I passed through the door. I was nearly at the elevator when Mr. Devlin's voice boomed through the corridor.

"Marliave! Noon!"

The door of the elevator almost closed on the words, "You be careful, sonny!"

10

I WAS TASTING THE ACID generated by the four sips I had taken of that barely remembered coffee, when I climbed the steps of the Suffolk County morgue. The burst of speed out of the gate at Mr. Devlin's office had trickled down to a crawl. Any morgue, to an outsider, is as pleasant as an IRS interviewing office. But this one in particular held the promise of an overwhelming cloud of guilt. The lining of my stomach ached at the thought of recognizing some aspect of the body that would tell me for the rest of my life that my dumb blundering had gotten Mei-Li killed.

Manny had done his thing. The man at the desk had my name. He gave me directions to the vault, a badge, and a slip of paper with numbers on it. I thanked God for the good brother. I have no idea what he told them, but it got me in without a police escort.

A man in green surgical clothes met me at the entrance. He took the slip in his latex-gloved hand and smiled. I smiled too. That was the extent of the conversation. I figured in his line of work he was used to the company of the less than chatty. He led the way into a room that looked like a bank vault, except that the safety deposit boxes could hold a sofa.

He checked the number on the slip against the numbers on the individual vaults until he found a match. He grabbed the handle and pulled. My heart went from one-twenty to two hundred. In the chill of that room, I was drenched.

I steeled myself for what I was about to see. I walked over beside the drawn metal pallet and looked down at what it held. I thought Manny's warning about the condition of the body had me prepared. I wasn't.

I hadn't eaten anything since the night before, so the only thing that could come up was pure stomach acid. It burned as I held my head over the stainless-steel sink that by some miracle I found in time. I wasn't sure my legs were not going to buckle, so I just hung on for a couple of minutes, trying to think of each piece of furniture in my apartment.

My silent guide held out a plastic cup of cold water. It helped. I could begin to focus on the reason I was there. In a few more minutes I could walk back to that disfigured, mangled body. If I had to identify it as Mei-Li or the old lady from the Ming Tree, or any female I had seen in a lifetime, I'd have had to say it could be any one of them. Most of the face was beaten into a nondescript mass of what I assumed to be flesh, and the body was the same. I couldn't even estimate the age.

I forced myself to look for any clue until I had to get out of there. I remember sitting in the outside room finishing the cup of water. There was the relief of not having made an identification of anyone whose life I'd touched on Monday, but it was soured with uncertainty.

The green-clad smiler was still there beside me.

"I know it's tough. I don't suppose you can make an ID?"

I shook my head. "Who could?"

His voice was soft and had a trace of unexpected compassion. "Who, indeed?"

He jotted something on a form and handed it to me.

"Give this to the man at the desk on the way out. Can you find it?"

An idea that I didn't want grabbed me before he cleared the door.

"Excuse me, do you have the clothes she was wearing when they brought her in?"

"Sure. Can you walk?"

I said, "Yes," but I wasn't all that sure till I tried it.

We came to another series of small lockers. He opened one of them. Everything was bagged and tagged in clear plastic baggies. He took the items out one by one. I was doing allright until he hit the bottom. My legs nearly buckled under me when I saw through the haze of the plastic a pair of bright red shoes.

Outside, a series of deep breaths of that cold sea-air that blows in from Boston Harbor when the wind's from the east helped clear the fog inside. I needed to think through my next move, because I could see myself on the witness stand trying to defend it sometime in the future.

It was pure instinct that told me to keep the identification, such as it was, to myself until I could put some thought behind it. If I had mentioned that the dead girl was probably the waitress from the Ming Tree, the next question would be, "How did you meet her?"

"I went there for dinner last night."

"What brought you there?"

"I felt like pork lo mein."

"Did you go there to see anyone in particular?"

I could bluff a "no," but it wouldn't hold up. They'd check and find out that I went there to see Mrs. Lee, their hidden witness. That could only lead to one question.

"How'd you find out about Mrs. Lee?"

Dead end. I couldn't turn in Manny for the tips he gave me, and our crusading DA could put me before a grand jury. My next appearance would be as a roommate of Anthony Bradley in the Suffolk County jail for contempt of court for refusing to answer the question.

My thought processes confirmed my instincts.

On the other hand, what could I do about the dead girl? How could I begin to unravel the ball of twine that tied together poor, dead Red Shoes, the prostitute she led me to, the Harvard student who happened into Chinatown and became a pawn of the Chinese Mafia, and the unfortunate old man who got caught in the line of fire? I needed a game plan more than the Boston Celtics, and nothing brilliant was coming to mind.

I let the thoughts bounce off each other in the back of a Checker cab while we cruised at the speed of morning traffic back toward the office.

The cabbie took Boylston Street up toward Washington. Last night's snow gave a peaceful, slumbering aspect to the Public Garden. I wondered where they kept the swan boats during the winter. I could see some of the webbed footprints of Canadian geese.

The cabbie was swinging into the right lane to continue up Boylston, when I came out of the seat and pounded on the glass.

"Hook a left on Charles! Over the bridge! I'll give you the lefts and rights. Let's move!"

Those damn goose prints in the snow. They brought back something I must have been too tired to understand, but not too tired to notice.

I had the cabbie up to fifty over the Longfellow Bridge. I rode him from behind the window all the way. I even appealed to his dark complexion in Spanish until I read his license and realized the dark complexion came from Beirut.

All the way I kept seeing what had never registered on my dream state the previous night—those three sets of fresh footprints in the snow coming out of the no-name coffee shop and tracking in Harry's direction.

I doubled the fare for a tip. He earned it, and I had no time to wait for change. I jumped out as he almost came to a stop at Harry's apartment house.

I took the stone steps in flying triplets in front of the brick-faced, four-story building. The whole layout was neat and precise enough to appeal to the MIT engineers who populated it. I'd have bet my life that the intercom was in perfect working order.

I hit the "Dr. Wong" button and prayed while waiting.

Nothing.

I pushed the button again and prayed a little harder.

The speaker system came on, but I couldn't understand the words.

"Harry, it's me. What're you saying?"

I heard the door buzz and grabbed the knob before it stopped. I double-timed the steps to the third floor. The door to Harry's apartment was standing open halfway down the hall, but there was no one behind it.

I walked into the well-laid-out living room. It was replete with white leather furniture, a stereo system that would have served Stevie Wonder, and a wet bar. Everything but Harry.

"Harry? Where the hell are you?"

A sound that made my skin crawl came from the sofa with its back to me. I looked over the back and saw a meatball sandwich.

The Harry I knew had a yellow-cream complexion with smooth, regular features. The face of the man on the couch looked like a Mr. Potato Head in the hands of a warped child. The colors ranged from raging purple to sallow. The stitches under the eyes looked vicious. It was the second identification that morning I couldn't make with certainty.

I gagged out, "Harry?"

One hand came up in a limp wave.

"Can you tell me what happened?"

He mumbled a few syllables, but I wasn't getting information.

"Harry, let me guess. Those three goons from the coffee shop caught up with you. Dear Lord, what did they hit you with?"

Something came out that sounded like "steel pipe" or "sledgehammer." I'd have believed either.

"Who sewed you up? Did someone get you to Mass General?"

He nodded slightly. What came out sounded like "cab driver."

I came around and dropped into the chair beside him.

"I'm not cut out for this line of work, Harry. So far I got one girl killed . . ." His eyes came up. "The little waitress from the Ming Tree. I just saw her at the morgue."

The eyelids came back down in internal pain.

"And now you."

When I said, "I'm sorry," it reached a record level of inadequacy.

"Can I get you something? Water, Scotch, hemlock?"

The cracked lips barely parted in a smile, and I had a feeling he might live.

He started to move, and I could tell from the contorted features that they had given equal attention to the ribs. In spite of the pain, he sat up against the pillows.

"I'm sorry I sucked you into this thing, Harry. I guess you were right about this white skin being insurance. The only ones who are getting it are Chinese."

"Don't count on it, Mike."

He was still mumbling, but I was learning to pull the words through.

"What do you mean?"

"You're pushing them." He waved vaguely at his face. "This is a warning to you. The girl had to go. She was your contact. Keep pushing, and they're going to run out of Chinese. Then it's your turn."

I leaned back against the folds of my overcoat.

"That's the problem, Harry. I don't know where to push next. So far all the points have gone to Yale."

Harry knew that was shorthand for the bad guys.

"I've got one more witness to see in Chinatown. Maybe I can do it without getting anyone killed."

Harry rolled slowly upright. I admired the effort.

"Who?"

"What's the difference? You're out of the game, buddy. You played well, but I'm putting you on the DL. It's not your fight."

He looked at me with what started as a scowl, but relaxed when it pulled the stitches.

"It's more my fight than it is yours."

The words were stronger, and as I looked at him, he had a point.

"The other witness runs a Chinese herbal medicine shop on Tyler Street."

Harry shook his head. "Not good."

"Why not? I've got to do it sooner or later."

"Later. Give it a couple of days. They'll be expecting you now. You'll be playing into their hands. You won't get anything now, except maybe hurt."

"Really. Any other reason?"

"Yeah. In a couple of days I'll go with you. You'd be as lost in Chinatown as I would in Puerto Rico. When's the trial?"

"Hasn't been set yet. The DA'd have it marked up tomorrow if she could. We've got a few weeks. I don't know about you going with me. They don't seem to value Chinese life. I don't want to lose you. Thanksgiving'd never be the same."

"I'm serious, Mike. It's my fight. I've seen a lot of my friends bend under their power. I've always told myself I'm a different kind of Chinese. I'm an MIT Chinese. Different world. It's the same world, Mike. No more hiding places."

I caught a look at the clock. I could just make the Marliave by noon.

"Gotta run, Harry. Whatever you need, let me know."

The last words I heard on the way out the door were, "Call me, Mike. You need me."

No argument.

11

THE MARLIAVE IS A TINY but authentic chunk of Rome, ripped out of the eternal city and dropped unspoiled onto a corner of the block between School and Bromfield Streets. The stone steps leading up to the entrance once led to the Royal Gardens when King George's royal governors were housed a block away.

Noon was a memory, but a recent memory, by the time I climbed those steps to the entrance.

The line of customers at the door suffered not gladly my weaving and squeezing my way close to the front of the line. I had a nodding acquaintance with the maitre d' from past occasions, which was usually good for a smile, a handshake, and a prediction of twenty minutes to the next table.

I caught his eye and mouthed the words, "Is Mr. Devlin here yet?"

I think he misunderstood and thought I said the pope was awaiting my arrival. He moved the head-of-the-liners out of my way and led me like the returning son to a small upstairs chamber in the back.

The room had the same Romanesque charm that pervaded the Marliave. It held one single table at which were gathered Lex Devlin, a dapper little dude of about the same vintage, whom I assumed to be Conrad Munsey, and a third, gaping chair.

Lex acknowledged my arrival with an eyebrow and a nod toward the chair, which I took as an invitation to join the fun. When he introduced me as "the late Mr. Knight," I realized that "noon" did not mean "or so, at your convenience." I was gratified, however, that though he may never use it to my face, he still remembered my name.

Conrad Munsey, our dinner companion, was another piece of work. Judging from his sitting position, I estimated that he'd come about up to my chin. He had bright eyes and a sharp little moustache. In fact, everything about him, from his salt-and-pepper hair, which looked as if it were trimmed hourly, to his diminutive but perfectly formed body, which he had tucked into a tidy, dark three-piece suit with the correct, conservative tie, bespoke nobody's fool.

I sensed comfort and probably more than mutual respect between Mr. Devlin and Mr. Munsey. I remembered Mr. Devlin saying they "go back."

I shook hands with Mr. Munsey and received a menu from the waiter. I was about to open it, when a red-haired man of about fifty years swept in from the kitchen and snatched the menus out of the hands of the three of us. Judging from the fine Italian wool of his suit, I figured he was not the busboy.

"Mr. Devlin, you never need a menu. What do you feel like? A little veal? A little pasta first, maybe a white sauce? You like my anti-pasto. I'll fix it myself. What do you think? You leave it to me?"

I saw the softest side of Lex Devlin I'd ever seen when he smiled and touched our host on the arm.

"We couldn't be in better hands, Vincenzo."

That widened the smile. Vincenzo gestured to the waiter and mentioned a particularly good *vino blanco*.

"Whoa, Vincenzo. No wine for this gentleman and myself. Connie, you suit yourself."

I didn't remember being consulted on the wine refusal, but apparently I was riding shotgun on Mr. Devlin's wagon. No sweat. If the boss was suggesting that I had two days' clear-headed work to do that afternoon, he was reading my mind.

When the room cleared and Vincenzo delicately closed the door to the outside room, Lex leaned across the table.

"Let's talk, Connie. There's a rumbling in the hills. I don't like it. I wanted to see if you're picking anything up."

Mr. Munsey's eyes were crackling, and his lips did something that put his moustache at a tilt, but nothing came out.

Mr. Devlin sat back. "You have no problem with Mr. Knight, Connie. We're on the same side. He needs to know where the shots are coming from, too. They could blindside either one of us."

Munsey took a couple of seconds on that one, but Mr. Devlin's confidence apparently won out. There was no one else in the room, but Mr. Munsey leaned in a bit before he spoke.

"Something's cooking. I'm getting more uncomfortable by the day. I remember the last time, and so do you. What tipped you this time, Lex?"

"The right honorable Mrs. Lamb. First she wanted to hang Bradley's fleece on the courthouse door. That was honest ambition. She'd convict Kermit the Frog if it'd get her to the statehouse. That side of her I believed. This morning she calls with an offer of a reduced charge. No headlines. Could even look like a slap in the face to the Chinese community—and every other minority community. And if you read what I think you do, you know that the whole Chinese community is torn up over this murder. That move didn't come from our Mrs. Lamb, Connie. Her lips were moving, but someone was feeding her the words. If it's true, I need to know who. I thought maybe those foxy ears of yours might have picked up something in the wind."

The moustache curled into a foxy grin.

"Could be that she heard that the redoubtable Lex Devlin was leading the defense, and she decided to withdraw to safer shoals."

Mr. Devlin leaned across the table. Only his eyes were smiling. "Could be that you're full of enough bovine feces to fertilize Ireland, Mr. Munsey."

They were six inches apart. "That would be *Northern Ireland,* Mr. Devlin. You could handle that rowdy southern province with no help from anyone."

For the second time since I'd known him, a smile cracked Mr. Devlin's lips. "It's not much of a compliment, Mr. Munsey, but I'll give it to you anyway. You're a credit to your race."

"I'll say the same for you, Mr. Devlin. And heaven knows your race needs all the credit it can get."

I could be wrong, but as I listened to this verbal tennis match, I could swear that the brogues of these two Boston-bred colonials thickened progressively, one from Dublin, the other from Ulster. It was the arrival of three antipastos in the hands of Vincenzo that called a halt. When the door closed, and the antipastos had been sampled, the smiles were gone.

"What have you heard, Connie?"

"Nothing concrete, Lex. Let me tell you what I've noticed. The boys have been restless. The morning that indictment came down against young Bradley, there were messages flying between them and little clusters of them meeting in each other's offices. The tone, you might say, was distinctly jubilant."

"I take it that's not their usual condition. Incidentally, sonny, 'the boys' are the esteemed justices of the Massachusetts Supreme Judicial Court, of which our Mr. Munsey has been the chief clerk since the memory of man runneth not to the contrary."

I nodded, not wanting to interrupt the flow.

"The 'usual condition' of the crowd I'm talking about is benign indifference to each other at best. Incidentally, I'm not talking about all of them. It's mainly Winston, Carter, Fulbright. Masterson and Chambers may be part of it. Carlyle doesn't show much emotion about anything, but he was in on some of the meetings. The others—Keefe, Samuels, and Reynolds—seemed unaffected. As I say, there was a big mood swing. This is why I tie it to the Bradley business. The morning of the indictment, they were a jolly little play group. Later in the day, when word had it that you were saddling up on the side of young Bradley—I'm serious about this—the mood changed. They were a bunch of tense little puppies. That was yesterday afternoon. I noticed little clusters of meetings erupting all afternoon. What does it mean?" He shrugged. "I don't know."

"That's interesting, Connie. I know your collection of Supreme Judicial conservatives isn't losing any sleep over the fate of our black defendant or the old Chinese man. Obviously, the focus is Judge Bradley's chances of joining their club. Does it really shake them that badly?"

"It's not so much Bradley himself. They could ignore him like they do Keefe and the rest. It's whom he'd replace. Fulbright's pushing eighty, and he appears less and less in chambers. I think his health is more of a problem than he's telling anyone. That means that if he goes and Bradley replaces him, you've got an old-guard conservative out and a confirmed civil rights liberal in. There goes the delicate balance of power, at least on civil rights issues."

"Come on, Connie. Do they still care that much about civil rights? What bastions are left to fall? We've got legislation on open housing, job discrimination, voting."

"And still the most segregated society north of Birmingham. For all of the legislation, how many blacks live in Brookline? How many whites live in Roxbury? If you had a child, would you send him to school in Roxbury?"

"Granted, and that's my point. You can't tell me those tired old men still think they're saving the world from the rising minorities. Hell, you could pack the court with Bradleys and in ten years Brookline still wouldn't send their kids to school in Roxbury. It'll take more than Bradley to change that."

Munsey held both palms up. "I'm only telling you what I see. But I'll tell you two more things."

He cut off the discourse while the antipasto plates were cleared and the finest magic I've ever seen worked on veal was placed before us. Vincenzo served it personally, and again remembered to close the door behind him. Munsey spoke before a bite of the veal was tasted.

"You've got two facts here. First fact, the boys go into a tizzy when this Bradley business breaks. Then there's another flurry of activity when the great Lex Devlin comes out of retirement for the defense. Fact two, coincidentally our crusading prosecutor offers a deal of leniency that runs against her personal best interests. Not in character. Can we agree on that?"

Munsey paused while Mr. Devlin nodded.

"Which leaves us with the question, is there a connection? And if so, what's the grip they have on her?"

"And more to the point, Connie, why would they care enough to pull that kind of string, if in fact they have influence over her to begin with? No, I don't see it. They may have a rooting interest in who joins their club, but I don't buy the civil rights angle as anything serious. They're not that afraid of Judge Bradley."

Munsey sat back with his eyebrows raised for dramatic effect.

"Correct me if I'm wrong, Mr. Devlin, but was it not yourself that called me out of concern over the strange turn of events?"

"I know, and I appreciate the information, Connie. I don't think that's the answer, though. You know, there's another possibility. We could be looking in the wrong direction. Maybe the DA found a serious hole in her case and dropped back to a charge she thought she could prove. A conviction on a lesser charge would still be better for her than losing the case outright."

Munsey dropped his voice a little, and I noticed he was looking right into Mr. Devlin's eyes.

"I'll say just one more thing. The last time I can remember the bees stirring in the hive this way goes back to the *Dolson* case."

I was looking at Mr. Munsey, but I could almost feel the effect of those words on Mr. Devlin. I could tell that Mr. Munsey was taking it in, too.

"You know yourself, Lex, there was a lot more to that case than ever came to the surface."

Mr. Devlin's voice was quiet and heavy, but not unsure.

"Let it rest, Connie. There's no connection. Is that all?"

"That's the best I can do, Lex. I'm one of their breed, so they're happy to have me as chief clerk. But they don't invite me to sit around the campfire."

Lex nodded. "Thanks, Connie. We'll carry on the war with an eye to our backs."

12

WE LEFT THE MARLIAVE at about one o'clock. The parting hand-shakes took place on School Street, with Mr. Munsey walking north toward Tremont Street, Mr. Devlin walking south toward Washington Street and ultimately the office, and me cutting behind Old City Hall, ostensibly to catch the train for Harvard Square to check out Bradley's friends. Actually, I doubled back and intercepted Mr. Munsey at the top of School Street. He was surprised and not altogether comfortable with the return engagement.

"Mr. Munsey, I wonder if I could walk along with you a bit."

"Public sidewalk, kid."

My estimate was right. He came about up to my chin, but self-assurance and the secure knowledge of who he was and who I was gave him another six inches.

"I think you touched a nerve back there, Mr. Munsey. I know you didn't want to aggravate it. I can understand. But I'd like to know more about the *Dolson* case."

He registered nothing. We kept walking.

"There's a reason, Mr. Munsey. There are two reasons. Like you, I think there's more to this change of heart by the DA than appears on the surface. It might be critical to Bradley's case. I get the feeling we're like little rodents in a maze. We're running after the cheese without knowing there's a technician who keeps changing the pattern."

I gave him a good gap before he said anything.

"You said there are two reasons."

"Mr. Devlin's tough, but I think he's tied up in knots over whatever this Dolson case is about. I guess I care that whatever happened to him before doesn't happen again. Maybe I could do some intercepting."

We reached the coffee shop in the Center Plaza complex without word one. Suddenly he beckoned with his head and turned into the coffee shop. I followed him to a table in the rear of the shop, clear of other customers.

"Sit down, kid."

Age or not, I figured it was time for some ground-standing.

"Mr. Munsey, I take it when Mr. Devlin calls me 'sonny.' But 'kid'? What do I have to do to get a name?"

"Earn it! They don't call him 'Mr. Devlin' for his age. It's respect for the man he made of himself. Sit down, will you, kid?"

I sat. There are some points even a lawyer doesn't argue.

"You want to hear about the *Dolson* case. Don't they talk about it over at Bilson?

"Never. At least not to the associates."

"Good. And you won't either. You understand me?"

He seemed to take one more look at me to confirm his decision. When he started, I had to strain to hear the words.

"This goes back more than ten years. Lex was, as a criminal trial lawyer . . . the master, the best."

"I know. I've heard."

"You know nothing. You haven't seen his likes at the bar in the last ten years. Anyway, he took on a client named Dolson. He was a petty hood. He had a few arrests on suspicion of arson, extortion. Couple of misdemeanor convictions. Nothing too serious. This time he's charged with a major arson, a vacant apartment building down in a run-down section of the South End. The job, if he did it, went bad. The fire spread to the two apartment buildings on either side. They went up like tinder. The clincher was an explosion that brought down most of the building.

"The police got a tip that Dolson lit the match. They picked him up, and he confessed to the arson. He pleaded guilty at the arraignment.

"Then it hit the fan. It took a couple of days to plow through the crumbled building. Everyone thought it was vacant. Anyway, they discovered a few bodies under the rubble. Probably street people who got in out of the cold.

"Now the charge is felony murder. Dolson didn't want to confess to that, so he reneged on his arson confession. He withdrew his guilty plea and hired Lex."

I didn't want to interrupt, but you never know if you'll think of the question again.

"How could a petty hood afford what Mr. Devlin must have been charging?"

"Well, that was part of the problem. The prosecution showed that a sizable deposit was made in an account set up in Dolson's name just after the arson. That was part of the prosecution's case. That, plus an eyewitness who spotted him around the building just before it went up.

"Dolson came up with an alibi. Another punk named Gallagher. I can't believe I remember that name after ten years. Anyway, he testified that Dolson was with him. On the other hand, he looked as if he'd testify that he was Jimmy Hoffa if there was a drink in it. Even Lex himself will tell you it was the weakest defense he ever had to present. Dolson came up with some story that he'd been hired to plead guilty to the arson. The money in his account was to take the fall and do a few years in prison for someone else."

I cut in again. "Who was the someone else?"

"Dolson said he never knew."

"Who paid him the money?"

"He said he never knew that, either. He said it was all arranged over the phone. Anyway, the case was tried, and went to the jury. Three days later, they came back hopelessly deadlocked. A hung jury. One juror held out.

"Now it gets sticky. The assistant DA has the case marked up for retrial before a new jury right away. The next thing Lex knows is that he gets an offer from the assistant DA to drop the felony-murder charge down to negligent homicide, go with the arson, and work a deal for a sentence of six years, probable parole in two. Dolson jumped at it.

"Lex had a couple of problems with the plea bargain. He had a client who first insisted that he was innocent and paid to plead guilty. Now the client insists on pleading guilty and is wishy-washy on whether he actually committed the crime. If he didn't do it, then the whole guilty plea was a fraud on the court."

"What other problem?"

Munsey was sitting close, but he checked the area and moved a bit closer.

"I'm going to tell you this, kid, because I want you to understand fact from rumor. First the rumor. Word got out that the first jury had been fixed. The hold-out juror was supposed to have been bought. The rumors hung it on Lex. There was talk of an investigation by the disciplinary committee of the bar, maybe even prosecution. The fact is that the whole thing, if there was anything to begin with, was dropped as soon as the plea bargain went down. The rumor going around was that Lex worked a deal to have the investigation into jury tampering quashed if he got his client to plead guilty."

"That's bull. Are you telling me that anyone believed Mr. Devlin would fix a jury?"

"Get off the stand, kid. I'm telling you what was going around the bars."

I knew that something had hit Mr. Devlin like a tank, but this was out of the range of my guesswork.

"Mr. Munsey, I've only known him a short time, but I'd sooner bet that my grandmother would fix the World Series."

"I don't know your grandmother, kid, but there was another reason for the rumor."

I knew I wouldn't like this one, but I asked anyway. Mr. Munsey gnawed his teeth a bit before he could get it out.

"It could have been true. Don't split a gut. Listen to me. Ten years ago, what I said about Lex being the best was true. He was a hell of a lawyer. Hell of a man. He was Darrow and Marshall. . . . After that, it wasn't the same Lex. Even Zeus can get pulled down from Olympus."

"I don't believe it." The words jumped out of me on instinct.

"You want to hear this or don't you? You got me this far. You're going to hear the rest of it. And open your eyes, kid. You do Lex a disservice if you think he's more than human."

I settled down and nodded.

"Ten years ago, Lex was going through hell. His wife, Dolly, they'd been married twenty-eight years. He idolized her, and with good reason. She went through a year of fighting cancer that wound up killing her. It killed most of him, too. It kicked the will out of him. Another thing. He'd always been a good-time drinker. It goes with the profession, but he always had it in control. After Dolly died, it got away from him. This Dolson thing came along when he was about three feet from the bottom. It wasn't the old Lex making the judgments."

I felt as if my heart had come to rest in the pit of my stomach. "I still don't believe it. Some things in a man just can't change."

He stood up and started buttoning his coat. I stood up too.

"Nobly spoken, kid. But as a Lex Devlin fan, you're new to the game. I've been at it for over sixty years. We both came from the same neighborhood in Charlestown. Did he tell you that? You might say I was his first client. At nine years old, he took on three tough Irish kids to get me out of a scrape. They didn't take much to a little Protestant kid in that neighborhood. We became like brothers, which, I must say, took a lot of guts on his part.

"When Dolly's illness came on, I was with him on the whole ride down. And during the years afterwards. When he got himself together, it took me five years before I could talk Old Man Dawes at your esteemed law firm into putting him back in harness. If you ever say that to Lex, I'll deny it, and probably have to punch you in the mouth. You understand, kid?"

As I looked down at him, his moustache came about up to my chest, but I believed him. I said it with a nod.

He shook his head. "Even at that, when he joined Dawes's firm, he wouldn't go near a criminal case. That Dolson business was the straw that broke his back. I hate to see him in this one."

"You said something about the reaction of the Massachusetts Supreme Judicial Court being the same on this case as in Dolson. What did you mean?"

"Not the court, kid. Just some of its inhabitants. It's hard to describe. The Dolson case never reached the court on appeal since it ended in a guilty plea, but if there'd been a conviction, Lex would have taken it up. He'd said as much. Lex believed Dolson was innocent during that first trial. The trial judge wouldn't allow Lex to put in evidence of the telephone conversations where Dolson claimed he made a deal to plead guilty. The judge ruled them out on hearsay. Lex said his ruling was dead wrong. He would have taken it up if there hadn't been a hung jury."

"So it never got to the court . . ."

"I know, but I remember the buzz that went on among those justices I was talking about. It was as if they were trying to decide the case *just in case* it went up. Anyway, I never saw anything like it before or since, until the Bradley case. Maybe I'm just superstitious. The last time, Lex almost went down for the count on a jury-tampering charge. I wish he'd never gotten into this one."

"You know better than I do, Mr. Munsey, but he seems to be thriving on it. Maybe it's what he needed."

Munsey looked at me as if he wanted to say something, but he just put on his Russian fur-ball hat and pulled the flaps down over his ears.

He was on his way out, when I thought I heard him mumble something like, "Watch his back, kid."

13

WHEN I LEFT MR. DEVLIN, the plan was that I'd take the train to Harvard to talk to Anthony Bradley's acquaintances, particularly the friend who went to Chinatown with him the day of the murder. After talking to Conrad Munsey, something seemed more pressing.

Since I was practically at the courthouse anyway, I went to the office of the clerk of the superior court. Trial records are public documents, which meant that I had the right to see the record of the Dolson case. Having the right is one thing; having the record of a ten-year-old trial excavated by a civil servant in the clerk's office can be another. In this case, the paper chase was cut to a minimum by an old tippling friendship with one of the docket clerks. I could always count on Tony Boyle to short-circuit procedures and fly direct. It was totally legal, but the occasional Jameson's on the rocks at the 77 after work hours never stood in the way of progress.

In an hour, I was at a side table, rifling through the familiar forms of indictment, bench warrant, pretrial motions, transcript of evidence, etc., through the dismissal of the hung jury. It read true to Mr. Munsey's telling of the tale.

I noticed in the transcript of testimony that Mr. Devlin had tried everything short of dynamite to get in evidence of the out-of-court statements of whoever it was that contacted Dolson by phone about buying his confession and service of the jail time. Judge Bennett, the trial judge, upheld every objection of the assistant district attorney on the grounds of hearsay. If the trial hadn't ended in a hung jury, I'd have bet my next paycheck that Mr. Devlin could have had the conviction reversed on appeal.

That came as no great shock. The Honorable Judge Bennett's qualifications for the bench had been that he had been a bagman for the right political party. It was no surprise that his track record on evidentiary rulings was as weak ten years ago as I'd experienced it in modern times.

One thing that never came out in the trial, mostly because of the suppression of Dolson's evidence, was who owned the building that was torched. That nagging question hung on after I had returned the file to Tony and hesitated over which direction to take from the clerk's office.

Curiosity won out. I followed the catacomb tunnels to the registry of deeds. I had to lean heavily on what I had learned in first-year real property to decipher the chain of title. Fortunately, it was uncomplicated. Unfortunately, it was a dead end. The building where the fire started was owned by a real-estate corporation that was already in bankruptcy at the time of the fire.

The bankruptcy clerk at federal court did a quick check for me while I held the phone and found that the creditors of the corporation—the only ones who could have profited from an insurance windfall—were many, widespread, and relatively insignificant. In other words, there was no motive for a risky torching there.

I was ready to pack it up, when an obtuse thought occurred. As long as I was in the registry of deeds anyway, could it hurt to check the owners of the two properties on either side of the torched building? Testimony in the Dolson trial indicated that they were "accidentally" burned out, too. Since it seemed irrelevant at the time, nobody questioned the "accidental" nature of the burning of two side buildings.

What I struck could have been gold dust. It could also have been pyrite. At the least, though, it was interesting. The building to the left of the torched building had been owned for a year by a corporation called Adams Leasing, Inc. So what? Well, nothing, until I saw that the building to the right of the said torched building had been purchased one month before the said torching by Adams Leasing, Inc. All three buildings had been totally destroyed. While the insurance payoff to the main torched building would have been held up because of the arson, the insurance company would have no grounds to hold up the payoff on the buildings to either side.

The question then became who owned Adams Leasing, Inc. That was not a matter of public record. That was a matter for private detection. It was now four o'clock and ticking, and I hadn't begun the day's work at Harvard. I decided to gain speed by doing what the bike racers call "drafting"—riding in the wake of a rider who has taken the trail ahead of me.

I went back to the superior court clerk's office to see if there was any pending litigation against Adams Leasing, Inc. The chances were good, since any company that leased apartments, particularly roach farms, was probably a familiar name on the court docket. True to form, Adams Leasing had a string of civil suits against it.

I ran the list until I came across a slip-and-fall case based on the dangerous condition of an apartment. The key factor was that the plaintiff's attorney was a law-school classmate to whom I had lost enough money over a two-hand poker deck during the third year of law school to claim him as a dependant.

Gene Martino was one of those ferreting kinds of lawyers, who keeps on ferreting long after most lawyers turn off the light. He ferrets for the sake of ferreting. He once told me that he can beat better lawyers because they learn *everything necessary* about a case. He learns *everything* about a case. I decided to "draft" on Gene's particular talent.

I got the number from the court records and made the call on my cell phone in the lower lobby of the courthouse. Gene's secretary buzzed him.

"Mike! How you doing? How about a little two-hand poker? My rent's due." He cackled.

I laughed at his little funny—not because I found it humorous, but because it was the best lead-in to a favor.

"Hi, Gene, you son of a gun. You're still looking for a fish."

"No way, Mike. I never thought of you that way. It was just a friendly way of passing the time."

"What I remember passing was money for lunches, carfare, dates . . ."

"Hey, we had fun, didn't we, Mikey?"

If I told him the truth, or for that matter told him that the next time he called me "Mikey" I'd feed that phone to him from one or both of two directions, he might have been inclined to deny me the favor. I wimped out.

"Hell of a time, Gene. I'll never forget it."

"So what've you been up to?"

"I've been up to getting myself into a position where I need to ask a favor, Gene. You've got a case against Adams Leasing, right?"

"That I do. Slip and fall. I'm gonna hammer 'em, Mikey. You're not representing those scum buckets?"

"No. No, no. No connection. Actually, I need some information. And if anybody has information, you're the man, Gene."

"You got that right, Mikey. Gimme a try. What do you need?"

"Did you ever find out from depositions or interrogatories who owns Adams Leasing?"

"Did I find out? It pains me that you ask. Would Gene Martino walk into a courtroom against a corporation without knowing who manicures the fingernails of every secretary in the place? Come on, Mikey. That's basics."

It was music to my ears to hear old self-deprecating Gene brag on because I knew he couldn't stop himself from backing up the bravado with his ferreted information. I had but to turn the spigot to open the flow.

"I know you, Gene, but that can be tough information to come by. Those people guard the names of the owners pretty carefully."

"Mikey. Listen to me. It's wholly owned by a holding company. Which tells you nothing, because it's just a dummy corporation owning the stock of another corporation. What you really want is who owns the stock of the holding company. That took some doing. It's wholly owned by a limited partnership. I can give you the name of the general partner of the limited partnership. It's right here. It's Robert Loring. Want his address? He's at 495 Federal Street."

I was writing on the back of an old Bruins ticket as fast as I could. "Gene, you're golden. Now for the big one. Who are the limited partners?"

"I'm working on it, Mikey. I got a deposition of Loring on Wednesday. I'll dig till I get it. You still at Bilson?"

"That's where I call home."

"I'll get you there."

"Geno, it was worth every dime, every penny I begrudgingly lost to you, every aggravating hour listening to that grinding East Boston accent of yours, to come to this moment."

Actually, I just thought that. What I said was, "You're a prince, Gene. I hope I can repay the favor."

I HAD TO TOUCH a couple of bases at the office. Harvard could wait another hour.

The old offices at Bilson, Dawes actually looked good. For some reason, the nods and smiles of the secretaries and paralegals carried a bit of what I self-indulgently sensed as respect. The usual attitude toward associates, particularly on the part of the fossilized queens of dictation of the more senior partners, is that of a day-care matron toward a child whose nose won't stop running. I silently thanked Judge Bradley for throwing me into a case and an association with Mr. Alexis Devlin that boosted my status three rungs on the food chain.

I was walking proudly by the time I reached Julie's desk. Needless to say, none of the above commentary went for Julie. I always thanked God for granting me a human being for a secretary. This particular blessing came with a concomitant curse.

Just as Julie was raising her eyebrows while she asked, "How are you and 'Lex' getting along?" I heard my name whined in the adenoidal tones of junior partner Whitney Caster.

"Knight, I want to see you."

I smiled at Julie and whispered, "Lex wants to adopt me. Would you prepare the forms?"

Julie's giggle was stepped on by a second whining outburst. "Now, Knight!"

I moved slowly backwards toward Caster's office while asking Julie, "Anything critical?"

She said, "Mr. Malone called three times about the Keilly case. He wants to set up a deposition."

"Tell him to give me a break. That case won't go to trial for two years. What else?"

"Mark Shuman wants a date for pretrial motions on the copyright case."

"When did he call?"

"Yesterday morning."

"No sweat. Mark's tuned in. He's heard what's going on. He won't press it. Anything else? I mean critical."

"Bob Casey just called about the Detroit Red Wings game tomorrow night."

"That's critical. And painful. Would you tell him it's impossible? Maybe the Black Hawks in two weeks."

From behind me, at a ten-decibel increase, "KNIGHT!"

Julie stifled a grin. "That man's gonna split a hemorrhoid if you don't get in there."

I smiled back. "Is that a promise?"

Caster was a nice shade of pink by the time I was looking across his desk at him. I'm sure the fear of losing the power of having me on voice commands had nearly driven him to distraction. My finally-obedient presence before him came just before he started sucking his thumb.

"Did you call me, Whitney?"

Any form of "yes" would have sent Julie into a case of the un-stiflable giggles. I think he appreciated that, because he finessed the question.

"Knight, I have an idea. I want you to go back and reargue that motion to suppress discovery before Judge Bradley."

I could see his weasely little mind working. He was salivating at the thought of Judge Bradley finding it difficult to deny my motion when I was in the midst of representing his son. More to the point, if I won the motion, Whitney could see himself garnering the credit with the seniors for coming up with the ploy.

"Whitney, baby, you don't have enough brains or ethics to realize that a man of Judge Bradley's character would recuse himself from the case before he'd play into your sniggering little plot."

I liked the sound of that, but it never actually passed these restrained lips. What came out was, "That's an idea, Whitney. I'll get on it."

"You do that, Knight," he whined as he busied himself with lofty legal issues in a brief. I was dismissed. I curtsied, and turned for the door.

I let him sink comfortably into the euphoria of self-admiration for his crafty little scheme before turning back.

"One more thing, Whitney. When Judge Bradley sees this motion marked up for rehearing, he'll probably think we're trying to put the squeeze play on him. My bet is that he'll be on the horn to Mr. Devlin in about six seconds to tell Mr. Devlin that he views the ethics of the rest of his law firm as beneath contempt. Mr. Devlin will be climbing up my back in about four seconds to find out whose idea this was in the first place. At that point . . ."

The pink had run from Whitney's cheeks. He was nothing if not protective of his little pinched posterior.

"Hold off on that, Knight. You've probably got other things more pressing."

"As a matter of fact, Whitney . . ." I thought of the Red Wings game I'd be missing.

14

I NEEDED THE PRIVACY of my office for what I was about to do. As I closed the door, I tried to think of the last time I had spent serious time there. It predated the Lothrop hearing before Judge Bradley, which seemed like a century ago.

Tom Burns was a private detective whom the firm used on a semi-regular basis. He was not inexpensive, but his rates still beat having a lawyer do certain types of legwork. He was also better than the rest of us when the information required serious private detection. I had worked with him enough to be able to play with the cards up.

"Hi, Mike. How goes?"

"Good, Tom. You alone?"

"Alone enough."

"I mean *alone* alone. This is really sensitive."

I heard him ask his secretary to type up what he had given her. I listened for the door to close in the background.

"What do you need, Mike?"

"I've got something for you, Tom, if you'll do it. I'm going to level with you. This is not authorized by anyone in the firm. A certain big guy down the hall would put me into a submarine sandwich if he knew I was doing this."

"I heard you were working with A.D. And you can still sit up and take nourishment. You're a survivor, Mike."

"You know what they say—that which doesn't kill us makes us strong. It could still go either way. Have you got some time free in the next day or so?"

"No. What do you need, Mike?"

"There was a case ten years ago this March, *Commonwealth v. Dolson*, Suffolk Superior Court. It was a hung jury. The names and addresses of the jurors on that case are in the record. I need to know if there were any radical changes in the lifestyle of any of the jurors, say in the next year after the case ended. You know what I'm looking for."

"I know what you want. Any cash windfalls that could be a payoff."

"You got it. I have a hunch it could be connected to this Bradley case. But it's just a hunch. I can't get you authorization from any of the partners. Lex Devlin's the only one involved in this case, and he'd split a gut if he knew what we were opening up."

"You're playing with dynamite here, Mike. That was the case where they said Lex Devlin . . ."

"I know. I don't believe it, Tom. It was never proven or disproven. It's been sucking the blood out of a great man for ten years. It's time it was cut open. Good or bad."

"You think that's your call to make, Mike?"

I felt the weight of it all of a sudden.

"Not if I weren't sure of the man. Can you spare some time, Tom?"

"No. But I will. When do you want it?"

"Ten years ago. Whenever you can. Listen, about payment, Tom. If there is a connection with this Bradley case, you can bill it to the Bradley file. I can't promise it, though. The best I can do is pick it up myself, but it could take me a while to pay it off."

"He really got to you, didn't he, Mike?"

"He's the class of this shop, Tom. The rest of them don't come up to his socks. It kills me to see him dying a slow death."

"I know, Mike. Don't worry about the bill. You'll never see it."

"That wasn't the idea, Tom."

"Hey, Mike, you're not the only one owes the old man."

IF I HAD THE OPTION of skipping any quarter hour of that particular day, the next fifteen minutes would have been goners. I knew I was skating on thin to no ice at all.

Mr. Devlin's secretary was at least not surprised to see me. She nodded to the open door. I started to knock, but he saw me and waved me in.

"What did you get from his Harvard buddies?"

Great start. For openers I got to tell him that I hadn't been there yet.

Let's face it. The only way through a difficult situation is to plough through the front door.

"I'm going over to Harvard after we finish here. I've got to talk to you about a couple of things."

I warmed up by telling about Red Shoes and Harry Wong. I could see the distress carved in the lines of his face. It needed more time to sink in, but there was no time. I had to get at the main event.

"I've got something very personal, Mr. Devlin. We've got to get it off the table." He pushed back in the heavy desk chair. Without doubt, I had his full attention. The thought of sitting down would have relieved a couple of shaking legs, but I had to do this one standing up.

"I went to the court clerk's office this afternoon. I dug out the Dolson file."

Those two beacons of eyes registered some mix of anger, pain, betrayal. I couldn't tell.

"I had to. I think there may be a connection. I need to ask you a question."

His expression was granite. But he didn't tell me not to.

"The assistant DA was going after Dolson for a felony-murder conviction. A life term. There was a hung jury. All of a sudden the charge was reduced to simple arson, and there was a deal for a sentence that may have let him out on parole in two years. I know that's not unusual, but there's always a quid pro quo. One possibility is that Dolson got off lightly for information on the people who hired him. I've got to ask it, Mr. Devlin. Is that what happened?"

I wasn't sure whether he was going to speak or not. I think he first had to decide whether he was going to dignify the question and the questioner with an answer or just squash me like an ant.

His expression never changed. When he spoke, it was quieter than I expected.

"No. There was no information. Dolson claimed he didn't know anything." He took a breath as if he were going to say more, but nothing followed.

"Then the other possibility was that the prosecutor was afraid of a weak case. I know that sometimes happens after a hung jury. But . . ." Now I was grasping for words. I finally decided no more grasping. *Say it, and put us both out of our misery.*

". . . I know there was rumor of a fixed jury on the first trial."

Our eyes were locked. If he flinched, I didn't see it. I didn't flinch either.

"They'll never fault you for guts, sonny. There isn't a lawyer or judge in this city that would brace me with that question. What the hell makes you think . . ."

"Because maybe I care more than they do, Mr. Devlin."

I didn't know what to follow that with, but it stopped the train. Those eyes were still riveted into mine, and I didn't have a clue what was going on behind them.

Six years went by in the next few seconds. Then his weight went back into the chair, and his head went back against the cushioned rest. I had the feeling that he was coming to a decision, and I gave him time to carry it out.

When he spoke, he was looking at the ceiling.

"You've just come about as close to the center of my sanity as anyone since my wife passed away. God rest her. I never said this before to anyone. I never had the chance. It was taken out of my hands, and then it just . . . festered away."

He rocked forward out of the chair and walked over to the window.

"Dolson had some kind of a deal going. He confessed once to arson. Then he pulled it back when they found bodies. I defended him. That was the case that ended in a hung jury.

"Two things happened after that. The assistant DA offered a plea with a light sentence. I never bargained for it. It was just dropped on the plate. Dolson was never required to ante up any information. It smelled. I didn't like it, but Dolson grabbed it. I think he was paid to take the fall—at least that much of a fall. He told me as much, but wouldn't or couldn't say who paid him. Then when I raised hell with him about fraud on the court, he said he was just joking about the payoff. I had nothing concrete to take to the court, so the plea was up to him."

He took a breath. I don't know what he was looking at out the window. I don't think he did. I didn't move.

"The other part . . ."

After a second, he walked back to the desk. He was looking me right in the eye. But that look couldn't have been meant just for me. I think he was looking at every bar-rail, gossip-mongering lawyer at the trial bar. The voice was strong, and it carried the weight of ten years' suffering.

"Get it out, sonny. You're the only one in ten years had the guts to ask me to my face if I fixed that jury. Give me the real question."

He was in court. He was on the stand, and he wanted the question to come from every one of his peers. The office door was open, but we both ignored it. I put the question.

"Mr. Devlin, did you have anything to do with fixing the jury in the Dolson case?"

He was at full height now, and it came from the bottom of his soul.

"I had nothing to do with it. Whether that hold-out juror was fixed or not, I never knew. Before Dolson pleaded guilty, there was supposed to be an investigation by the disciplinary committee of the bar, or the DA, or both. After the plea, they were both squelched. I went to both offices and demanded a full investigation to clear the rumors. I couldn't get to first base. The case was closed. Nobody wanted to hear about it, except in the bars and the chambers when I wasn't there to speak in my own defense. I'll say it now, for the first time in ten years, in the hearing of another lawyer. *I had nothing to do with it.*"

When he sat down, he didn't fall into the chair. He sat down. The dignity and the immensity of the man's aura poured over me until I felt a knot the size of an orange in my throat.

There were no more words to say, if, in fact, I could have gotten them out. I could see in his face, as he could see in mine, there was no question of belief.

My voice croaked when I reached the door and said, "Thank you, Mr. Devlin. I'll do that Harvard run."

There was a ten-ton silence in the corridor as I walked to the elevator, but it wasn't tension. They had just heard the sound of justice, and it overwhelmed them.

15

IT WAS PUSHING FIVE by the time the train pulled into Harvard Square. The afternoon chill had dipped into an early-evening freeze. Crossing Mass. Avenue at rush hour from the island that houses the "T" station took skill, cunning, and the pretense of not looking. The trick, of course, was not to face a driver who was also pretending not to look.

There was always the alternate course of waiting for the light at the crosswalk, but then, why stand out from the crowd? It would only confuse the drivers.

I walked down Dunster Street, which led to the student houses on the Charles River. I found the door of a relatively modern building that housed the offices of tutors and PhD candidates. Barry Salmon fit the latter category.

I had heard from classmates over the years that after we graduated, Barry had practiced his acquired art of classical philosophy for some years at a private high school. Inevitably he came back to John Harvard for a PhD He was well into his second year at this point.

The plug-in letters on the directory board told me that they had filed Barry in room 412B.

I remembered the first time I met Barry. He was a well-shined, skinny, bow-tied, tweed-sport-coated (still bearing the frays of his older brother's wearing) freshman at Chambers Academy. He was smiling then, and he was smiling the last time I saw him, which was the day we graduated from Harvard College. As a freshman at Chambers, he smiled out of a deep-rooted good nature. His smiles at Harvard emanated from chemical substances that the chief chemist at Dupont couldn't have identified.

When Barry came to Harvard, he fell in love with three institutions: classical philosophy, some dredged-up cult of the old sixties' hippie culture, and Cynthia Wallingford. The only one of the three that ever did him any good was classical philosophy. For all of his daffiness, Barry was probably the brightest individual, strictly in terms of raw intellect, that I have ever known. I would probably score Barry: Intelligence—ten; Common Sense—point three.

The funny thing was that Barry never lived in the sixties. He was born in '77. On the other hand, he never *outlived* the sixties.

Barry was a hippie in the nineties, when our classmates didn't understand the meaning of the word, and they certainly didn't understand Barry. We traveled in different circles, I'm happy to say, but there was always something warm in our acquaintanceship that harkened back to Chambers days.

I found room 412B with its door open. I peered inside. The room was about the size of Anthony Bradley's cell, but it seemed a great deal smaller. There was a tiny footpath that led through mounds of books, papers, lecture notes, fruit, and sneakers. At the end was a wooden desk chair with no one in it. Then there was a desk with Barry on it, semireclined and reading. At least I suspected that what was behind the salt-and-pepper beard and under the Don King hairdo was Barry. I caught the aroma of the sneakers, and I knew it was Barry.

I knocked, but it took a yell to get his attention.

"Barry! Michael Knight. You remember?"

He squinted for a second, then sprang like a cat over the chair to the floor. I was amazed that whatever was cooking his brain cells at that point in his life had done nothing to his athletic prowess.

"Mike! I don't believe it."

He just laughed, and I did too. It seemed to cover all the trite, conventional questions and answers that would otherwise have been necessary to bring us up to date. There we were, and the last ten or so years were blown away.

"Barry, I want to ask you a question."

"Shoot, Mike. Hey, would you like some coffee or something?"

I smiled and declined. Much as I still liked Barry, I wouldn't drink coffee out of any receptacle in the room, and what "or something" meant I'd have needed a degree in pharmacology to figure out.

"I'm a lawyer, Barry. I have a client who's on trial for murder. He's a Harvard student. Anthony Bradley. Sophomore. African American."

I don't know why I was looking for recognition. If Plato didn't report on the event, it was unlikely that it would have taken Barry's attention. Nonetheless, I pressed on.

"He was a football player his freshman year. He lives in Dunster. His father's a judge."

Suddenly the beard parted as if to speak. I wondered which of the facts I had ticked off struck the chord.

"He's a black kid. Runs that group. What do they call them? 'The Point,' right?"

"You lost me, Barry. I never heard of the group. What are they?"

"Yeah, well, it's a group of students. They do some good volunteer things. Mostly they help freshmen get up to speed with their study habits. They help them make the crossover to college." He grinned. "They help the kids that never went to Chambers."

"I didn't realize he was into that, Barry. How long?"

He ruffled the beard. I looked to see what would fly out, but nothing did.

"I don't know. I heard it eighth-hand. I don't know Bradley personally. I think he got heavily involved in the spring term last year. This year I think I heard he was running it."

"Do they have an office?"

"Are you kidding? They're showcase. The president moved them into the Yard so they could be close to the freshman. I think they're in Dunlevy."

I thanked Barry with a wave instead of a shake and promised to keep in touch.

DUNLEVY IS A NEOMODERN, neo-utilitarian, neogrotesque building in the northeast corner of Harvard Yard. Architecturally, Harvard is much like its faculty. By the time an individual has reached the level of scholarship necessary to be invited to join the faculty, there is usually an independence and self-assurance that has evolved in the mix that makes the individual defiantly unique. To say that a Harvard professor doesn't fit into a pattern falls somewhere between an irrelevancy and a compliment. The same is true of the architecture.

Unlike Barry's sign at the front door, the *permanently* lettered sign at Dunlevy proclaimed that The Point was in suite 203. In this case, "suite" meant two adjoining rooms with identical neo-Ikea desks and chairs in each.

The door was open. There were two students, both white, hovering over a sheaf of papers at a desk. I gathered that one was the tutor, the other was the tutee, and the subject was my old nemesis, calculus. I mercifully decided not to break the train of logic and passed through to the second room. Feeling less intrusive there, I got the attention of what looked like two junior-aged students, both African American, one male, one female, both attractive in spite of the oversized collegey garb they were draped in.

The woman smiled and offered a hand.

"Hi. I'm Gail Warden."

"Michael Knight." I shook the hand, and also that of the man who offered his, together with the words, "Rasheed Maslin. What can we do for you? You from the college?"

"No. I'm a lawyer. I'm Anthony Bradley's lawyer. Can I talk to you?"

They exchanged the kind of positive lip and eye signals that meant, "Well, all right."

They swung a chair around for me and settled down to offer anything they could to help.

"Tell me something about Anthony."

Gail was the first to speak. "He's a man, Mr. Knight."

My look said I didn't grasp her meaning.

"That's not slang, Mr. Knight. I mean he's mature, more than you'd think from his age. He came through a lot of growing up in the last year."

"How so?"

Gail nodded to Rasheed and gestured at the door next to him leading to the other room. Rasheed closed it.

"You know about his father? I mean being a judge and a football hero and gonna be on the Supreme Judicial Court? All that was a heavy burden for Anthony."

"Burden?"

"That's right. Anthony felt he had to be just as good at the same things. He couldn't do it. Anthony's got a lot of talents, but they're different. Like last year, he had to play football. But he couldn't *just* play football. He had to be as good as his father, or maybe his father's legend."

"Did his father put pressure on him?"

"I don't know, but he didn't have to. Anthony put pressure on himself that nobody could live up to. When he knew he wasn't making it at football, he went into a depression. He couldn't study, then his grades started going to pieces. Then he got more depressed."

Rasheed got into the conversation with a quiet voice. "Did he tell you about the attempted suicide?"

Gail caught his eye and his voice clutched. It was apparently not a well-known fact. We needed some ground rules.

"Listen, folks. Anthony's on trial for murder. Nobody's going to fight for his side but me and the lawyer I work for. I need to know everything I can about him. I'll sift out what I need. And all of it's confidential."

Rasheed stole a quick look at Gail like a batter getting the sign from the third-base coach. She apparently gave him the green light.

"Last year, about finals time in the spring, we were supposed to have a meeting about setting up finals tutorials for some of the people we were helping. Anthony didn't show up."

I jumped in for a quick one. "Was Anthony a helper or being helped?"

Gail took it. "He was a helper from day one. He had a good prep-school education, which is different from a lot of the kids they admit. He got involved with us right away, in spite of the time football was taking."

I nodded. "Go back to the meeting, Rasheed."

"When he didn't show up, we called him, but no answer. A little while later we decided to go check out his room."

He stopped for a moment. I wasn't sure why, but it gave me a chance to ask, "Why were you worried about him? I mean, anything could have kept him from one meeting."

"Not Anthony." They said it together, and Gail went on. "He took these helping sessions very seriously."

Rasheed went on. "Besides, he'd been getting more and more into depression. We kind of . . ." He glanced at Gail. ". . . kept an eye on him. We tried to talk to him, like build up his confidence. But we weren't getting anywhere. We wanted him to get some help."

"So did you find him?"

Rasheed looked down at the bracelet he was fidgeting with.

"Yeah. He was in his room."

The pause indicated the need for urging. "Was it the suicide at-tempt?"

Rasheed just nodded. Gail's eyes watered over, and I thought about dropping it, but I needed to learn all I could.

"How?" Neither one was looking at me, but Rasheed made a ges-ture across his wrist.

"What did you do?"

"We put pressure on it. Got him to the hospital. He did OK. We got him in time."

I thought I heard Gail say almost under her breath, "No, we didn't."

I looked at her. She was so sincere she had my heart as well as my attention. When our eyes met, maybe it showed.

"How was he afterwards?"

"He was OK." Rasheed's version.

"No, he wasn't." Gail didn't need the third-base coach. "He never really recovered from it."

I said, "He seemed to be healthy when I saw him recently."

"You mean physically. Yes, the stitches healed, and he got his energy back. But there was something missing."

"Like what?"

"I don't know. You know how sometimes there's something about a person that almost defines them. You can't put your finger on it, but when it's not there, it's like emptiness."

I wondered if Gail could have had more than a passing affection for whatever that something was. Rasheed looked at her gently with what could have been either agreement or empathy, or maybe more.

There was a jolt that brought us all out of it when the door to the other room swung open. A string of high-pitched jive rolled like a babbling stream off the lips of a six-foot, rail-thin dude who came through the door in full swing. He had a walk that had arms, feet, hips, and head syncopating with each other to a beat somewhere in his own universe.

The gist of the jive, as nearly as I could put it together, was the registration of a complaint that the local rap station had been put to rest. It flowed until he spotted the unexpected visitor. Then I saw "the freeze."

It took me back through the past, and it's like bike riding. You never forget. I learned it when I spent some time with kids in a Puerto Rican settlement house. I was seriously Puerto Rican at that time and looking for cultural identity, not the well-adjusted biracial of current times. That was when I learned about "the freeze."

It's like a babbling brook, where all of the happy molecules are monolithic and bouncing in easy rhythm with each other. Then a molecule from another kind of brook is introduced, and in a sort of instant chemical reaction, the brook freezes solid, but only under the top layer. On the surface, to the untrained eye, the brook babbles on.

My white face was the molecule from another brook. I was tuned to the snap freeze, as I'm sure Gail and Rasheed were. I was equally sure that none of the three gave me credit for being in on the phenomenon.

I didn't sense it at all when I walked in on Gail and Rasheed, but the meter was pinning with our new arrival. What it meant was that the surface bopping would go on, but any information I would get from then on would be carefully screened for white ears. With him present, I'd probably had the best of the harvest from the others as well.

Gail took the lead. "Abdul, this is Mr. Knight. He's Anthony's lawyer. This is Abdul Shabaz."

I pegged him at about the junior year, but somehow the Harvard accent had not adulterated his singy-swingy dialect.

"Hey, Anthony's ma man. Please to make your acquaintance, Mr. Knight."

I couldn't tell if he wanted to shake or high-five, so I just nodded. "Nice to meet you, Abdul."

"How's ma man doin'?"

I suddenly realized that I didn't really know. I mentally filled that in as my next appointment.

"He's all right, considering."

"Whachu want us to do? You name it. You got it."

"Give me six Phi Beta Kappa divinity students who'll swear they were with Anthony all day Sunday."

I thought it, but I didn't say it. If I had, I had a feeling that Abdul would have had them at my doorstep in the morning.

"I need to find a friend of Anthony's by the name of Terry Blocher. Do you know him?"

"Terry's a member. You just cool it. I'll get him up here."

I cooled it, while Abdul walked the walk into the next room. I could hear phone sounds and a pause. Then I heard Abdul in a semimuffled tone that only carried through both rooms. Abdul was not cut out for espionage.

"Terry, ma man. Git yourself over here. We got Anthony's mouth-piece. He wants to see you."

With my eyebrows up and a restrained smile, I looked at Gail. "'*Mouthpiece*'? Are they running a forties' film festival? I haven't heard that since *Little Caesar* on AMC."

Her eyes went to the ceiling, and she just shook her head.

In about five minutes, a white student of about nineteen, shorter and heftier than Abdul, walked in. He had a roundish face crowned with the kind of dull blond curls that never seem to need a comb.

Introductions were made, and I got down to it.

"Terry, Anthony tells me that you went with him to Chinatown on Sunday. He said you suggested having dinner there."

"It was his idea, but that's right. I went with him."

I was slightly jangled by the correction, but it was a minor point.

"Tell me about it."

"Well, we went in on the train about two. We went to a place called the Ming Tree."

"Did you pick the restaurant or did Anthony?"

"No, he did. I'd never been there before."

"Had he?"

"I don't know. He just picked it."

"OK. Then what?"

"We had dinner. Then we went down to the street. It was like . . . pandemonium. I had to get out of there."

"So you left him where?"

"Outside the restaurant. I walked to Park Street."

"Did Anthony have a gun?"

He gave me one of those whose-side-are-you-on looks and silence.

"I'd be happy to hear, 'no.'"

"OK, no."

"Did you see anyone there with a gun?"

"No."

I racked my brain for any nugget of gold that I should dig while

I was still at the mine. None occurred at the moment, but now I knew where I could find him.

I turned my mind to surviving the recrossing of Mass. Avenue. If I made it, I was going to take the train to the Suffolk County prison.

16

OVER THE YEARS, I've found that visits to clients in prison fall roughly into two categories. First, there are those where the visitee shows some combination of hostility, fear, sullenness, whatever, but also a hefty flavoring of embarrassment at being confined in housing that does not exactly reek of honor. The second involves those where the disgrace aspect of the confines is as far removed from the outlook of the client as anchovies from a chocolate milkshake. My guess is that the second group has its own moral code that exists on a nonintersecting plane with that of "the system." They have therefore not *failed* under the system; they've merely been caught by it.

When Anthony walked into that sterile interviewing room, he still looked like a classic example of the first type. While some slip into prison garb like a loose bathrobe, it seemed to clash with every aspect of Anthony's bearing, as if the clerk had dressed the mannequin in the wrong suit. He was beginning to show the wear of confinement with an excess of time to suffer the bombardment of negative thoughts. He forced a smile that said acting was not his forte.

"All things considered, Anthony, how're you doing?"

"I'm OK, Mr. Knight. How are you?"

I was impressed that he asked.

"Good. We're covering all the bases. I hope you know that Mr. Devlin is the best there is. And this is the only case I'm working on. So you have our full attention. Have you heard from your dad?"

"He's been in every day." His voice was full of something that I took for shame.

"How's he taking it?"

"I don't know. I couldn't see him."

"What do you mean?"

He shook his head. He was looking somewhere between the table and his shoes, and I think if he looked up, I'd have seen drops of moisture.

"I can't . . . I let him down so much. I just can't be what he is."

"Did he ever say you should?"

He thought about it and shook his head rather than try an unsteady voice.

"Did you ever think that what he wants is a son, not a clone? Maybe he just wants you at your best, whatever direction you take."

He looked up, past me to the ceiling. I was right about the moisture. There was some despair in there, too.

"I guess my direction is pretty clear now."

I caught his eyes and brought them back to mine.

"Anthony. Did you murder Mr. Chen?"

He seemed surprised at the question. "No, Mr. Knight. I didn't."

"Then don't even consider giving up. Mr. Devlin and I can do everything for you except keep your spirits up. That's your full-time job right now. Maybe seeing your father would help both of you."

I can't say that I made any inroads, but he looked as if he was thinking.

"Anthony, I'd like to have the luxury of being able to lead up to this slowly, but I've got to make every minute count. For your sake. I was over at Harvard. I talked to Gail and Rasheed."

For the first time in the conversation I saw the lights go on. "And the Big Bopper, Abdul."

I even caught the makings of a grin on that one. I regretted having to get heavy.

"They told me about the suicide attempt." So much for the grin. "You don't have to explain it. I just feel terribly sorry about the pain you must have been in at the time. What I've got to ask you now is this. Is there any chance at all that you could be there again?"

The tears had dried. He was looking right at me, which helped with the belief factor.

"No." He shook his head for emphasis. "Whatever pain my dad's going through, I won't put him through that."

I had to make a judgment. I came down on the side of running the risk. "OK, Anthony. I haven't said anything to anyone here. I won't."

He just nodded, but I think the trust meant something.

"Do you need anything?"

He shook his head. "I appreciate everything you're doing, Mr. Knight."

You have no idea, Anthony. I was thinking about Harry and Red Shoes.

I stood up and reached across to put a hand on his shoulder.

"I know that between the two of us, you have the tougher job, Anthony. But try to keep up your confidence. You might use some of that heavy time for praying."

"I do, Mr. Knight. A lot."

"Then you've got three of us working for you. And think about what I said about your father."

He stood up, too. Before we went in opposite directions, I thought I'd double-check something.

"Last Sunday. You said you went into Chinatown about two. You wanted Chinese food?"

"Terry came by. He wanted to go in. So I went with him."

"His idea."

"Yes, sir."

"And you picked the Ming Tree Restaurant. Why?"

"No, sir. He did."

For some reason it wrangled me that the two disagreed on the probably minor point of who suggested the Chinatown trip.

"Had you been there before?"

"Not that I can remember. It was just convenient to everything that was going on."

"The New Year's business."

"That's right."

I toyed with the idea of confronting him with the disparity between their stories, but on intuition I decided to file it for another day. While I had him, I thought I'd get out a thought that had been making shuttle trips between my conscious and subconscious.

"Assuming you didn't do it, which I do, and there are two witnesses who say they saw you do it, it's got to be either a mistake or a frame-up. I have trouble with mistake. In that neighborhood, you don't exactly blend. That means frame-up. Why you?"

"Maybe that's why. I've been thinking about it. I stood out like a sore thumb. People would believe the witnesses if they said they noticed anything I did, even with everything going on. I was convenient."

"That's true. But if someone were planning to murder the old Chinese man, they really lucked out to have you pass through the neighborhood at the right moment."

"If it weren't me, I guess they would have picked someone else."

"I guess." *And someone else would be on trial, and I'd still be doing nasty little errands for Whitney Caster.*

I REPLAYED EVERY CARD, shuffled the deck, and re-replayed them again and again in my mind over a good scrod dinner at the 99 down by the *Boston Globe* offices. I was up to my eyeballs in nagging little questions and inconsistencies, like, Whose idea was it to go to Chinatown? Who picked the restaurant? And who cares? Except, why do they disagree on such a minor point?

ASSUMING ANTHONY WAS NOT GUILTY, why would someone decide to frame him, when it was mere chance that brought him to that neighborhood, let alone to the right spot on the right street at the right time? Why in the world would anyone shoot the old man anyway? Was the old man the real target, or a means of getting at Anthony—or Judge Bradley? Another possibility was that the shooting was what Mike Loftus's column in the *Globe* intimated—another act of random violence. On the other hand, I've never seen random violence result in a carefully constructed, almost airtight frame-up.

Then there was the card I didn't want to turn up, but it was certainly there in the deck. What if Anthony were guilty? That would, in fact, simplify things by giving simple answers to most of the other questions, leaving only the question, "Why?"

Two eyewitnesses with no apparent reason to lie, plus Anthony's having the perfect opportunity in the middle of Chinese New Year's pandemonium, were on the side of "guilty."

As I chased the raisins through a bread pudding for dessert, I realized that the only real argument on the side of "innocent" was the straight-up look in Anthony's eyes when he said he didn't do it. And even lie detectors can be fooled by a clever subject.

There was one other thing, and this was the itch I couldn't scratch. Why would poor, sweet, defenseless Red Shoes risk, and in fact give, her life to get me to help cool, together, unruffled Mei-Li, who seemed about as blissfully problem-free as Barney?

WHEN I GOT HOME, I called Harry Wong.

He was slightly out of breath. I gathered it was not from jogging—more likely from getting to the phone while keeping his breathing as shallow as possible not to disturb the rib cage.

"How's the recovery? Those ribs must be painful."

"I've seen healthier ribs with barbecue sauce. What're you up to, Michael? How's the case going?"

"Well, it's like this, Harry. I've got enough questions to keep *Jeopardy* on the air for a year. But there's one in particular. I have just a hunch that if I can find an answer to this one, a lot of other things will fall in line."

"Mei-Li."

"Bothers you, too."

"That girl actually died to get that fortune cookie to you. And for what? It was certainly wasted on Mei-Li."

"I keep wondering what kind of help the fortune-cookie waitress was promising me. She knew I was there about the murder of Mr. Chen. She was listening to my conversation with the witness through the interpreter. Three-quarters of it was in Chinese. I think there's only one way to find out."

"We go back to Mei-Li."

"One of us does. I don't think you're ready for another round."

"Really, Mike? How're you going to talk your way past the Dragon Lady?"

"I haven't worked that one out yet."

"I think I have. It's going to take nerve. I know you've got plenty of that."

"So tell me the plan. I'm open to suggestion."

"It's also going to take a knowledge of Chinese. How're you fixed in that department?"

"Less than adequate. You're still on the bench, Harry."

"There's no way you can do this without me, Mike. You're stuck with me."

I thought about the way Harry looked the last time I saw him. He'd have had to improve to die.

"I don't think so. Out of curiosity, what's the plan?"

"Here it is. You pick me up here tomorrow morning about nine."

"Yeah."

"That's it. You pick me up about nine."

"And then what?"

"And then I tell you the rest of the plan."

"You could tell me the rest now."

"That's right, I could. Then I could pick up the *Globe* in the morning and read about how parts of some unidentified Puerto Rican–WASP were found in six different places. When they put the jigsaw puzzle together—guess who?"

"I'll pick you up about nine."

17

THE *GLOBE* HAD A SPREAD the next morning covering half a page in the city section devoted to the funeral of Mr. Chen. The silent procession of mourners through Chinatown gave testimony to how deeply a quiet, good soul can move the heart of an entire community. I found myself wishing that he could feel the outpouring of love. The funeral mass was said by the auxiliary bishop for the Chinatown area. It was an honor, but I think he would have been even more deeply touched by the tears on the faces of the line of children that extended the length of Tyler Street.

HARRY WAS ON THE SIDEWALK outside of his apartment house at nine sharp, as advertised, bundled up in layers of clothing until only his eyes showed below the fur cap. As he got into the car, I watched him move to see how much mobility had come back. If I were a scout for the Patriots, I'd be more likely to draft Barbara Walters.

He muffled a groan as he slid his rib cage into the front seat as if it were Ming dynasty porcelain.

"So how're you feeling, Harry?"

He turned his head three degrees. "Terrific. You want to wrestle?"

I sat there looking at him. "This is crazy."

"Just drive, Mike. It's early. I get better as the morning goes on. Drive to Chinatown. Come at it from the South Station side. Just park as close as you can. I want to get to that place on Beach Street without walking past the no-name coffee shop."

I put the car in gear and looked for a way to make a U-turn on Memorial Drive.

"Harry, what's with the outfit? Is it that cold? You look like Nanook of the North End."

He squinted crosswise at me. "You're saying I look Italian?"

I took another look and had the first good laugh I'd had since I gave up laughing—around the time this case began. He was referring to the fact that the North End of Boston is the domain primarily of people with more vowels in their names than Harry could buy on *Wheel of Fortune*.

"What you look like is Outer Mongolian."

"It's partly disguise. The idea is to get through to the Dragon Lady for five minutes before the boys come out to play. Actually, three minutes would do it. Do you have a hat with you?"

"In the back. I only wear it if it's below zero."

"Why?"

"Because it makes me look like Henry Osterwald, Harvard, class of '94. You remember our classmate, the king of hats?"

He managed to look at me sideways. His neck had loosened up a good ten degrees. "Is it that bad?"

"I don't wear it until everyone else's eyelids are frozen shut."

"How about when a Chinese street gang would like to separate your ears by about six feet?"

"Then, too. Tell me the plan."

Harry didn't start right away. He seemed to be checking the extent of ice that rimmed the sides of the Charles River.

"I think it's time you knew a little more about the culture you're invading, Mike. This goes back a ways. You've heard of the tongs."

"Sure."

"You know much about them?"

"No."

"A tong was like a club, an association. The word 'tong' means 'hall,' 'gathering place.' They were first set up in San Francisco. There was a wave of immigrants that came over to work on the railroads and the gold mines. They were pretty close to slave labor. They had to look to each other for protection. Some of the large families banded together for mutual support. Anyone with a name like 'Lee' or 'Liu' had plenty of relatives to form a family association. But the ones who didn't belong to a large family were out of luck. They formed the first tongs. They grew pretty fast, because they could recruit anyone, regardless of family name. You've heard of the tong wars."

"Long time ago."

"Right. Originally, the purpose of the tongs was pretty good. Mutual protection and help. And heaven knows they needed it. They were in a strange country, and not exactly embraced with open arms.

"Then some years later there came a time when the tongs were taken over by leaders who got them almost exclusively into organized crime. The biggest moneymaker was gambling. Probably second was prostitution. Everything from shacks to 'parlors' were supplied by the open buying of girls from age two to twenty. They were smuggled in from China, usually through Canada first. Then, of course, there were drugs—opium being the big one. This goes back to the late nineteenth century."

"Is this what we're playing with in Boston?"

"Bear with me, Mike. I want you to know it all. You have to know where it came from. You drive, I'll talk. At different times, there were wars among the tongs, especially in San Francisco and New York. Sometimes it was over a killing, sometimes over control of territories, particularly in New York and San Francisco. The warriors were usually the professional hit men of the tong called the *boo how doy*. In the early days they used to use ceremonial hatchets to split skulls. That's where we got the word 'hatchetmen.'

"There were so many killings over the fifty or so years of the wars that the tongs got a bad name. You almost never hear the name used by the Chinese. That doesn't mean the organizations are gone.

"Many of the tongs are controlled by leaders from triads back in Hong Kong. Some of them are actually American branches of triads."

"You've got a new word there, Harry. By the way, do you want the heat on, or would you fry in that get-up?"

"I'm fine. Just drive and listen."

Harry shifted his position with meticulous care. I wondered if his plan for the brothel involved a lot of broken-field running.

"The triads go back into Chinese history. It's an interesting story. After the Manchus conquered China, they set up the Ch'ing dynasty. They ruled China for over three hundred years. In 1672, the Ch'ing emperor, Kang Xi, got help from the monks in a monastery called Shaolin in Fukien. They were experts in the martial arts. Did you ever watch reruns of the television series called *Kung Fu*?"

"Sometimes. In my high-school days."

"Then you understand something about the idea of Shaolin. The emperor needed help to drive off the invading Xi Lu barbarians. There were only 108 Shaolin monks, but they repelled the Xi Lu barbarians. The emperor rewarded the monks, and they went back to the Shaolin monastery.

"Two of the senior officials in the emperor's court wanted to overthrow him, but they were afraid of the Shaolin monks, who were obviously loyal to the emperor. So they convinced the emperor that the Shaolin could be dangerous to him as revolutionaries. The emperor fell for it. He had the monastery burned, and all but five of the monks were killed. Those five are supposed to be the 'Five Ancestors' who created the first triad. They called the triad 'Hung'—'red'—because of a red light that appeared in the sky during their first ceremony. It was later called a 'triad' from their idea of the relationship between heaven, earth, and man. By adopting heaven as their father and earth as their mother, they were free to ignore the bonds of their real families and country and give their loyalty to each other as brothers and to the organization.

"The Chinese officials from the old Ming dynasty who were thrown out by the Ch'ings and even the poor classes joined into triads patterned after that first 'red' society. They used secret oaths and ceremonies and all the trappings. The whole purpose of the triad was patriotic—the overthrow of the Ch'ing dynasty.

"Then in 1912, Sun Yat-Sen's revolution finally overthrew the Ch'ings and established the Republic of China. Most of the old triad leaders who weren't absorbed into the new government stayed with the triads for the status and power. The problem was that there was no patriotic cause left. So they turned to organized criminal activity. The old triad values of patriotism, brotherhood, and righteousness of the last three centuries got warped into pure loyalty to the triad. And the triads became purely criminal organizations.

"After the communists took over in China, most of the triads moved to Hong Kong. There were about thirty of them there when the mainland took back Hong Kong, in spite of the fact that a Hong Kong statute makes it a crime to belong to a triad. They're probably mostly still intact."

We were passing the Museum of Science, heading in the direction of the once and former Boston Garden and North Station to come into Chinatown from the North End.

"Interesting, Harry. What does it have to do with the Dragon Lady's brothel?"

"I'm getting to that. Listen to me. There are thirty-six oaths of loyalty that every new member swears on the night he's inducted. Like, they promise not to disclose any of the secrets of the Hung family to anyone, parents, brothers and spouses included. If they do, they agree to be killed by many swords. They also swear that if a brother goes away or is arrested or killed, they will help his wife and children. They agree to be killed by thunderbolts if they don't do this.

"They're quite amazing. None of the thirty-six oaths ever mentions criminal activity. But when they pledge complete loyalty to the brethren, it pulls them away from all of the norms and values of the rest of society. There's no room for other loyalties. Robbing, beating, killing—it's all allowed if it serves the purpose of the organization. And if it's done to someone outside the circle."

The more he got into it, the more animated Harry became, and the less restricted he seemed in his motion.

"You're telling me we're dealing with fanatics here."

He shook his head. I was glad to see that he could.

"Not in the sense of being crazies. Just in the sense of being totally dedicated to the cause—which is the business of the tong."

"What's the difference between a tong and a triad?"

"The tongs originated in the United States or Canada. In many cases they were formed as branches of a triad by people who left Hong Kong or Taiwan."

I was surprised. "Are they big in Canada?"

"Enormous. It's easier to do the smuggling into Canada first and then into the United States."

"Smuggling what?"

"Aliens, drugs, whatever. They bring over girls for the prostitution houses. They recruit young men, usually already criminals over there, for the youth gangs that are affiliated with the tongs. These people are illegal aliens, so the tong has a good grip on them."

"What else are they into?"

"Every type of crime that's profitable in the Chinese community. Extortion is everywhere. Everyone pays *lomo*, 'lucky money'—shop-keepers, restaurants, even famous entertainers who come over from China to play in the Chinese theatres here. They also pander to the vices that exist in the community. Gambling has always been a way to escape the present with a chance for a different future. Drugs, particularly opium, go back centuries. It's certainly not a large percentage of the people. But it's enough for the tong to turn a good profit.

"The greatest protection the tongs have is that as long as they don't bother anyone outside of Chinatown, whatever police and politicians they haven't bought don't get too excited about law enforcement. Then, too, they have the Chinese community so frightened of reprisals from their muscle, the youth gangs, that they won't go to the police. Anyway, it's sort of inbred in the Chinese to deal with their problems in their own community. They've learned not to expect much from the white system."

I maneuvered through the circle of traffic that leads, for those who survive it, to the new openings of the so-called Big Dig that replaced the old Southeast Expressway.

"What percentage of the people are involved in the tongs?"

"Minimal. I don't now the exact numbers, but it's like asking what percentage of the Italian people are in the Mafia. The percentage is tiny. Most Chinese are incredibly peaceful, hardworking. They send their children to the best schools they can. They lead good, moral lives. There are infinitely more Chinese victims than criminals."

"Tell me about the youth gangs, Harry. Were those gang members that got you?"

He nodded slowly. "That's another institution. The tongs need enforcers, primarily for two purposes. They need protection for the gambling dens, and they need muscle for their extortion rackets. They're like the replacement for the old hatchetmen.

"The youth gangs are perfect for that. They take in young recruits beginning anywhere from thirteen years old, up. Most poor communities have juvenile delinquents. But what makes these gangs especially powerful and controllable is the mystique of the triad trappings. They're recruited by the tongs with the old triad initiation ceremonies and oaths of loyalty. Everything has a triad twist to it. For example, when they demand ransom or extortion money, the amount is generally in some multiple of 36 for the 36 oaths, or 108 for the original 108

Shaolin monks. This 'secret society' mystique is effective. It not only instills fear in the community, but it forges these delinquents into a disciplined gang.

"The way it works, each tong usually has its own youth gang as an affiliate of the tong. For example, one tong in New York had the Ghost Shadows. Another tong had the Flying Dragons. You don't want to mess with either one."

I pulled into a parking lot close to the Washington Street end of Beach Street. I liked the park-and-lock policy. Just in case we came out of that brothel at a dead run, ten steps ahead of thirty-six teenagers with hatchets, I didn't want to wait for an attendant to fetch the car from the bowels of some garage.

We sat in the car for a minute. I wanted to get the plan straight before we walked into the neighborhood.

"So how do we do it, Harry?"

He turned slightly toward me and realized he was still better off looking straight ahead.

"There are a lot of little low-stakes gambling dens in Chinatown. They're like family businesses. But the tong always runs one major high-stakes gambling den. It's a twenty-four-hour-a-day operation. It's like a giant bank for very serious gambling, drug deals, whatever. There's a lot of money floating around inside. That's where the tong is most vulnerable. That's why a major function of the youth gang is guarding the den. I think I know where it is."

"How?"

"I read the signals. Young, tough kids around the building. There's usually just one slip of paper somewhere on the outside with two Chinese characters meaning 'in action.' I think I saw it."

"Where?"

"The building down the block from the no-name coffee shop."

"All right, suppose you're right. How do you use it?"

"We use the weapon of choice in Chinatown."

"Which is?"

"Fear. That's what gives the tong control over the community. Maybe it'll give us some control over the tong. First we reach the Dragon Lady. Let's go."

"Wait a minute, Harry. Are you going to threaten to go to the police?"

"Hardly. The police are useless. Once in a while they'll raid a gambling den to appear to be doing something. They arrest some of the old people the den keeps around. The judge'll fine them a hundred dollars, and it's on with the show. I don't know what it's like here in Boston, but the tong usually has some of the police tied up."

"So if they're not afraid of the police, what?"

"The tong has a rival. The *Dai Huen Jai*. The Big Circle Boys. They're a bunch of loose-knit bands of criminals from around the southern provincial capital of Canton. In Hong Kong, that area's called the "Big Circle" because that's what it looks like on a map.

"These babies are tough. They run about twenty to forty years old, and they're seasoned fighters. Most of them are out of the Chinese military or are former members of the top-gun Red Guard. A lot of them are wanted criminals in China.

"Their organization smuggles them out of China into Canada, then to the United States. They're brought in specifically to commit crimes, usually robbery of everything from jewelry stores to gambling dens. When things get hot, they're smuggled somewhere else. They're violent enough to be feared even by the tongs."

"And exactly how are you going to use this?"

"Follow this inscrutable Chinese and learn."

He opened the door, but I couldn't let one question hang. I grabbed his elbow.

"One question, Harry. How do you know all this? I mean the oaths and all that."

I think he wanted to be out of the car before I asked the question. I could see his lips tighten.

"What's the difference?"

It came out harsher than he'd intended. He saw my expression and softened his.

"Sometime I'll tell you, Mike. I will. This isn't the time. We've got business."

I nodded.

He was out of the car with both feet on the sidewalk in around sixty seconds flat. I said a prayer that "the plan" did not call for blistering speed. I followed him, but not without grabbing and donning my Henry Osterwald hat from the back seat.

18

THE WIND OUT OF THE EAST was whipping twenty-one-degree air salted with snow particles into our faces. In spite of it, I could feel the beading of perspiration on my forehead and upper lip.

We moved down Beach Street from the opposite direction of the no-name coffee shop. I was about four paces behind Harry in case they recognized us together. There was no trouble keeping up.

I had no idea what kind of watch the youth gang would keep on a brothel at nine-thirty in the morning. There was hardly anyone in sight on the street.

The only activity we saw was in the poultry shop that we passed on our right. Ancient wooden cages along the walls held a dusty, feathery collection of live chickens and ducks. Three old Chinese women seemed to be singing the morning gossip to each other while they waited their turn. A fourth watched a rail-thin clerk of somewhere between twenty and forty years grab the quacking duck she pointed to out of the cage and lock one wing behind the other. They were as oblivious to us as I prayed the rest of the local citizenry might be.

When we reached the door of the brothel, I felt the same grappling sensation in the stomach that I had two nights before. Harry neither speeded up nor slowed down as he turned right and pushed open the door. I checked the street one last time. No one.

I scuttled in and closed the door. I was a step behind Harry as we crossed through that mangy hallway to the stairs. The only light was still what fought its way through a century of grime on the door glass, but as far as I could see, there was no one inside. My observation was confirmed by the fact that no one had killed us. Yet.

We climbed. I've heard steps creak, but these roared. I'm sure it was magnified in my mind, but every step was like jumping on the tail of another cat.

Harry stopped a step from the top. I was crowding him from behind, squinting to squeeze every bit of information out of the pitiful rays of light that made it to the top of the stairs.

There were two doors. I couldn't remember which one we used two nights before. I remembered the story, "The Lady or the Tiger," and thought of the clear possibility of finding "two tigers, no lady."

I whispered, "Which door?"

Harry turned to make what I suppose was a guess, but instead drove an elbow into my chest so hard I had to grab for what I hoped was a rail to keep from taking the stairs backwards. He was recoiling from a blast of daylight that hit him with surprise harder than he hit me. The first door had swung open. From the gasp of the figure that stood framed in the door, Harry and I had thrown as much of a shock as we received.

From the bulk of the black shadow, I had instant fear that we were dealing with the sumo hulk we'd run into there before. Then I saw the edges of the shadow billowing and showing light. The silhouette under the billowing was massive, but not gargantuan.

A flood of hot Chinese poured like staccato little fireworks out of whoever it was we were looking at. Whatever it meant didn't slow Harry in the slightest. He was a pace behind the figure that was attempting to disappear behind the door. He kicked back the door and grabbed the elbow of the Dragon Lady who had been our effusive hostess of two nights previous. Once he had her stopped, he leaned back to let the wave of pain he must have unleashed in his ribs subside. I was inside with the door shut by the time the hot lava began pouring out of her mouth again.

In a tight sheath, she had been merely obese. In a free-flowing robe, she expanded to fill the material.

Harry bellowed, "*Silence!*"

Not "Quiet," or "Could you hold it down?" or even "Stifle it." Just plain "Silence!" I thought I had warped into a classic Charlie Chan movie.

Harry knew what he was doing. She froze.

He took off the hat and opened the coat so she could see who she was dealing with. I was sure that by that time she knew we were not immigration officers. Harry was back working from ground zero.

"Listen to me, Old Mother. You can do yourself great good or great harm in the next few minutes. You would do well to pay attention." He kept it in English.

She looked stunned. At least she left a gap for Harry to speak.

"I have information. I assume you can reach the *Fu Shan Chu?*"

Whatever it meant, it grabbed her attention. She didn't move. She didn't answer, either.

Harry grabbed a piece of white paper off a desk to his left. He took a pen out of his pocket and wrote in large numerals, "438." He pushed it in front of her to emphasize the question.

Her mouth seemed stuck. She just nodded.

"Then tell him this. I have inside information on the Big Circle Boys. There's a robbery planned. I know when. The high-stakes gambling den."

He pointed in the general direction of Beach Street. She was stone still. But her eyes flared a little when he pointed in what must have been the right direction.

"You have two choices, Mother. You can pass the information to the *Fu Shan Chu* so he can set up an ambush. You'll gain much face. They'll be very grateful. Or . . ."

She gave it a second before breaking her silence.

"What?" Their eyes were deadlocked.

"Or when the raid occurs, I can get word to the *Fu Shan Chu* that you were the one who tipped the Big Circle boys to the location of the den." He touched her cheek. "You may not take those pretty features to an old age, Mother."

"Why you want to tell me about the raid?"

Harry set the hook. "For a very low price. It has nothing to do with you. I want to see the girl, Ku Mei-Li, right now. When we've seen her, we leave. You won't see us again."

"Why you want Mei-Li?"

"As the price for making you a hero instead of another dead madam. That's all you need to know. It's time to choose."

"Who you really?"

"That doesn't affect your decision. If they ask where you got the information, you can tell them one of your customers got drunk and talked too much to one of the girls."

She looked from Harry to me. I was purely backup. I gave her my best Clint Eastwood stone face. In the seconds that followed, I could almost hear her brain cells searching for a third alternative. The one that occurred to me was to call out the enforcers and watch us being cut into stir-fry.

Time was not on our side. Harry knew it. He stuffed on the hat and headed for the door.

"I have no time for this. You've obviously lived long enough, Mother. The thought of pleasing your employer no longer appeals to you."

"Wait. Come back. How I know you have good information?"

"You don't. But you can only win. If my information is good, you save your employer a great loss. He'll be very grateful. If it isn't, they'll just think the raid was called off for some reason. They'll know you did your best. On the other hand, if there is a raid and they hear later that you tipped off the *Dai Huen Jai* to the location . . ." He pulled down his hat for emphasis and turned toward the door.

"Wait! Why you always run off?"

"I have precious little time, Mother. Which way will it be?"

The furrows in her little fat brow deepened each time she clenched her teeth. She was trying to thread a path between survival on one side and death, or at least very serious pain, on the other. I was sorry for her. I was even more sorry for poor little Red Shoes. In a way, this old woman was part of the machine that ground up little innocent Red Shoes. I left it with Harry. He grabbed the doorknob. That did it.

"You tell me when raid. Then I call girl."

"You've got that in reverse, Mother. You call the girl first. We want to see her in private. Right here. But not like last time. This time she comes with orders from you to tell the truth. I know half the story. If she gets it wrong or holds out, no deal."

As Harry talked, I could see her getting squinty and cool. I was afraid Harry was losing her. The worst thing for us was for her to have time to think.

"Maybe no deal anyway. If I yell, boys come. They make you tell for nothing."

Harry peeled around from the door. He grabbed the telephone on the desk and drilled in ten numbers. I knew it was for show, but it had even me on edge. Big Mama just stared. Harry held the receiver out to her while it rang.

"Ask the man who answers what I told him to do if I'm not back in an hour. The message goes out that you betrayed the tong. When the raid occurs, there won't be a hole big enough to hide you in China-town. Go ahead. Ask!"

She stared at the thing that was making "hello" noises in front of her. She pushed it away. "All right, I do it."

Harry said into the phone, "The same plan is still on. One hour." He hung up.

"That's it, Mother. Call Mei-Li."

Harry had the momentum back. She hustled through the door in the back of the room. I moved close enough to Harry to whisper.

"Did you set that up with someone?"

He whispered back. "That was my research assistant. I intended to tell him this morning. It skipped my mind. It'll give him something to think about."

IN A FEW MINUTES, Mei-Li came through the back door. She was still beautiful, even in slacks and a blouse, but she was less perfectly composed than previously.

She looked from one of us to the other without knowing which of us to please or how to do it. It was my turn at bat. I stepped over to her, took her hand, and brought her to a chair. I pulled a chair over to sit in front of her.

"I don't want to frighten you, Mei-Li. I just want the truth. Did the woman tell you to tell us the truth?"

"Yes." It was meek.

"Did she tell you to answer our questions?"

She looked over at Harry, but she said "yes" to me.

"Then listen carefully. The girl who worked in the restaurant, the one who gave me the note I showed you, did you know her?"

She looked confused by the question, and I realized it could have been the past tense. "I saw her yesterday in the morgue. They killed her."

The little gasp was the first sincere thing I had heard out of her.

"She was killed, Mei-Li, because she gave me the note to help you. Now tell me the truth. Why did she think you needed help?"

First the tears started, and then her face was buried in her hands. I took her as gently as I could by the shoulders and lifted her to look at me.

"Why did she want me to help you?"

There was gentle sobbing that almost muffled the words. "I don't know."

"Mei-Li, I have to know . . ."

"I am not Mei-Li."

I heard it clearly, but it took a second to sink in.

"I don't understand."

"They brought me here two days ago. I saw her then."

"Mei-Li?"

"Yes. They were sending her away. When you came two nights ago, they told me to pretend to be Mei-Li, but to tell you nothing wrong."

"When you saw her, before they sent her away, did you speak to her?"

"Only a little. She was crying. Very frightened."

"Frightened of what?"

"She did not say."

"Did you ask her?"

"It would do no good. She would not know she could trust me."

Harry and I exchanged a look that said frustration. I had little or no hope for the next question.

"Do you have any idea where they sent her?"

She shook her head. Harry touched my shoulder, and I leaned back to give him room. He squatted down to catch her eyes.

"What is your name?"

"I called Xiao-Wen."

"Xiao-Wen, where did they bring you from when you came here?"

"It is place like this in a different country. In Toronto."

"Do you know the address?"

"Yes. It is on Columbia Street. It is above grocery store in middle of block."

Harry looked at me and we were in sync. The easiest way they could get Mei-Li out of reach would be to exchange her for a girl from another brothel out of the country. That made it likely that Mei-Li was Xiao-Wen's replacement in Toronto.

I didn't like the question that raised. Wouldn't it be easier still to simply kill her? Like Red Shoes? The answer was so clearly "yes" that my heart froze at the prospect of seeing another mutilated victim in the morgue. Why go to the trouble of a double alien-smuggling just to keep her alive? On the other hand—and this was the only hand I wanted to consider—maybe, if Mei-Li was still alive, it had to do with the dollar value of an exceptional prostitute. Maybe more.

Before we left, Harry took a piece of paper from the desk and wrote, "Raid—this Friday—9:00 PM" He showed it to me and handed it to the girl.

"Give this to the old lady. She'll be waiting for it."

In the hallway downstairs we bundled against the cold, as well as recognition, before going out into the street. I pulled Harry's earflap up for a question before leaving.

"What was that you asked the old lady? Did she know 'Fu'—something or other? Then you showed her three numbers."

"The *Fu Shan Chu*. I was asking if she knew the second in command of the tong. The big boy. These tongs and triads are crazy about numbers and symbols. Every officer has a code number. The number for the *Fu Shan Chu* is 438. She got the point that I was not an outsider."

"Why the number two man? Why not number one?"

"Nobody in the tong knows who he is. They call him the Dragon Head. Only the number two man knows who he is."

He started out the door, but I had one last point.

"Harry, I've got one more stop to make. You can come with me or wait for me."

"What stop?"

"There's one more witness to the shooting. He's the old man who runs the Chinese herbal medicine shop on Tyler Street. I've got to talk to him. This is as good a time as there's going to be. I don't want to have to come back here. We're getting too well known."

I could have predicted his decision. He pulled down his earflap.

"Let's go."

19

TUCKED AWAY DOWN six worn, stone steps beside the Ming Tree restaurant on Tyler Street, we found the anomaly of the twenty-first century. It was a time warp. Those steps carried Harry and me out of the age of laser surgery into the middle ages of Chinese medicine.

This was no tourist haunt. The sign over the door was in untranslated Chinese. I would bet that mine were the first white feet to cross that threshold in a century. Dangling from a black, cloth-covered cord, a single weak bulb that wouldn't have passed inspection in a chicken coop created shadows out of blackness.

I was aware of bundles of unidentifiable somethings or other piled up on both sides of the narrow shop. Faded Chinese newspapers were stacked intermittently with nearly biodegraded cardboard cartons that seemed to hold old Chinese magazines.

When we came in, I saw a shadow move in the back. It approached until I could make out an elderly Chinese man, somewhat stooped with age, but not emaciated as I would have predicted from the surroundings.

Thin, wispy strands of white face hair, which were about as close as the old gentleman could come to a full beard, sprouted below an otherwise hairless head. He wore Chinese-style pants and top which were sewn out of coarse black material. They had long since taken the permanent press of his natural folds and bends. He padded along on black cloth Chinese slippers. I was overwhelmingly grateful to have Harry along to translate for me.

I knew we were in a different world when Harry bowed. The old man returned it immediately. They exchanged what even I could tell were polite well-wishes in non-English. Harry must have used his full Chinese name, because I didn't hear "Harry" in any of it.

The first words that I recognized came when Harry held out his hand toward me and said in Chinese "*Something . . . something . . .* Michael Knight."

It seemed perfectly natural to bow. I did. He returned it graciously. I figured it didn't matter what I said as long as it sounded polite.

"Good morning, sir. It's a pleasure to meet you."

He smiled at me with a warmth I could feel and said without a trace of an accent, "Good morning, Mr. Knight. The pleasure and the honor are mine. I thank you for gracing my humble shop."

There was no condescension in it, just a very beautiful style of expressing welcome. So much for translation.

Harry added, "This is Mr. Qian An-Yong. He deals in a type of medicine that predates by centuries the time when the most scientific instrument of the West was a leech. Isn't that right, Mr. Qian?"

He nodded. I wondered if the sparkle in his eyes that accompanied the smile was because someone of Harry's age appreciated his art, or because he assumed that I wouldn't.

"You have a familiarity with the ancient medicinal arts, Mr. Wong?"

Harry seemed at ease with the old gentleman. I was getting that way.

"I remember my mother used to go to the herbal medicine doctor before we left China. She had great faith in him. I don't know whether or not she ever found one in this country."

"Then you might not take offense at my noticing the obvious. You're in great pain. I wonder if you would permit me to help you."

"In what way, Mr. Qian?"

"Would you do me the kindness to excuse me? I'll be just a moment."

He bowed slightly and shuffled back through a curtain at the back of the shop.

I looked at Harry with an apology for getting him into an embarrassing situation. He seemed undisturbed.

In a few minutes, the old man was back. He had a handleless Chinese cup in each hand. The light caught steam rising from each of them. He handed one to Harry.

"I think you will find this more satisfying than anything you might have tried. By the time you leave, your pain will be substantially less."

I'm sure he noticed the look on my face. I had no idea how Harry could refuse without offense. On the other hand, this brew could have ingredients that even Barry Salmon never tested. Equally disturbing was the likelihood that the other steaming cup was for me.

Harry had taken his first hot sip, apparently without qualms, before Mr. Qian said to me, "Don't be afraid for your friend. It contains combinations of herbs that are perfectly natural. There is no narcotic. There is no need for a narcotic other than what the body produces for itself. These herbs will simply allow the body to produce its own cure."

Harry finished the liquid and handed the empty cup back to Mr. Qian, who, in turn, held the second cup out to me. I took it, but only to hold. He was smiling an ingenuous smile.

"Mr. Knight, what you are holding is simply a cup of tea. Please permit an old man to be hospitable."

The old gentleman affected me with his warmth. My fear of offending him grew stronger than my doubts about the contents of the cup. I stole a quick look at Harry. He was still standing. I took a sip, and the comforting warmth flowed through every quarter of my body. The second was just as good. I had finished the cup by the time I remembered what everyone's mother tells them about taking food from strangers.

The old man looked pleased, and I could feel the warm tea untangling the knots of tense muscles.

"Thank you. That was wonderful, Mr. Qian."

He bowed. Amazing how many thoughts a bow, properly done, can express. "It is only an inadequate effort at hospitality."

I was coming to realize that I could sooner get this properly schooled Chinese gentleman to accept hemlock than a compliment without deflecting it with humility.

It was time to get to business.

"Mr. Qian, I'm an attorney. I represent the man who's charged with killing Mr. Chen."

He nodded. I felt a touch of sadness in his nod.

"I'm sorry for his death, Mr. Qian."

He nodded again. "There is no doubt that we are diminished by the loss of his gentle presence. Others would have difficulty understanding . . ."

He seemed hesitant to go further, but I wanted to hear it.

"Would you finish your thought, Mr. Qian? I want to understand."

He gathered his words for a moment. I think it was sensitivity to the feelings of this Occidental.

"We see old age not as a flaw but an accomplishment. We respect our elderly for suffering all that life can bring for their many years. They give us their patience and knowledge and even wisdom that are like our rock. Mr. Chen, with his patient love for our children of all ages—myself included—was our rock."

I wanted to say something deep and understanding, but all I had was conflicting thoughts. I still represented the one whom he said killed his Mr. Chen. I simply said, "Yes," in the kindest way I could, and moved on.

"Mr. Qian, I understand that you were a witness."

He looked down, and a troubled look crossed those serene features.

"Am I right? Did you see the shooting?"

There seemed to be a sadness that settled in when he looked at me.

"An old man should be used to violence. It's a part of life. It should no longer be disturbing."

"I've been sorry to find so much of it in the Chinese community in the last few days, Mr. Qian. I didn't realize it was here, too."

"Oh, we have everything that every other culture has, Mr. Knight. Good and bad. In fact, we've had it longer. The form of medicine that

I practice goes back not centuries, as Mr. Wong said, but millennia. As does a highly developed spiritual philosophy and morality. Do you know, Mr. Knight, why the Chinese still use chopsticks instead of your knives and forks?"

"No." But if the truth were told, I suppose, without giving it much thought, I considered it evidence of backwardness.

"Because from our earliest civilization, the Chinese have considered a meal to be more than nourishment for the body. It is a social experience that bonds the family together in spirit and affection. To use instruments of war and fighting like knives and forks would be disruptive to an atmosphere of harmony and peace."

"That's very beautiful." I started to add, "But . . . ," but the words mercifully stayed in.

"Go on, Mr. Knight. There was more."

"Well, since you ask, I was just wondering how a community that brings such a beautiful philosophy into every meal can be as riddled with fear and intimidation from within as I've seen lately."

"For every *yin* there must be a *yang*, Mr. Knight. It's the coexistence and attraction of opposites that holds the universe together."

I nodded, "And since that violent element exists, I guess we have to deal with it. I understand that you identified my client, Anthony Bradley, as the man who shot Mr. Chen."

"I did not know your client's name, but I made the identification."

"And do you still stand by that identification?"

"I do."

"Could I ask where you were standing when the shot was fired?"

"I was outside my shop on the sidewalk."

"What view did you have of Anthony?"

"I saw him from the front when he came out of the Ming Tree restaurant next door. Then I saw him from the side while he was on the sidewalk."

"Is that where you say the shot was fired?"

"Yes."

"You say you saw him when he came out of the restaurant. In all the confusion of the New Year's celebration, how would you notice or remember him?"

"Because I had seen him a number of times before."

I wasn't sure I could have heard him right. "You saw him before? Where?"

"At the Ming Tree restaurant."

It was like seeing the pieces of a jigsaw puzzle pull apart.

"How many times?"

"Perhaps five or six over the last six months. He would come alone, but others would join him."

"Could you tell me who?"

He thought about it. "Most frequently Mr. Liu. He is called Kip Liu. He is the manager of the restaurant. They would eat together. Sometimes others would join them. I don't know their names. They are from the community."

I was really rocked by the way the conversation was going. One familiar note rang in my mind.

"This Kip Liu. Is he tall, expensively dressed, hair slicked back, speaks good English?" I could have added, "Looks like Dick Clark?" but I might have lost him on that one.

"That is Mr. Liu."

I had hit a wall. I realized that I had done just what Mr. Devlin warned me about. I had taken as a given the truthfulness of the client. I could hear Anthony say at least three times that he'd never been to the Ming Tree before. With his story as base information, I thought I knew where I was headed. All of a sudden, the road signs were spinning. I wasn't sure where to go from there.

I thought of an old Lewis Carroll line from one of the *Alice* stories— "If you don't know where you're going, any road will take you there."

"Had you ever spoken to Anthony, Mr. Qian?"

"No. He was just a familiar face. You seem suddenly troubled, Mr. Knight. I'm sorry."

"It's not your fault. Mr. Qian. I'm just running into a credibility problem. Between the two versions I've heard, I'm inclined to believe you're telling me the truth. Sometimes the truth takes us by surprise."

I had run out of questions for the moment. We all exchanged amenities before he saw us to the door. He wouldn't accept payment for whatever it was he gave Harry, who, I had to admit, went up the stairs with a great deal more spring than he had shown all morning.

BY THE TIME WE REACHED the street, I felt as if a wrecking ball had gone through my stomach. I had been dealing with the nagging question of why Terry and Anthony disagreed about whose idea it was to go to Chinatown. That was minor. Now I had to face the more devastating fact that good old straight-up Anthony had been jerking my chain about the fact that he was a regular at the Ming Tree restaurant, and more than that, a frequent diner with Dick Clark, whom I trusted as far as I could throw a refrigerator.

"It's been a beaut of a morning, Harry. All things considered. How're you feeling?"

We walked together down Tyler Street toward the parking lot. He thought for a second before answering.

"Better." He even said it with a bit of a smile.

My thoughts were racing from random to what was taking shape as a pattern. In terms of a next move, conscience and logic were forcing me into a decision I did not want to make. There were a number of other bases I had to touch, but a nagging and unwelcome voice kept insisting that when I gathered all the pieces, there would be one large, central piece missing. Like it or not, the voice kept repeating that the key to the puzzle was Mei-Li.

We turned right onto Beach Street before I got up the courage to put it into words.

"I'm thinking out loud here, Harry. You're my sounding board."

"Think on, brother."

I pulled Harry into a decrepit doorway, out of the wind, and out of the sight of spying eyes, if any.

"No matter how I piece it together, I get one name. I'd give my Bruins play-off tickets for five minutes of conversation with that little waitress with the red shoes. I'd throw in your play-off tickets to find out what she meant by helping me. That's not going to happen. I'm sure she died trying to get me to help this Mei-Li. Help her what? What's her problem? I've got a voice inside that's screaming in high C that there's a serious connection to this murder. Is my little voice whacko or what?"

Harry pulled his coat tighter against the cold.

"My voice is saying the same thing in Chinese. Could we talk a little faster? It's freezing out here."

"No. I'm at warp speed now. Anthony's obviously been lying to me. I could have it out with him, but I couldn't trust anything he said at this point anyway. One thing I can't finesse. He's no complete by-stander in this business. If little Red Shoes could have helped him as promised, there must be a connection. If he's connected to her, he could be connected to Mei-Li. Does that make sense?"

Harry looked like he was getting the shivers. "Could we talk and walk at the same time?"

"In a second, Harry. Does that make sense?"

He nodded.

"There's no one here in Chinatown that won't freeze me out at the least—kill me at the most. I know this is off-the-chart nuts, but I keep coming back to Mei-Li."

"I know, Michael."

"I've got to find her."

"I know. That's why we're going to Toronto."

"I said 'I,' not 'we.' You're still on the DL."

He grabbed the front of my jacket and pulled my ear close to his mouth. The physical effort made him wince.

"Listen, Michael. I'm going to say this once before my ears freeze off. She's in a brothel in a foreign country, probably surrounded by Chinese of the non-English-speaking variety. If there is one hint of what you're there for, they'll kill you faster than they could roll a wonton. You want to commit suicide, there are easier ways."

I was silent for lack of an answer.

"With me you've got half a chance. Maybe half of a half of a chance. It beats no chance. When do we leave?"

I just shook my head.

"Michael, nothing personal but you're one *low faan* against a small Chinese army. Why not just mail your body to the morgue and eliminate the middle man? If you've got an alternative, I'm all ears, unless they've frozen off."

"This is my job. It's not yours. And what's a *low faan?*"

"It's you, Michael. It's a non-Chinese. And this is my community. It's not yours."

I felt guilt and gratitude in one rush. I knew he was in no condition to make the trip, but he was right. Without him, I didn't have a clue.

"How about day after tomorrow, Harry?"

20

IT WAS JUST AFTER NOON when I got back to Franklin Street. My first port of call was Mr. Devlin's office. The Cerberus at the door no longer even looked up as I passed. She did flick the end of a pencil in the direction of the high chamber, just to show that I entered with her permission and that she still had the power to bar the door. I blew her a kiss, which she accepted with all the effusion of a kindergarten teacher when little Winston brings her a dead mouse from recess.

I briefed Mr. Devlin on what I'd learned since our last meeting. He just listened through my account of the Harvard group, nodded in what I took for approval of my visit to our client, scowled at me for re-running the gauntlet of the Chinese Mafia at the Beach Street brothel, and paced to the window when I told him that Mr. Qian, witness for the prosecution, had seen our client on multiple occasions dining with a Chinese gentleman of questionable honor at the Ming Tree—counter to our Mr. Bradley's consistent recitation of the facts.

"How's your confidence in that look in young Bradley's eyes now, sonny?"

"Waning. Not gone, but waning."

"This could be the best thing that happened to Bradley."

"You lost me, Mr. Devlin."

"Any time you base a defense on your belief in your client's inno-cence because he told you so, you're a loose cannon. Often as not, you'll wind up exploding in your client's face. Go with the facts as you find them. You'll do the best job for your client."

"Yes, sir. I remember you said that."

He gave me a sharp look when he caught the lawyer's difference between agreeing with him and noting that he'd said it.

"Mm. What about this Mr. Qian? Is he a solid witness?"

"In the worst way. Mrs. Lee is strung tight as piano wire. She could fold under pressure. But Mr. Qian is . . . gentle, intelligent, confident, humble . . . wise. He won't be shaken."

He was leaning against the chair, but his eyes came up.

"Wise?"

I thought about it. How many people do you meet in a lifetime that fit that description?

"Yes, sir. Wise."

"What about the Harvard group? Anything there?"

"Nothing substantive. Couple of possible character witnesses. One in particular. I think she has a crush."

"Then she's useless. The jury'll see it. Anything she says'll be considered biased. The only remote possibility for an affirmative defense seems to be this girl, Mei-Li. And she's an unknown. The rest of it's blowing smoke."

I was pleased in a frightening sort of way that we had reached the same conclusion.

"I want you to get a detective up to Toronto. Get Tom Burns on it."

"No, sir."

I think the last one to say the *n* word to him was his mother. He hadn't heard it in so long, he looked as if he wanted me to define it for him.

"What I mean, Mr. Devlin, is he's good, but not for this. This is an outfit that runs on secret code words, and numbers, and mostly well-orchestrated fear. It's a matter of always touching the right buttons. I couldn't have gotten this far without a Chinese friend who runs interference for me."

"What are you suggesting?"

"My friend and I are going up to Toronto tomorrow."

That lit a fuse and raised the decibel level to where I'm sure Julie could hear it comfortably.

"The hell you are, sonny! You're not going outside of this commonwealth. You've gone far enough. Too far. No more foolish risks. Get Burns on this. And do it now. I want a statement from that girl. Do you hear me?"

"Yes, sir."

He swung the chair around and focused the full Devlin heat at me from three feet.

"Let's get this straight, sonny. Do we understand who's running this show?"

"Yes, sir."

"All right then. You stay put."

He eased back a bit, and I felt the furnace subside. The change of subject was a relief.

"I got a call from Judge Posner's chambers. The case has been assigned to him. He's called a pretrial conference for three days from now at two. I want you there. He's going to be pushing for an early trial date before the press and the Chinese community get more revved up than they are already. The DA has the cards, so she wants a quick showdown too."

"We need time, Mr. Devlin. This case is not shaping up fast. It gets more complicated every time I talk to a witness."

"I'll do what I can at the conference to buy us some time."

"How do you feel about Judge Posner?"

He grabbed a pair of reading glasses and paced to the window.

"I don't know. I haven't had a criminal case before him in ten years. He's good on evidence. Tough on lawyers, at least the young ones."

"That's not what I mean, sir."

"I know what you mean, sonny. In plain English, is he going to give Bradley a fair trial? I wish I knew. You know what they say in Chicago. 'If the fix is equal, justice prevails.'"

"And is the fix equal here, Mr. Devlin?"

He rubbed the morning shadow of regrowth on his chin. I knew we were both thinking of the DA's sudden reversal on a plea bargain and Conrad Munsey's warning about unrest upstairs.

"Let's hope so, sonny. Without solid grounds for a motion to have him recuse himself, that's the best we can do at this point. Let's get on with it."

He came back to the papers on his desk. I was halfway to the door when his voice caught me.

"Sonny! *You be damned careful in Toronto.*"

I was caught flat-footed. "But didn't you just say . . ."

"I know what I said." He stood up, and the chair spun. "And I know you. I could order you to hell and back, and you'd still go to Toronto, wouldn't you?"

There was no point in not telling him the truth.

"Yes, sir."

"And you'll probably go on taking these foolish chances for the rest of your life. You're too damn much like me."

I was grinning, and I didn't hide it. I think inside maybe he was, too, in spite of the fierceness of the scowl.

"If you get hurt up there, you'll get it double from me when you get back! You understand?"

"Yes, sir. I'll watch it."

"I want to see you right here the instant you get back."

I nodded. "The instant I get back."

I walked out of there on six clouds. I got looks of sympathy from the corridor dwellers who heard the ruckus and thought Mr. D. had devoured another associate. I sensed that back of the bellowing, the man cared whether I lived or died. I never got that feeling from anyone else at Bilson, Dawes.

I DECIDED TO CHECK into my office, as briefly as possible. Julie held out a pink please-call-back slip.

"Are you and 'Lex' still tight? Sounds like there's trouble in Paradise."

I said it quietly while I checked the slip. Tom Burns wanted me to call him back at his office. "We're cool. I've got him right where I want him."

"Right. On your back, taking bites out of your neck."

I just shook my head and smiled. I looked back down the corridor. "Did you ever notice something, Julie? When you walk down toward that office, the floor seems to rise. You know why that is?"

She looked blank and curious, and I just winked.

TOM BURNS PICKED UP ON the second ring. It was his private line with no secretarial intermediaries.

"Any pay dirt, Tom?"

"I checked the twelve jurors. The twelve of them continued on with about the same lifestyle they had before the Dolson trial. The only exception was that one of them died about a year after the trial."

"Of what?"

"Heart attack. Nothing suspicious. He had heart problems before the trial."

"So we struck out."

"Did I say that, Mike? Hold your horses. I checked probate. The one who died left the usual things a carpenter from South Boston would leave his daughter in his will. Plus a three-hundred-thousand-dollar bank account."

"Bingo."

"There's more. I checked with the other jurors personally. The guy who died was the holdout that made the hung jury. The others were ready to convict. I also checked to see if any of the others were approached with a bribe. None. But they only needed one."

"You're a thing of beauty, Thomas. What kind of an account was it?"

"According to the will, it was a regular savings account. South Boston Savings."

"In his name?"

"Right."

"Which was?"

"Ronald Perry."

"I need to get some information on the account. Do you know who the executor was under the will?"

"By coincidence, the daughter who came into the three hundred grand. Joyce Perry Frank. She works at the Shaughnessy Funeral Home in Southie."

"You're too good, Tom. I'll get back to you on the bill."

"Not this time, Mike. Just go with it."

I CHECKED THE PHONE BOOK for the address of the Shaughnessy Funeral Home. I called and made an appointment with Joyce Perry

Frank for two o'clock. I didn't give any specifics. I didn't want her to lose that sympathetic, consoling tone of voice until I had a chance to explain what I needed.

There was just time to dash through two hot dogs from one of the Washington Street vendors and pick up a package of Tums for desert. Then out to Southie.

It was nearly two by the time I found the D Street address. I had passed six similar establishments before I found the Shaughnessy Funeral Home. Not surprising, since Southie is still overwhelmingly Irish, and among the Irish, funeral homes are a bustling industry. It's not that they die more frequently than anyone else. They just seem to do it with more panache. An Irish friend of mine used to refer to the obituary column in the *Globe* as the "Irish Sports Section."

JOYCE PERRY FRANK was a roundish woman in her late forties, early fifties. She was neatly attired in a suitably colorless dress. She had that mortician's ability to smile with her mouth while her eyes conveyed empathy with the bereaved.

"Mrs. Frank, this is a bit difficult. I hope you'll understand. First, the good news. Nobody died."

From her expression, I wasn't sure she considered that good news.

The question was whether to go with the truth and ruffle some feathers, or spin a yarn that would get the same result without ruffling feathers. The problem was that the truth might later become public, and it could be devastating if it took her by surprise. I opted for the truth up front.

"I'm going to be honest with you, Mrs. Frank. I'm investigating an incident of possible jury tampering. It occurred in a criminal case some ten years ago. I'm afraid that the juror was your father."

She stiffened.

"I believe there was a payoff. A big payoff. Something in the range of three hundred thousand dollars. That's water over the dam. Nobody wants the money back. There's something more important at stake. The wrong man was blamed for it. It nearly destroyed him. He still lives under the weight of it. It was a great injustice. He deserves to be cleared."

"What will this do to my father's reputation?"

"Well, it may bring it all up again. Apparently, everyone considered it jury tampering ten years ago, anyway. My investigation could confirm it. It would also pinpoint your father as the juror."

I could see the concern on her face. "What is it you want, Mr. Knight?"

"You were the executrix under the will. I'd like to get your permission to see the records of your father's bank account. I need to know if a major deposit was made around the time of the trial. If it was, the next step is to find out who paid the money."

"How will you do that?"

"I haven't figured that out yet. One step at a time."

"And this will mean my father's name in the paper?"

"It could. And I know that'd be painful. And I don't mean to seem insensitive, but your father's at rest now. The man I mentioned has been in sort of a living death for the past ten years. He can't shake the suspicion."

"Are you his son?"

"No."

"But you seem to have a son's feeling for him."

I had a shot of recollection of how much Mr. Devlin reminded me of the only father I'd known from the age of fourteen.

"Something like that."

She stood up. "I'll have to think about it, Mr. Knight."

I stood, but I didn't move. I needed one more attempt.

"Mrs. Frank, two things. First, if you help me with this, I'll do everything in my power to see that the juror is not named. All that's even suspected now is that it was just one of the twelve."

"Can you do that?"

"I don't know. I'll do my best. The second thing is hard to say without seeming overly dramatic. I'm the only one who cares enough to see this through. I have to go on a trip day after tomorrow. I may not be coming back. Today could be my last chance to work on this."

She took a deep breath that ended in a sigh. When she looked at me, I could see that whatever she'd decided had cost her emotionally.

"I'm going to give you what you want, Mr. Knight. My father was never happy since that trial ended. It changed him terribly. I think it finally brought on the heart attack that killed him. I believe he'd want me to do this."

I nodded. "I understand. If I could have a sheet of paper, I'll draft a consent form. Do you have something showing that you were your father's executrix?"

"Yes, in my desk. I'll get it for you."

BY THREE O'CLOCK, I was getting cozy with one of the officers of South Boston Savings. I was referred to "our Mr. Dunwoody" for this special request. Our Mr. Dunwoody turned out to be one of those people who finds excitement in neatness.

My heart leaped when I checked out his desk with the pad of unsullied paper squared off with the corner of the desk. One silver pen was at attention in its little holder. No fistful of half-sharpened pencils rammed into a Skippy jar here.

The reason this brought joy to my heart was that this was exactly the kind of puppy who might take it as a challenge to his prowess to come up with a copy of a ten-year-old bank statement.

And so he did, but not until he went over the documents I handed him as if they were commanding him to release the Queen's diary. Fortunately, he found that "Everything seems to be in order."

I had a printout of activity of the account in hand in fifteen minutes. Looking at items occurring shortly before the start of the Dolson trial, I checked for any out-of-line deposit.

I thought the fixer might have been subtle enough to spread payments out over a period of time, but he wasn't. It was bold enough to knock your eye out. Three days after the hung jury came in, the sum of three hundred thousand dollars was deposited in the account. As a matter of fact, other than the opening of the account and the monthly addition of interest, that was the sum total of activity in the account. Either he was afraid or ashamed to dip into the funds, or maybe he just wanted it all to go to his daughter.

That settled for me the question of whether or not the jury had been fixed. It left hanging the big one—who was the fixer?

IT WAS ABOUT THREE THIRTY when I made a cell-phone call to Julie from the bank. I thought I'd save a trip back to the office if there was nothing pressing.

Julie told me that Gene Martino had called about three. He wanted me to get back to him around four thirty. That meant he was on trial, probably in Suffolk Superior Court. He'd be back in his office by that time, after court adjourned at four o'clock. Any other county court would have taken him until closer to five.

I asked Julie if he mentioned which courtroom. He hadn't, but he mentioned suffering the slings and arrows of the outrageous Judge Mandoski. I decided to fly direct to the courthouse to catch Gene in person in case there was something he'd rather whisper in my ear than in a phone.

I was more than familiar with the Right Honorable Judge Mandoski. Before the Suffolk Superior Court took up residence in the federal court building, His Honor was the ruling titan of the equity session held in the east wing of the *olde* Suffolk County Courthouse. I believe the first case pleaded in that courtroom was pleaded by Cicero personally—quite possibly before Judge Mandoski. He was a crusty old tyrant, who peered through glasses that looked like thermopane. He had an acerbic wit that could strip an argument down to its naked essence and leave counsel bleeding from lashes to the ego. I could show the scars.

Gene was wrapping up a plea for a preliminary injunction. His argument was pockmarked with craters created by scud missiles hurled from the bench. Defense counsel would have enjoyed the bombardment but for the realization that as soon as she rose to defend, the missile launcher would be turned in her direction.

At four o'clock precisely—and typical of the old boy—out of the clear blue, without a prior hint of which side was ahead on points, Mandoski, J., awarded the decision to Gene.

I caught Gene at counsel table, somewhat stunned but just beginning to realize that he'd won.

"Congratulations, Gene."

"Mike. You got my message. What, were you in the courthouse?"

"Close enough. Hey, you had the old boy eating out of your hand."

"Actually he was eating my hand. Let's get the hell out of here before he comes back for dessert."

We found a spot at the end of the corridor that leads to the world beyond the realm of Mandoski.

"What have you got for me, Gene?"

His voice came down to a lawyer's whisper.

"This is the damndest thing, Mike. You wanted the names of the limited partners behind that apartment house in the South End. I sent interrogatories to the general partner, Robert Loring. He refused to answer. OK, I figure I'll get him at the deposition. So, he refuses to answer the question at the deposition. I take him to court on a motion to compel him to answer. It's a mail-in motion. I've got a right to the information. Get this. The judge denies the motion."

"On what grounds?"

"No grounds. He just writes 'Denied' and scribbles his initials on the motion and calls the next case. I say, 'I beg your pardon, Your Honor.' He says, 'You're out of order, Mr. Martino. I've called the next case.' This is crazy, Mikey. They're guarding the names of these limited partners like the recipe for Coke."

"So it would seem. Who was the judge?"

"Judge Montark. You know him?"

"I've been before him a couple of times. Very low-key. He's always seemed straight."

"He did to me, too, until this. I'm sorry I don't have anything for you, Mike."

"Thanks for trying, Gene. Actually, it helps. I owe you one."

It did help. It told me that the usual channels of court procedure were, for some reason, closed. If I was going to get the information, it would have to be through less orthodox methods.

21

IT WAS WEDNESDAY EVENING about seven-thirty. I'd told Lanny Wells I'd pick her up for our first official date at eight o'clock, which was rapidly approaching. I'd fumbled through two shirts and four ties before coming up with the perfect combination. Then I threw the tie out altogether.

It was not in the least calming to realize that my current state of advanced jitters was my own fault. I'd spent what seemed like decades squeezing eight days into every week just to keep even with my self-imposed demands. The last thing on my weekly list, and the one that always got pushed off the list, was the kind of boy-girl mixing that keeps most people's lives in balance.

The last serious date I could remember was with Emily Snipes. I'm not demeaning it. She was the cutest girl in kindergarten. It went nowhere, however. The ardor had cooled by first grade.

The clear result of an imbalanced social life was a case of nerves that for some reason beat my usual pretrial shakes. I was well beyond the age of acne panic, but I had so many razor cuts that I looked like I'd tried to kiss a pissed-off alley cat.

With the full and certain conviction that I would probably find a way to mess things up, I put the tie back on, took it off, and drove to Lanny's apartment house on Commonwealth Avenue around Clarendon.

Without having much to measure it by, I had the feeling that Lanny and I had probably come as close to developing a feeling for each other, at least from my perspective, as two people can in casual meetings over a piano at Daddy's.

I hit the button for apartment 603 at about eight, give or take four seconds. The warring hoard of butterflies in my stomach could have defoliated an apple orchard.

Then the door opened, and Lanny beamed a smile that blew everything out of my consciousness except the incredible thought that this angel had chosen to spend the evening with just me. The butterflies scattered. I burst into a grin that just seemed to bubble out of everything within me.

She gave me a little kiss on the cheek as I took her hand. I tried to remember the exact date—because I didn't ever want to forget it.

She wore a deep-blue dress with some kind of glitter around the shoulders. It was the first time I'd seen her hair up, which to my untrained eye added a sweet sophistication to natural beauty. When we came together, her three-inch spike heels brought her just under my cheekbone.

I held her hand on the way down the steps, and I was still holding it while I opened the passenger door of my blue Corvette—my one excess in life. When she held my hand a little longer than necessary, I realized that the primary love of my life had been replaced. I apologized to my Corvette.

For some reason, God chose to remove the clouds and sweep the sky with stars. A new moon stayed ahead of us on the drive up the coast along the North Shore, above Boston. I realized by the time we passed through the chain of seacoast towns from Marblehead and Salem to Beverly and Beverly Farms that never had a stomachful of butterflies raised a ruckus more needlessly. We fell into conversation and laughs and the comfort of each other's company as if all this had been waiting to happen.

We arrived in Manchester-by-the-Sea a little before nine. There was a little time to watch the waves spread white foam across Singing Beach before dinner. I mentioned that it got its name from the sound that particular sand makes when you walk on it in bare feet. We agreed to test it next summer.

Danny had held our reservations at the Circolo. We were a little late, but he welcomed us, as he did everyone, as if our presence had made his entire evening. He had a table by the fireplace for us, and insisted on choosing the wine himself.

I discovered through dinner that among the many loves we had in common, excellent food was high on the list. Calories and cholesterol played no part in our selections, guided by Danny's intuitive suggestions, and every inspired opus of his chef brought unabashed smiles and raves from us both.

To improve on perfection, a pianist close by was giving the most tender, loving treatment to some of Jerome Kern's and Cole Porter's gifts to humanity. Before the final coffee, he smiled at us and nodded toward the small dance floor. There was no one there, but the lights were dim, and we had never danced together—until then.

It was midnight when he played "The Way You Look Tonight." I think I was born knowing those beautiful Dorothy Fields lyrics, but I asked Lanny how it went. She sang it to me in a whisper. When she sang those moving lyrics, I could scarcely breathe. We danced the last chorus in a kiss.

IT WAS NEARLY ONE when we bundled up and left the warmth of the fireplace. The main street of Manchester was vacant except for my trusty Corvette, waiting about fifty feet from the door. A light powdering of snow had brought back an almost Christmas softness.

I clicked open the doors of the car and let Lanny slide into the passenger seat. Just before I closed the door, she got that look that says "I forgot my . . ." In this case it was her sweater over the back of one of the chairs at the table. I said, "Stay there. I'll get it."

I handed her the keys before heading back to the restaurant. I said, "Here, Lanny. You start the car and get the heater going. It's that button in the center."

I was about to go into the restaurant when I heard her call. I turned around and she was leaning out of the passenger door to ask, "Which button?"

I had to laugh. It was a fair question since the dashboard looks like the cockpit of a 757.

I yelled, "Right in the center."

She turned back to look at it. I could see a smile of recognition when she must have read the label. She waved out the open door to me as she turned the starter key.

I can't really describe any of the emotions after that. What I felt was mainly numbness. I can barely describe the facts. There was an explosion. The car seemed to come apart. I could see Lanny's body hurled out onto the sidewalk.

I ran as fast as lead legs could get me there. Her body was twisted and her limbs were at odd angles. She was unconscious. There was a pool of blood spreading from where her head lay on the sidewalk.

I dropped down beside her somewhere between panic and shock. I tried to hold her head, but I had no idea what not to move. Danny ran out of the restaurant.

I yelled to him, "911!" He ran back inside.

It was about four or five minutes before we were surrounded by white vehicles with rotating lights. Someone lifted me out of the way, and three men in green overalls and coats went to work on her. I was totally useless except to pray harder than I ever had in my life.

When they had Lanny in the ambulance, I jumped in without asking. They understood. We made record time to whatever the nearest hospital was. The only thing I can remember is seeing a monitor with wires running to Lanny's chest. I think I took my first breath when I saw the sawtooth squiggles running across the green screen. It got my hope machine going.

They wheeled Lanny into a room in the emergency section and three doctors went to work. One of them came out in about twenty minutes. He asked if I was a relative. It was no time to tiptoe around privacy laws. I said, "Yes."

He said she had a broken leg, and possible broken ribs. That plus the cleanup they could handle. She also had a concussion and possible cranial fracture. For that they wanted to get her to the Mass General as soon as possible.

I rode with her on the full-throttle race to the emergency entrance of the Mass General. This time the wait was until about four in the morning, when I saw her being wheeled out of surgery with bandaging around her head. I stopped one of the doctors and caught hold of my heart.

"How is she, Doctor?"

"Are you . . .?"

"Yes. How is she?"

"We don't know yet. She has a hairline cranial fracture. Concussion. She's still unconscious. The next twenty-four hours are the important ones. The sooner she regains consciousness the better. We can let you know."

"Actually, I'll let you know. I'll stay with her."

He thought for a second. "That'll be all right. What relation did . . .?"

"There's another complication, Doctor. Her injuries were caused by a car bomb. She's going to need security. What room will she be in?"

"She'll be in the Phillips wing, room 504. I can notify the police."

"Thanks, Doctor. I can do better than that. I'll take care of it."

I CALLED TOM BURNS'S private number. Fortunately he can come out of a sound sleep ready to listen. I explained what had happened. He said he'd have a good man at the room in twenty minutes. I told him this was connected with the Bradley case so he could start the meter running. He said he was more concerned about something else.

"What's that, Tom?"

"You. You were the target, not the girl. How about if I put a man on you, too?"

"No, just her, Tom. It'd just get in the way. I'll be careful. I've had the wake-up call."

I SPENT THE REST of the night and well into the morning beside her, holding her hand and talking to her. The nurses came and went, and I felt like an idiot, but I heard somewhere that the talking might do some good. I thought there might be something inside that was listening and wanted to come back to my voice.

Around ten o'clock I went out into the corridor and used my cell phone to call Mr. Devlin. I was relieved to see a tall man in nonmedical clothing sitting in the corridor with a good view of Lanny's door. He had the indefinable but unmistakable stamp of private security about him. I knew Tom Burns had come through.

I relayed what had happened to Mr. Devlin. He was grim and grouchy, but there was no mistaking the tone of deep concern.

"What do the doctors say?"

"They say it's important that she wake up. So far she hasn't. I'm staying here with her at the hospital."

"You do that. And call me as soon as there's a change."

"Thank you, Mr. Devlin. I will."

"Another thing, sonny. I'm calling Tom Burns. I want you covered, too. This is getting way out of hand."

It was hard to say no, but the last thing I wanted was a tail. I didn't know where the next few days would take me, and speed and invisibility could be my two best friends. A tail could interfere with both. I said it and kept at it until Mr. Devlin backed off.

I later found out why.

22

BEFORE GOING BACK to Lanny, I checked my messages. Nothing at the office, but there was one at home. It was from Daddy. I returned the call and got him at the club.

"Hey, Mickey, it's like this. There were two men in here yesterday. They were asking questions about you."

"Like what, Daddy?"

"When you be in, where you live, stuff like that."

"What'd they look like?"

"Both Orientals. Maybe Chinese. One a big guy. He's no sumo wrestler. A little smaller'n me. The other one's a little guy. About your size."

I realized anyone of normal proportions would be "a little guy" to Daddy.

"Thanks, Daddy. I know what you told them."

"Right. Nothin'."

It was painful, but I told Daddy about Lanny. He felt the pain, too. He, of course, asked what he could do. I told him same as me. Sit tight and pray.

I WAS MORE CERTAIN than ever that all of this could be traced back to Kip Liu, my personal perversion of Dick Clark. The gaping hole was the lack of proof. More than ever I wanted five minutes with Mei-Li.

I called Harry to see if we were still on for the next morning. After I filled him in, he was on with a vengeance.

There was no change through the day. I held Lanny's hand and babbled on, but there was no response. Around four in the afternoon, my mind was numb. I was out of one-way conversation. The best I could do was recite song lyrics. At some point I told her I was going to say the words to one of my favorite Harry Arlen songs, "My Ship." I got to the part where it says that the pearls and all the treasures my ship will bring will mean nothing "if the ship I sing doesn't also bring my own true love to me."

I could feel the wetness on my face as my head rested down on the pillow beside her. I must have fallen asleep, because I came up sharp when I thought I heard a hoarse whisper say, "Weill . . . Curt Weill."

I jumped up and looked at her. Her eyes were at half-mast, but they were open.

"What? Lanny, did you say something?"

I bent down close and I could hear her say, "Curt Weill. You said it was Harry Arlen. Curt Weill wrote it."

I grabbed her hand and almost yelled, "You came back! Lanny, stay here. Don't move. And don't go back to sleep!"

I ran out the door and down the corridor to the nurses' station.

"Get the doctor! She's awake!"

The nurse was on the pager, and the doctor arrived just after I was back beside her. I read encouragement in his face, and I started to come back to life. He checked her signs, asked her some questions, and gave orders to the nurse. He came over to me before leaving.

"That's the big one, but there are a couple more. She seems alert and that's the best sign. We're treating her primarily for concussion. We'll know a lot more in a couple of days. Were you there when it happened?"

I filled him in. "If that car door hadn't been open and she hadn't been leaning out. That blast . . ."

He just shook his head. "She had something working for her all right. I'll tell you something else. She had to want to come back just now. You must have been saying the right things."

I STAYED ANOTHER HOUR just holding her hand and talking. This time it was two ways. A team of nurses and younger doctors came to do some tests, so I left them alone.

I called Mr. Devlin to give him the news. It was a lift to hear that it really meant something to him. I told him I was coming back to the office and I'd check in with him. One more call to Daddy to let him know she was awake, and I was on my way.

IT WAS DARK, AND THE NIGHT air felt so good that I decided to walk. I came up Cambridge Street and took my usual shortcut through Pi Alley. I always loved that little paved pathway. It was actually where the newspaper trade in New England began. Printers used to throw their printing type, called "pi," into the street, whence the name.

It was dark, but I knew every inch of the rough pavement. Fifty feet into the alley I might have heard something or just sensed that someone was behind me and gaining. I looked back and saw the outline of a man moving directly toward me.

I couldn't tell if it was paranoia or just good, solid fear, but I picked up the pace anyway. The pace of the footsteps behind me came up, too. It was a good seventy feet to the end of the alley ahead of me. I'd have given next year's pay for just one more human being in that alley.

I looked up and my prayer was granted double. I could see two figures coming toward me about fifty feet away, and the comfort it brought cannot be overstated. They were clearly men, which, under the circumstances was all to the good, although any form of humanity would have done.

The comfort was short-lived. The steps behind me were beginning to gain speed. I was tempted to call out to the approaching pair, but I had no idea what to say.

In what seemed like a second, the steps behind me were up to a dead run and no more than twenty feet away. The other two were still a good forty feet ahead. Even if I yelled, what could they do? I was tempted to run toward them, but it was too late.

I spun around with both fists ready. A glint of light from above played on the barrel of a gun. I braced for the shot and crouched. What I felt was a kick in the ankles that sent me sprawling. I hit the ground in a gangly lump just as I heard a forced whisper, "Stay down! Stay down!"

The form went flying past me. It stopped and crouched and fired a volley of four shots. I saw the two figures that were coming down the alley drop where they were. The man who fired was standing over them, gun pointed, checking for signs of life.

That same raspy whisper said, "Come up here."

He still had the gun, so it seemed like a good idea to follow orders. When I was beside him, he pulled out a small flashlight and shone it on the two bodies at our feet. There were two large, running holes in the chest area of both of them, and neither man showed any sign of movement.

The light moved to the area of their arms. Both had forty-five-caliber automatic weapons in hand. Most chilling of all, they were both Chinese, one a little less than Daddy's size and one about my size.

The voice beside me said, "You better get out of here unless you want to spend the night answering police questions."

"Who are you?"

"It doesn't matter. I work for someone who works for someone who wants you to stay alive."

That meant Lex Devlin. Now I knew why he agreed not to call Tom Burns to have me protected. He was going to do it anyway.

"How did you know about these two?"

"I spotted the guns in their hands when they turned into the alley."

"I didn't see anything."

"You weren't looking. You were more worried about me."

I still had the shakes, but the panic was rapidly turning to anger. Someone had turned the legal battle into all-out terroristic war, with the worst possible casualties so far being Lanny and Red Shoes.

I figured I had two clear choices. The first was to go underground and hide or depend on rescuers for the rest of my life. That was unacceptable. The second might well result in a seriously shortened season, but anything was better than the first. I chose the second, and knew I'd better do it while I was still white-hot angry enough to overcome abject fear.

I searched through the pockets of the two dead Chinese until I found what I was looking for. I turned around to thank the man beside me, but he was nowhere in sight. I ran down to the Washington Street end of Pi Alley and turned right up toward Chinatown.

I WAS ACTING ON INSTINCT, but without time and proof, it was all I had. At that moment, I'd have bet the pot that the one behind the attacks on me and Red Shoes was that slick dude I first met at the Ming Tree. He was the only one who knew both of us, and he set off alarms the first time I met him.

I ran or jogged most of the way to Tyler Steet. I knew I could never bring off what I had in mind if I were cool and rational. I climbed the steps of the Ming Tree restaurant and walked straight in.

I was just inside the door when I spotted Kip Liu seated at a table at the far end with his back to me. There was no one else in the restaurant. I made a direct line at quick march. He must have heard determined footsteps, because he spun around when I was ten feet away. I hovered over him so that he couldn't stand if he wanted to.

His first expression told it all. He was looking into the face of an Occidental ghost. I was supposed to be dead—twice.

While he was still off balance, I snapped down on the table in front of him, picture-side up, the two driver's licenses I had taken from the bodies in the alley. I let him recognize the faces and draw his own conclusions before I grabbed them back. I was not irrational enough to leave the evidence of two homicides in his hands.

I leaned over him to say it directly into his ear.

"Listen to me, you cowardly son of a bitch. The word is out. If one more incident, even an accident, happens to me or anyone close to me you'll have every cop in the city of Boston and one particular detective on your personal ass. You and that parasitic pack of bastards you run will be hung out to dry. Every one of you. That's a promise."

He just stared. I don't think he'd had a personal threat since the day he was born. It was all bluff, but I was raging enough to carry it off. I had no idea how he'd handle it. I didn't have to wait long. I turned around and saw two muscular teenagers coming down the aisle with blood in their eyes.

I turned back to him. "You want to test the system? It's up to you."

He looked in my eyes, which must have been as cold as the steel I was feeling inside. He made a living trading on the fear he put in others. Now it was his turn. They were five feet away when he waved them back.

I straightened up and looked at the two of them. They were completely blocking the only way to the door. The big shot hesitated just long enough to give me chills from toes to nose. I could only wait. I put every bit of concentration I could muster into holding the bluff. I knew he was weighing the loss of face in front of his men—no small item—against loss of his whole seedy empire if I could pull off what I threatened.

It took five of the longest seconds of my life right then, and probably ten years off the back end of my life, before he made the decision. He finally gave a signal. They stood aside.

I walked between them with every ounce of deliberate cool I could muster. I figured that if I made it alive to the door, we'd have established a stalemate. At least for the moment.

I've never smelled or tasted air as sweet as the air I breathed outside the door of the Ming Tree. I caught a cab on Beach Street to get back to room 504 at the Mass General Hospital.

23

FRIDAY MORNING I was up and off early in a rental to pick up Harry and catch a direct flight from Logan Airport to Toronto. I decided to take advantage of the dead time during the flight to get a handle on the game plan. Obviously Harry had given it some thought.

"The first thing we've got to do is to get inside the place alive. If we do that, we have to find someone who'll trust us to see Mei-Li alone."

"Right on, Harry. How?"

"I'll do the talking until we're alone with Mei-Li. It'll all be in Chinese. So I'll let you know now what I hope is going to happen. When we find the building, I think it'll be pretty much the same layout as the Beach Street house. I'm going to try to get us in by telling them I was sent by Kip Liu, the man you met at the Ming Tree restaurant. You'll be a business associate of mine."

"Why Kip Liu?"

"From what you and Mr. Qian said, my intuition tells me he's the man in the Boston tong. Not the Dragon Head, but probably the *Fu Shan Chu*, the number two man."

That reinforced my instinct.

"Will that carry weight in Toronto?"

"It's the same tong. They have branches in New York and Toronto. That way they can shuttle prostitutes among the three. They do the same with soldiers in the gang when one of them gets in trouble."

"Suppose whoever you talk to decides to call Kip Liu to check on the Chinese Batman and his white Robin?"

"Then they'll probably kill us. Have you got a better plan?"

"Nothing concrete."

"I've got another ace in case things get dicey."

"Which is?"

"Somehow I slip into the conversation the number 489. That's the code number for the Dragon Head, the *Shan Chu*. They'll figure I wouldn't know it if I weren't a member of the tong. And no one who's a member would use it lightly. It might get immediate respect. They might not want to risk offending the Dragon Head by questioning anyone he sent."

"Where did they get 489?"

"It goes back centuries. I told you they were big on symbolic numbers. If you add four and eight and nine, you get twenty-one. Add the two and the one and you get three, which was the most significant number to the old triads. Also, twenty-one is the big three times lucky seven."

I must have looked at him a bit doubtfully. "Are you by chance pulling this straight out of your ass?"

"Michael, those three digits could be the only thing standing between us and the kind of death I'm not even going to tell you about. Believe me, I'm not making it up."

We had a window and an aisle seat. Fortunately there was no one between us. I unbuckled and slipped over to the middle seat.

"Harry, when you put it that way, I've got to ask you a personal question. If this stuff is so secret, how do you know about it?"

Harry looked out the window as the pilot announced that we were passing Niagra Falls on our right. He was still looking after we passed the falls. I knew he hadn't forgotten the question.

We've been close friends since we were seventeen, but obviously there was a gap in my knowledge of his background.

When he turned back, he leaned closer. I could just hear him over the drone of the engines.

"I guess you need to know this, Mike. You're putting a lot of trust in what must sound like Dungeons and Dragons."

He took a breath before saying something I think he had never told another soul.

"My father was drafted into the Chinese Red Army just before my mother came to this country. My mother and grandmother and I lived in Chinatown in Boston before we moved to Brookline. They both worked twelve, fourteen hours a day, seven days a week at their restaurants in the suburbs. I never really saw them. I was twelve years old. I resented it. I was too dumb to realize they were earning money for me to go to Harvard and MIT. I was the hope of the family for something better.

"I used to spend time with a bunch of kids in Chinatown. We started hanging around a martial arts school. They'd let us work out with the mats. It's actually the tong's recruitment place for the youth gangs. I didn't know it at the time. I didn't know much."

"I knew I couldn't afford the classes. I couldn't ask my mother for the money. She wouldn't have wanted me to hang around there anyway. One of the older kids saw that I was catching onto kung fu pretty fast. He said he'd pay for my lessons. I was dumb enough to let him. I guess I was getting back at my mother and grandmother. The older kid always said not to worry about the money. Someday he'd ask me a favor.

"The favor came when I was thirteen. It was the turning point in my life. I hated it, but I did it. I was afraid of losing face with the other kids. I've been ashamed of it every day since."

He looked me in the eyes and saw something that made him keep going.

"There was an old man on Tyler Street. He ran a grocery store. It was a dismal sort of place. I don't think there was anything in his life that wasn't drudgery. Except he had one thing in the shop. It was a tank of exotic goldfish. It was the prize of his life.

"The older boy who paid for my lessons told me the old man kept servants in the basement and he beat and tortured them. He said he and his friends were vigilantes. They were going to teach the old man a lesson.

"I went with a couple of sixteen-year-olds to the grocery shop one day after school. We ransacked the store. When we finished, they gave me a rock and told me to break the glass fish tank. The old man was looking at me while the others held him. He was pleading with me. I can still see it in his eyes. It was like he was pleading for his life. The other boys were yelling at me to do what I promised.

"In all my life, I wish I had that one moment back. I smashed the tank. The old man crumbled. I could hear him sobbing when I ran out of the store. I cried all the way home.

"The next day, the boy who'd paid for my lessons told me I was going to join the gang. I told him I couldn't. He said they'd tell my mother what I'd done. I couldn't do that to her, so I joined the youth gang.

"Every time I passed the old man on the street, he got older, more feeble. Of course I knew by that time that it wasn't true about the servants in the cellar. He was just an old man who wouldn't pay *lomo*— "lucky money"—to the tong.

"They started having me go on other jobs. I did it because of my shame before my mother.

"Six months later, the old man died. I knew I had killed him. He started dying the instant I smashed that tank of fish. I took away the only thing in his life that gave him pleasure.

"I couldn't stand it anymore. I had to get out. Actually, I was lucky. The number two man in the tong had noticed me. I think it was because I was the only one in the gang in a college-prep course in a decent high school. It was unusual. Most of the kids in the gangs don't get educated beyond high school.

"He seemed to like me. I became almost like a son. He'd take me along to meetings that none of the other gang members went to. He told me things that were part of the tong. Secret things. I think he was grooming me to move up in the organization.

"When the old man died, I couldn't live with myself. I went to him for the supreme favor. I wanted out. It had never been done as far as I know. He wasn't happy about it, but he said he'd plead for me to the *Shan Chu.*

"A week later, he sent for me. He seemed very sad. He said that I was released from my oaths. I have no idea what he had to do to pay for my freedom. I never saw him again. He just disappeared. He might have been sent back to Hong Kong. I know he forfeited something.

"The other gang members froze me out completely. That was all right. It wasn't long before we moved to Brookline. The way they move around, none of the gang that I knew back then is left in Chinatown."

Harry looked at me directly. He looked more stricken than relieved.

"That's a part of my life I'm not proud of, Michael. I live with it every day. I'm only telling you so you'll know I'm not guessing about the tong."

He turned back to the window. I nudged his elbow.

"Harry, you remember what Jesus said about letting the one who is without sin cast the first stone?"

He looked around at me. I looked him in the eye when I said, "I'm in no position to cast any stones, brother."

He waited in case I had more to tell him. Somehow I wasn't up to filling in the details. Maybe another time. I thought, God grant there'd be another time.

24

BY TWO IN THE AFTERNOON, Harry and I were in a taxi, weaving our way through the streets of Toronto's Chinatown. The driver found Columbia Street, and we walked from there. We spotted a grocery shop in the middle of a block that fit Xiao-Wen's description.

Two Chinese boys, in the range of about sixteen to seventeen years, bracketed the doorway beside the grocery shop. I'd never have given them a second look, but now I noticed the lean, muscular builds and the eyes that scanned everyone and seemed to take in more than I'd expect from a couple of kids just hanging out.

I felt a slight nudge and barely heard Harry whisper, "That's the place, Mike. From here on, it's my show. We don't panic, no matter what happens. Believe the bluff. We've got friends in the tong so powerful these bozos don't dare to mess with us."

We picked up the pace, like a couple of businessmen on a mission. Harry breezed past the two at the door without dignifying their existence with so much as a nod. I realized that there is a lot of implied power in looking like you know where you're going.

Both of them turned around. One of them started to speak, but the other one grabbed his arm. I noticed he also touched a button beside the door.

The outside door led to an inside flight of stairs that ran beside the grocery store. At the top, there was a door with an opaque glass center and Chinese embossed figures in the glass. While the layout was similar to that of the brothel on Beach Street in Boston, the approach looked far more sterile and bright. It could have been the entryway to a good orthodontist.

We climbed the stairs without haste or hesitation, and Harry knocked on the door at the top.

A slender woman of about fifty opened the door. She wore a sheath dress of emerald silk that bespoke feminine allure and dignity at the same time. I got the impression that she was one of the few survivors of the trade who went on to rise as far as a woman could go in management.

Her bow and smile to Harry were gracious. There was a bit of stiffness that translated to chill when she saw my *low faan* face. Harry matched her graciousness in both bow and smile. I did my best to keep the shivers from rippling my clothes.

Harry spoke to her softly in Chinese, while I took in the silk-suited dude at the carved mahogany desk across the room. He was about the age and cut of the Ming Tree's Dick Clark. If scorpions came with slick black hair and manicured fingernails, I'd have looked for his stinger.

His perusal of Harry seemed almost nonchalant, but there was a distinct toning of the senses when he spotted me.

It was also hard to ignore the bulky six-footer standing by the wall to the left of the desk. He had one of those muscle developments that prevented him from fully dropping his arms or bringing his knees together.

As nearly as I could follow, the woman introduced herself to Harry as Mrs. Woo Yo-Si. Harry became Wong On-Lee, which I think was actually his Chinese name. I was getting used to the Chinese custom of placing the family name first.

Harry introduced me as Peter Frathing, which was the name of one of our classmates at Harvard, who never, to the knowledge of either of us, said more than three words in an evening. I got the hint.

Mrs. Woo brought us over to the desk and graciously introduced us to Mr. Sun Yu-Ming. Everyone ignored the stack of muscles to Mr. Sun's right, which suited me fine.

Mr. Sun addressed me first, in English.

"Mr. Frathing, we see so few Occidentals in our humble establishment. How did you happen to hear of us?"

I did some fast computing. I knew I was supposed to be an associate of Harry's, but I didn't have a clue as to what business we were supposed to be in. I tried to lead something neutral to avoid finessing my partner.

"On-Lee has told me many times that there is no beauty on earth to compare with Chinese beauty. He kindly invited me to accompany him on his business."

The Chinese Batman flew to my rescue. "Actually, Mr. Frathing is too modest. He has been of immense assistance to our Boston family in helping us with the guidance of our children. We would be hard-put to function without his wise advice in certain matters of their up-bringing, such as the one that brings us here. In that regard, I bring you greetings from our Mr. Liu."

The name "Liu" cracked a polite smile of recognition from Mr. Sun and slightly flared his pencil moustache. He waved an invitation to two chairs in front of the desk.

"Ah, yes. Mr. Liu and I have had many mutually beneficial deal-ings. I trust he is well."

"He is, and wishes the same for you. As a matter of fact, I've come in regard to your most recent dealing. I believe you received a flower from Mr. Liu by special delivery. It was a very delicate flower. Mr. Liu is very grateful that you would give it room in your house."

"I was honored to be able to accommodate Mr. Liu. Is there a ques-tion about this particular flower?"

"Only the desire to see and learn what we can from this unique specimen. As I mentioned, Mr. Frathing is instrumental in guiding Mr. Liu's children. If we could see this flower, we might learn something essential to furthering their education."

I stood there with a knowing smile, totally clueless. I figured the flower was Mei-Li, but who these children might be escaped me en-tirely. It was like playing a tennis match when you can't see the ball.

All I knew was that Mr. Sun was unflustered. He was also making no apparent move to produce Mei-Li. He played with a tiny piece of ornamental jade sculpture on his desk for a moment before speaking. I was moving from seriously concerned to seriously terrified that my white presence was shooting the plausibility out of Harry's cover. Mr. Sun opened the center drawer of his desk to check something before picking up the telephone.

"I'm sure you appreciate what a delicate flower this is, Mr. Wong. I'm certain you'll understand my checking carefully before exposing it to sunlight."

Panic bubbled close to the surface, but we both held it in check. Harry must have been as sure as I was that the silk scorpion was dialing up Kip Liu, who would probably give the execution order on the spot.

He pressed enough digits for long distance, the first three of which were "617"—Boston area code—and then swung back in his chair. I counted the rings. By the third, my pulse hit one hundred and eighty. Each ring after that brought it down ten beats. When it hit six, he placed the receiver back in its cradle, and I breathed "Thank you, Lord"—not necessarily out loud.

The scorpion swung back to look at us. He was talking to Harry, but in my honor, he kept it in English.

"I'm afraid we'll just have to wait. In the meantime, you'll be my guests. May we bring you tea or whatever you desire?"

Harry was on his feet with his right hand in the breast pocket of his suitcoat. "Muscles" was beside him faster than I thought that much bulk could move. He eased off when Harry took out his wallet. Harry pulled out a hundred-dollar bill and a pen.

"That is not acceptable, Mr. Sun. My time is not limitless. I come representing a certain gentleman who requests a courtesy of your *er pao*. If your *er pao* wishes to deny or delay the courtesy, I'll return that message to the gentleman."

Harry inscribed three small digits with a felt pen on the hundred-dollar bill. I figured the hundred was some multiple of something significant. The digits were "489"—the symbol of the Dragon Head of the tong.

Harry folded the bill and handed it to Mr. Sun, who looked quickly at the digits. He rose immediately and bowed. The greaseball polish had dropped out of his tone of voice. He sounded like a man who had been on the verge of making a colossal mistake and had pulled back in time.

"Mrs. Woo will escort you to a suitable room. The flower will be brought to you immediately."

Harry bowed curtly, not to lose the momentum. We followed Mrs. Woo through a door in the back of the office to an expensively and tastefully appointed sitting room toward the back of the building. The white silk brocade in the upholstery matched that of the wallpaper, and the tapestries looked authentic and ancient.

I noticed the lack of a bed. Mr. Sun apparently took us seriously about being there for information.

I caught Harry by the arm as soon as Mrs. Woo closed the door with the promise of an immediate return. I whispered.

"Can we speak?"

"Do it quietly. I don't think they have the gall to eavesdrop on the Dragon Head's business, but don't broadcast it."

"Right." I kept it low. "Who are these children I'm supposed to be guiding?"

Harry leaned close. "One of the things that keeps these bozos in business is that it does no good to plant microphones or tap their phones. They always speak in code. Sometimes just the way someone sets down a pair of chopsticks means he has a shipment of hot money to exchange."

He glanced at the door, but nothing yet.

"The word 'children' usually refers to a shipment of narcotics. Like, 'I'm happy to say my fourth son is home,' means 'I just received a shipment of pure number four heroin.' When I told Sun that you help guide our children, I was saying that you help the tong bring shipments of narcotics across the border."

"I'm impressed that you speak the language, On-Lee."

"You're impressed, Mr. Frathing, because you don't know what they'd do to us if we make one slip. We're not back in Cambridge yet, Toto."

There was a slight knock on the door before it opened. Mrs. Woo walked in ahead of a young Chinese woman of about twenty.

I thought that I'd never seen beauty to compare to that of Xiao-Wen, the girl we first thought was Mei-Li; but the real Mei-Li—on a scale of one to ten, you could forget the scale. No finite number that I could think of came close.

The grace with which the jet-black silk of her hair flowed into the long, deep blue sheath that outlined her flawless form was arresting; but the indefinable beauty of every perfect facial feature from eyes, nose, mouth, to chin actually constricted the breath at first sight.

Features and form aside—although they were the absolute apex of everything desirable in a woman—there was something far more striking. Xiao-Wen's beauty could have been captured in a wax doll without losing anything but motion. She had been molded into a sort of Stepford consort, where every word, look, and gesture was a pre-programmed answer to the desires of the client. Nothing human, nothing that was "Xiao-Wen" showed through.

Mei-Li was different. Her spirit glowed through her large, almond eyes. This was a woman that anyone could not just love, but fall in love with.

Mrs. Woo performed the introductions and beat a bowing retreat, closing the door softly on her way out. Mei-Li's responses to the introductions showed a smooth grasp of English.

I took her hand and led her to a corner where three chairs were clustered. As a second-thought precaution against electronic ears, Harry and I moved the chairs to the middle of the room before we sat down.

I cut to the chase.

"Mei-Li. We may not have much time together. I'm a lawyer in Boston. I represent a client by the name of Anthony Bradley."

A bat at high noon could have seen the reaction. Her mouth dropped open, and a gasp told me she was taken completely unaware. She came forward in the chair and uncharacteristically interrupted before I could go on. Her voice was low but crowded with tension.

"When did you see Anthony? Is he all right?"

"Yes. So far he's all right. I saw him yesterday afternoon."

"Did he ask for me? He must have been worried."

I wasn't sure how to handle that one.

"He had no idea that I'd see you, Mei-Li. He's in the Suffolk County jail. He's charged with murder."

The gasp this time squeezed a tear out of the corner of one eye.

"Whom do they say he murdered?"

"An old man in Chinatown. His name was Chen An-Yong."

That brought on the flood. I gave her a handkerchief and let it run its course. When she looked up, her precise makeup was in streams, and I thought she was more beautiful than when she had walked into the room.

"How can I help Anthony?"

"I need information, Mei-Li. I need the truth. If you lie because you think it'll help Anthony, it might put him in prison for the rest of his life. Do you understand?"

She nodded and blotted one more escaping tear.

"How did you meet Anthony?"

"I met him through the man I worked for in Chinatown."

"His name?"

"Mr. Liu. He is called Kip Liu."

There was a slight sense of satisfaction in the confirmation of my instincts about him. Very slight. Mostly I disliked the entire direction this seemed to be taking.

"Tell me about it."

"When I was first brought to America from China, I was sixteen. I was commanded to be Mr. Liu's . . . mistress, for some time. I met Anthony when he would come to a restaurant in Chinatown to meet with Mr. Liu. Mr. Liu ordered me to . . . become friendly with Anthony. I did, and . . . we became much more than friends. We saw each other frequently, even when Anthony was not meeting with Mr. Liu."

"Why would they meet?"

"It was business."

"What business?"

She lowered her head. There was no response.

"Mei-Li, Anthony's charged with murder. His only hope right now lies in my knowing everything there is to know about Anthony—good or bad."

She nodded and said something I couldn't make out. I leaned closer to hear it again.

"Drugs. Heroin and cocaine mostly."

"Was he addicted?"

She said it even more softly, but I caught it.

"Yes. Once. But then he stopped."

I looked at Harry. "Why would he go to Chinatown? He could get anything he wanted in Cambridge." I was thinking of Barry Salmon.

Harry had a gray look in his face.

"There's a reason, Mike. Think about it. Kip Liu doesn't deal with addicts one on one."

I looked back at Mei-Li. "Was he buying narcotics in large quantities?"

She nodded "I think so. Yes."

"How would he dispose of them?"

"I don't know. He began doing business with Mr. Liu after his first year of college. He was very depressed. He began using cocaine heavily. But he stopped last fall."

"Did he keep on doing business with Mr. Liu after he stopped using cocaine?"

"Yes. Until after Christmas."

"What happened then?"

"Anthony and I were in love. He wanted to stop what he was doing with narcotics. He wanted to end it. He wanted to buy my freedom so we could be together, be married. Mr. Liu first told him he could never get out. Then, after Christmas, he told Anthony there was a way, but he would have to do a big favor. There would be a big price, but he could get out, and I could be free."

"What was the price?"

"I don't know. He called Anthony just before the Chinese New Year. He told him to meet him on Sunday afternoon at the Ming Tree restaurant. He would tell him then."

"Were you at that meeting on Sunday?"

"No. I was living at a house on Beach Street. That Sunday morning, two men came for me. I never saw them before. They brought me here. They would not let me see Anthony before we left."

I looked at Harry. His look back said that he agreed that the pieces were falling together in an unfortunate pattern.

"Did you know the old man who was killed, Chen An-Yong? He had a grocery shop on Tyler Street."

"I would see him outside of his shop. He was always kind to me when I saw him. But he was kind to everyone."

Tears escaped from both of her eyes, and I couldn't tell if it was for Anthony or Mr. Chen.

Mei-Li brought us back from the pause. "How did you find me?"

"It's a long story. I don't have time to tell you the whole thing, but it started with a girl about your age. She worked in the Ming Tree restaurant as a waitress. Short girl. That's about all I know about her. Except that she wore bright red Chinese slippers."

"That's my little friend, Lee Mei-Hua. We are closest friends. We confide everything to each other. But how did she know where I was?"

"She didn't. I was at the restaurant Monday. She overheard that I was Anthony's lawyer. She wrote in a note that she'd help me if I'd help you."

"She must have known that if Anthony was in trouble, I'd be in trouble, too. She was risking her life."

"I'm sorry, Mei-Li. I'm really sorry. I believe she's dead. She was murdered. I saw the body in the morgue. I couldn't really identify her, but there were the red shoes."

Mei-Li turned away and the tears started again. The sobs seemed to let out what was building up. I was out of handkerchiefs, but I held her against my shoulder until the sobbing stopped.

Harry gave me a nudge.

"Mike, we've got to wrap this up. Our friend could be out there making another phone call."

I gave him a "just one more minute" nod.

"Mei-Li, I can't think of an easy way to ask this. I'm sure that somehow your friend's murder is tied in to Anthony's case. It leaves so many questions. This is a difficult one to ask. They seemed to have killed your friend without a thought. Why do you suppose they didn't do the same to you?"

She blushed. "I believe I was very expensive when they acquired me. They didn't want to lose their investment. My friend, Lee Mei-Hua, was a waitress. She was of value only to her mother . . . and to me."

"Who was her mother?"

"Mrs. Lee."

"The owner of the Ming Tree restaurant?"

"She is not the owner. They own the restaurant. They only put the restaurant in her name to make it look respectable."

That dropped a piece in place. No wonder they were free to conduct business at the Ming Tree. Harry gave me an emphatic look, but I had one more question.

"Mei-Li, I'm sorry to ask this. If your friend were too badly beaten to recognize by her face, could you identify her any other way?"

"Yes. She has a scar between the fingers of her left hand. It was a broken dish. I was with her when it happened."

I filed that away. I began to see the dimmest light at the end of the tunnel.

When she could straighten up, I held her by the shoulders.

"Listen to me, Mei-Li. I need you to come back with me. I don't know what's left to save for Anthony. There may be nothing. I don't know. I can only promise you it'll be dangerous, but I believe you can help Anthony."

I looked at Harry. His eyebrows had climbed a solid inch at the realization that I had promised the impossible. On the other hand, Mei-Li had no hesitation.

"I'll do whatever you say. Can you take me to Anthony?"

Harry was shaking his head vigorously while I said, "I'll try."

Harry lifted me by the arm while bowing slightly to Mei-Li. He nearly carried me six feet away in spite of the toll it took on his ribs.

"Michael, are you suddenly suicidal? You got the information. If God chooses to grant a miracle, you and I will get out of here before that cockroach changes his mind about the phone call."

I got Harry to ease his grip before speaking in the softest tone I could manage.

"I need her, Harry. I have a feeling she can tie this thing together."

Harry was so furious he was hissing out the words.

"You don't need her. You got the facts. You can find people in Boston to testify. Besides, she digs your client in deeper. Can't you figure out what the 'price' was Anthony had to pay? And when he killed the old man, they weren't going to let him out. They don't do that. They were going to use the court to send him to prison for life with their witnesses. He was an example to any of their people who got frisky."

"Maybe, maybe not. I know this. I can't leave her here, Harry. This is too pathetic. This is slavery. They can't get away with it. Dammit, this isn't third-century China! It's the United States." The hot steam seemed to go out of Harry's words.

"Actually, it's Canada, Michael."

"So what? You said it's your community. Look at her. You like this?"

He had no response, but he let go of his grip. I went back to Mei-Li.

"Do you ever get to leave this place?"

"Only to go downstairs to the grocery store. I go in the morning to shop for rice and vegetables for the house. They never let me go outside."

Harry came back to our tight little circle, and I had the feeling that he was back in the lineup. He picked up on my thought.

"What time in the morning, Mei-Li?"

"Around ten o'clock."

"Make it exactly ten o'clock tomorrow."

We put together an idea so sketchy, and iffy, and dependent on circumstances, that it started everything from my tonsils to my toes vibrating with fear. A lifetime of reading James Bond novels, and a fat lot of good it did me when the chips were down.

25

HARRY AND I SHOPPED THAT NIGHT for some essentials for the following morning. We checked into a motel, and each fought a war with our nerves for an hour or two of sleep.

At nine forty-five in the morning, we were sitting in a rented van, a block from the grocery shop on Columbia Street. Toronto was putting on a gray bluster that promised snow. The temperature had dropped to the low teens. I prayed that the snow would hold off until we had finished business, in case we needed traction.

The coffee was hot in our hands through the plastic. We'd talked a lot the night before about what we were up to, but we never got to the heart of the matter. Harry finally got the words out through the plume of steam rising from the cup next to his lips.

"I know now why I'm doing this, Mike. This really is more my cause than yours. This is my chance for a payback."

He looked for a reaction, but I waited to see where this was going.

"You're just here for your client. I'm not a lawyer, but I think you could get killed doing him more harm than good."

I was still listening.

"You heard Mei-Li. What do you think of your client's innocence now?"

I took a hot sip and still had no real answer. "It's more complicated than that."

"Well, then, let me tell you how I see it, Mike. That business about your client's getting out of his deal with the tong is pure fiction. Maybe Mei-Li believed it. Maybe even he believed it at the time. But it doesn't happen. They don't let you out. It would set a very bad precedent."

I looked at him. "Harry, they let you out."

"That's why I know how special the circumstances would have to be. You want to hear what happened with your client? This is my version, and I'm in a better position to guess than you are. Anthony fell in love with Mei-Li. He straightened out his addiction. So now he's in control of the pressures that got him into the drug-selling deal in the first place. He wants out. Clean.

"He goes to his contact man in the tong, Kip Liu. Liu sets him up. He tells your client that the price of freedom for him and Mei-Li is one little murder of an old man. He has your client meet him at the restaurant at the height of Chinese New Year. He knows the target will be in the window across the street. He convinces your client that one pop of a pistol in that din will never be noticed, and he and the girl are free.

"Your client buys it. Liu gives him the pistol in the restaurant. Your client goes down on the street and shoots the old man. Now Liu has him arrested by the police with two ready-made, honorable witnesses.

"The news media goes crazy over this new violence in peaceful Chinatown. The Chinese community naturally goes into a frenzy over the murder of one of its most beloved fathers. The whole thing is a gift to the DA. And Liu's clear. And the precedent is right. The kid was *not* let out. He winds up put away at the hands of the state. The kid can claim that Liu had him do it, but it's the kid's word against Liu's.

"In fact, it turned out even better than that for Liu. Your client is sticking to the story that he didn't do it, probably because he doesn't want to admit the whole thing to his father. So Liu doesn't even get implicated."

Harry raised his hands and looked to me to find a hole in the theory. I took a long sip of coffee while my computer was spinning.

"I thought you told me the Chinese don't look to the white establishment for help."

"They don't, Mike. This is not some Chinese victim going to the police because he's been robbed or extorted. This is the tong using the white system as a tool to get what they want done."

I had no immediate answer. Everything in me wanted to disbelieve Harry's theory. I wanted Anthony to be innocent. But I'd be doing what Mr. Devlin warned me about. I'd be playing the game with my own fantasy facts. I could miss getting the best outcome for the client on the real facts.

Harry brought me back. "You didn't answer my question. If your client's guilty, is it worth it for you to risk getting killed here?"

I gave it some thought before answering.

"I've got to go through with it, Harry. Just because I can't find a hole in your theory doesn't mean it's right. Either way, I'm committed. Mei-Li is the only one I can get to identify little Red Shoes. Mrs. Lee could do it, but Liu's got her tied up so tight I'll probably never even see her before trial. I still have a gut feeling there's a connection between Red Shoes's death and Anthony's case. If I could open up her murder, it could unravel a lot that I'm just not seeing. If I don't try, I'll never know if it cost Anthony his freedom."

Harry had no answer.

"I know I'm grasping at straws here, Harry. But Mei-Li's my last straw. Everyone else is hostile or dead."

I looked over at my faithful coconspirator. "How about you, Harry? Last chance out."

Harry drained the final bit of coffee and set the cup down. He checked his watch. "Maybe I can score one for the ancestors. Anyway, you'd be like a splayed duck in there without me. Let's go. It's time."

WE PARKED THE VAN CLOSER to the grocery shop. Harry went first. He started down the street toward the store with a large shopping bag in his hand. He was bundled in an oversized overcoat, a wool scarf around his mouth and nose, and a floppy fur hat down over his ears. It could all pass as protection against the cold, and at the same time he could have been anyone from Mao Tse-Tung to Boy George. He put on a limp and a slouch that added age.

I watched from the van as he passed slowly between two young turks at the door. They were different from the two of the previous day. They eyed him but gave no sign of alarm. That cleared the first hurdle—one of many.

I gave him a few minutes to browse around the shelves of the grocery store before I waddled in, attired in a similarly fetching outfit. The fear of the moment was that the two young toughs would notice that the steam had stopped coming out of my mouth when I passed between them. It stopped because I was so scared I couldn't breathe.

One of them mumbled something to me in Chinese. I tapped my ear and shook my head, which, thank God, they took for a sign that I was hard of hearing. They said something to each other and laughed. I was never so happy to be the butt of a joke.

It was exactly 10:01. There was no one else in the store but Harry in mufti, an old woman in Chinese garb shopping in the back, and the elderly clerk at the front counter absorbed in a Chinese newspaper.

The store was laid out the way Mei-Li described it. The counter with the cash register was to the left of the door as you came in. One dimly lit aisle crowded with merchandise in sacks and cans labeled in Chinese led back to a storeroom twenty feet to the rear. Beaded strings hung as a separation between the two rooms, but I could see into the storeroom.

I got a slight nod from Harry and played my part. I took a can of what looked like water chestnuts from one of the shelves in the front and approached the old man behind the counter. I asked for a detailed translation of the Chinese labeling to check out the sugar content, the amount of salt, whether they added elephant tusks, anything I could think of.

He understood everything I said up to "Good morning." I, in turn, understood even less of what he was saying. Together we got into a hot debate over water chestnuts without ever exchanging a thought; but more to the point, Harry had free access to the back room.

It took about three hour-long minutes for Harry to locate what he was looking for. Then all hell broke loose. It started with one loud *pop!* in the back room that brought the old man's head up and sent his glasses flying off his head. I knew then that Harry had located the stash of fireworks left over from the Chinese New Year. Mei-li had told us where they were.

The second and third pops turned into what sounded like continual bursts from an automatic rifle. Then crates of fireworks exploded in such rapid succession that it sounded like rolling thunder. Sparks spit in every direction, and a cloud of gray smoke billowed out into the store.

Seconds later there was a flash that lit up the rear half of the room. The blasts became deafening as the flames in the back room reached the cherry bombs and possibly M-8os.

The old man was frozen in panic. The two galoots at the front door made a charge for the back room that carried them past Harry and the old lady. They started beating away at flames with old burlap bags until the bags themselves caught fire.

As soon as they passed, Harry hustled the old lady down the aisle toward the front door. As he ran, I noticed he held a razor blade against the fifty-pound sacks of rice on the shelves. It was a beautiful sight to see a waterfall of rice consuming the floor behind him.

When I saw Harry coming, it was my turn to bolt for the door and get the van. I got to within two feet of the door when I ran smack into a wall of flesh. The door was crammed full of the muscle-bound goon we'd seen in the office the day before. He stood there like a zombie, watching the Fourth of July blow the back off the store, while the old man screamed in high-pitched Chinese.

There was no way past him. I heard Harry yell, "Do it, Mike!"

The zombie focused on me. Before he could move, I dropped on my back in a crouch. I kicked both heels straight out with a thrust that came from the spine. I caught him square in the crotch. He doubled over with a groan that drowned out the screaming old man. He fell forward, inside the door. I figured if he ever turned out to be an innocent bystander, I owed him one whale of an apology.

I looked back and saw the two punks in the rear. They'd seen what happened up front and made a charge up the aisle that looked to me like the entire Chinese army coming down on us. They got about to the canned bean sprouts when they both did an upender as if someone had cut their feet out from under them. The rice that covered the floor made it like running on ball bearings. They tumbled in lopsided cartwheels, spewing out Chinese that I didn't want translated.

I was on my feet and through the open door by the time Harry closed the gap. The old woman was somewhere in between.

I cut left to get to the van and ran head-on into the arms of the two punks that had been at the door of the brothel the day before. One of them grabbed me in a grip that pinned my arms. I could feel my feet leaving the ground. My legs just waved in the air as the grip around my chest tightened.

I could feel the breath squeezed out of me, and I couldn't get air back in. Everything was going from color to black-and-white. My only conscious thought was of the pain that meant that in another instant ribs would start cracking.

Just before that instant, everything came loose. As fast as I was gripped, I was released. I heard the sound of Harry's slicing hand on his neck just before I dropped to the ground like a rock. The kid who had the grip fell to the ground beside me. I lurched away from him, but I could see he was unconscious.

I saw Harry standing behind him. Harry spun around to square off for combat with the other punk.

Harry shouted, "Get out of here, Mike!"

I ran for the van.

Fortunately I had left the keys in it for a quick start. I pulled up to the sidewalk beside the shop. I saw Harry exchanging open-fist blows with the second boy. I knew he was in no condition to take on the Karate Kid. I jumped out of the van to help.

Harry yelled, "Get back in the van!"

I was torn between the two, but Harry yelled, "Do what I said, Michael!"

At that moment, Harry took a step back and dropped his arms to his sides with his hands behind his back. He stood still and waited.

The young enforcer froze in confusion for an instant, then seized the moment. He drove in close enough to go for a chop to the base of Harry's neck. Harry's hands moved so fast I could hardly see them. He twisted left so the blow glanced off his shoulder. In the same fraction of an instant he grabbed the top of the coat of the attacker in his right fist. He pulled it open with the right while he stuffed something inside with the left. Meanwhile the kid used his position to chop away at Harry's ribs.

Orders or not, I was about to bolt for the neck of the kid when there was an explosion that sounded like a muffled stick of dynamite. The kid was blown halfway across the street.

Harry half–straightened up, clutching his ribs. He was heading for the van, when I caught sight of three more punks of the same cut as the two Harry had just leveled coming at a full charge down the sidewalk. They were at twenty-five yards and closing. I rammed the van into first and floored it. I swerved around Harry onto the sidewalk and played the three like making an easy spare. They jumped, but I made enough contact to put them out of commission.

I threw the van into reverse and backed up to the shop. Harry pulled open the back hatch. He grabbed the arm of the old woman who had been following close behind and practically threw her into the back of the van before jumping in himself. I floored it again—this time on the street.

We made two right turns on the left two tires and one left turn on the right two tires before I let up on the gas. I brought it down to cruising speed once we were clear of Chinatown.

I headed south, as we'd planned. When we stopped at the next light I checked the backseat. Mei-Li had pulled off the gray wig and bulky clothes that had turned her into an old lady. She had found them in the aisle at the back of the grocery shop where Harry had set them down in the shopping bag he brought in. She was able to slip into the back room long enough to age forty or fifty years.

I yelled back, "Stay down, Mei-Li. Just in case."

I looked over at Harry, who was leaning heavily to his right. "You OK, Harry?"

He let out the breath he was holding. His voice sounded strained. "Why do they always go for the ribs? I'll be all right. Keep moving."

"My every wish. What did you drop in that kid's jacket? It blew him halfway to Montreal."

"I kept a couple of cherry bombs from the fireworks box. I thought they might be useful."

I just whistled at the thought.

WE DROVE ALONG an open roadway south and west of Toronto along Lake Ontario. I found the small motel in a lakeside village where I'd made a reservation the night before.

I went in and registered in my name while Mei-Li got back in costume. I hustled her into the motel room while Harry rested his ribs in the front seat of the van. I'd bought a few things for her for overnight, since I knew she'd be traveling fast and light. I left some money for meals through the next day.

She was obviously still shaken by the escape, but she seemed to have no injuries or regrets.

"I'll be back for you tomorrow sometime, Mei-Li. Stay in the room till I get here. You can order out for lunch and dinner from the pizza shop. Just don't call a Chinese restaurant. I'll give you a call tonight to see if you're all right. Here's the number at my office if you need me. Don't speak to anyone else. You understand?"

"Yes. Will you be seeing Anthony?"

"I don't know. Time's short."

"If you see him, would you tell him I'm safe?"

"Sure."

The wind bit on the walk back to the van. We could have used breakfast, lunch, Scotch, any number of things. Harry could probably have used a doctor. But more important was catching the earliest plane back to Boston.

26

HARRY AND I CAME OFF the flight ramp at Logan airport a little after one o'clock. I had less than an hour before meeting Mr. Devlin for the pretrial conference at the courthouse. The judge had accommodated the DA by holding the hearing on Saturday. My first move when I hit solid ground was to call Lanny's room at the Mass General. My heart nearly came through my ribs when she answered the phone herself.

She said she was doing fine, all things considered. I thought it was pretty gutsy, considering all the things there were to be considered. It was not your average first date.

I promised to get over to see her as soon as possible. She understood the necessary flexibility in the schedule since I had filled her in on most of what was going on.

HARRY WAS STILL HOBBLING a bit, but he had managed to straighten up. I had one last favor to ask.

Before we left the airport, I called information for the number of the Ming Tree restaurant. I dialed it and handed the phone to Harry.

"Harry, see if you can get Mrs. Lee on the phone. I'll need you to interpret. I'll tell you what to say when you get her."

I listened to the exchange. I guessed by the inflection of Harry's Chinese that she wasn't there. Harry hung up, and we headed for the taxi stand.

"Not only is she not there, Mike. I asked, and they haven't seen her at the restaurant for the last couple of days. No idea when she'll be in. Is that a surprise?"

"It's a disappointment, not a surprise. They've got her hidden away. She'll be back for the trial."

"You're starting to think like they do, Mike. You've been paying attention."

"I had a good professor. I figure they realized we could get to her at the restaurant. She's Kip Liu's insurance policy as long as she doesn't change her testimony."

We split into separate taxis. I headed directly for the courthouse. I led the driver to believe the tip would be doubled if she beat her best time through the tunnel. She apparently took me seriously. She burned a route through back streets of East Boston that don't appear on maps. They brought us to the very head of the killer line of airport traffic at the entrance to the tunnel. She squeezed into line with a horn and an endangered left fender. I made good on the tip, and jotted down her name for future needs—Carlotta something.

I GOT THROUGH SECURITY at the courthouse as soon as possible and met Mr. Devlin at the bank of elevators. We rode in silence up to the eighth floor.

Before going into courtroom 809, Mr. Devlin hustled me into a small, unoccupied lawyer's conference room. We had five minutes. I used four of them to fill him in on the Toronto details.

He took in every word with his chin on his fist and his eyes locked on mine. There were no interruptions, but two veins were pulsing in his temples by the time I finished.

He looked me over.

"Are you all right?"

"Yes, sir. Harry's a bit under, but he'll come around."

The veins were hammering at this point. It took him three seconds to spit out, "*If you ever . . .*"

"I won't, sir. I won't. The rest is easy." It seemed an injudicious moment to mention that I still had to get Mei-Li across the U.S. border.

He just looked at me. I had no clue what was going on in his mind, but it seemed a good time to break the train of thought by filling him in on Harry's call to the Ming Tree.

He spent another twenty seconds in thought after I ran out of words. I gave him the space until he bounced up and checked his watch. He grabbed his briefcase.

"You have to make up tactics as you go along, sonny. Sometimes a good hunch is better than logic. This one should get their attention. Let's go."

WE WADED THROUGH THE BUZZ of newspaper and TV people who packed the six-row spectator section to SRO. Pretrial conferences are generally held in a judge's chambers. I assumed that this trial was drawing so much public attention, especially among the people in Chinatown, that the judge wanted everything done in the open.

Ms. Lamb was sitting expectantly at prosecution's table. She bared her teeth in her version of a smile for Mr. Devlin's benefit. He cast a slight bow in her general direction, and we took up residence at defense counsel's table.

We were just seated, when the "All rise!" brought us back up. Judge Posner mounted the bench with a sprightly step. He was just shy of fifty, with the neat, graying look of dignity that befits the bench.

He had the reputation for being a no-nonsense, down-the-middle, neither defense- nor prosecution-oriented judge. He held a tight rein, but let the lawyers try the case.

The clerk called the case of *Commonwealth v. Bradley*. There was little to deal with at this particular pretrial, since there was not much by way of scientific evidence to exchange and no evidence that called for motions for suppression. The defendant admitted being at the scene at about the time of the killing. The only question was whether or not he pulled the trigger. The actual murder weapon had not been recovered.

The primary business of the conference was to fix a trial date. The court called for counsel to state their preferences. Ms. Lamb was first on her feet. She came out swinging. Mr. Devlin kept his peace during her impassioned plea for swift justice—the swifter the better. The people were ready "at any moment" to bring the defendant to justice.

I thought to myself, "If we could try him this afternoon, waive the appeal, and sentence him at dawn, she could file her candidacy for the governorship in time for a campaign breakfast tomorrow morning."

The real translation of Ms. Lamb's position was that she had her ducks in a row and ready to quack—they being the two eyewitnesses. The sooner she could get the case to trial, the less time we'd have to find counterwitnesses or work on her two stars.

When she had run her course, Mr. Devlin rose slowly and addressed the court quietly. She had neatly laid the burden on the defense to come up with a good reason for delaying the trial.

"May it please the court, Ms. Lamb is zealous as always in her representation of the people. I think her zealousness carried her beyond her intentions this time. She couldn't possibly mean that the commonwealth is ready to try this case."

He paused, as if groping for the next word. I knew something was up. Mr. Devlin had never groped for a word in his life.

Ms. Lamb jumped into the pause with both feet.

"Mr. Devlin underestimates the commonwealth's sense of duty in preparing this case, Your Honor. This is a vicious crime that has the entire Chinese community watching and waiting to see if justice will be done. I want it on the record that any delay will be the result of the failure of defense counsel to put his case in order."

Mr. Devlin took the grandstanding in better grace than I would have predicted. In fact, he seemed to enjoy it.

"I'm impressed, Your Honor, but I can't believe the district attorney would consent to anything short of a two-month period before trial."

She was on her feet, grinning a grin that I last saw on the lips of a trout just before I set the hook. "Your Honor, I assure you and Mr. Devlin that the people are ready to begin this case this afternoon."

She was looking at the judge, but her insufferably smug body language was aimed at Mr. Devlin. The eyes of the judge and every reporter in the courtroom were on Mr. Devlin, while he played with the papers in front of him. I was more anxious than the rest to see what delaying tactic he could pull out of the air.

He looked up from the counsel table with an almost imperceptible grin.

"Your Honor, let's call her bluff. I move for a trial date of this coming Tuesday."

My eyes shot to Ms. Lamb. It was as if she had asked for a toy and got the toy store. Her eyes bulged. She had to forcibly close her mouth. I have to admit, it took me a few seconds to get my own breathing started again.

The judge registered something between controlled shock and indignation.

He was on his feet and heading for his side door when he issued the command, "I'll see counsel in my chambers."

He was at his desk, in robes, drumming a tattoo on the arm of his chair with his fingers, when our little band of Ms. Lamb, Mr. Devlin, and me paraded in. He didn't bother to invite us to make ourselves comfortable.

"I don't know what you're up to, Mr. Devlin, but I'll give you the ground rule. No one plays games in my court. This case is going to be tried by the book."

Mr. Devlin accepted the noninvitation and sat down. Mr. Lamb followed suit. As for me, there were only two chairs.

Mr. Devlin calmly bit the words off in dead earnest. There was not a trace of a smile.

"This is no game, Your Honor. I've got a boy who could be sentenced to life here. There isn't anything on earth I take more seriously. You say we try it by the book. The book says that defense counsel has the right to decide how his case is to be tried, as long as he isn't shown to be incompetent. I've never been accused of that."

The judge's steam subsided.

"What's this business about beginning this case on Tuesday?"

Mr. Devlin leaned back. "Anthony Bradley is the son of Judge Bradley. I'm sure you know that. I say that not to ask for special favors. But it does create a problem. The longer he remains incarcerated with men his father may have sentenced, the greater the chance he could be executed before the trial. Prison precautions are never perfect."

Mr. Devlin nodded to Ms. Lamb, who was perched like a raven on the edge of her seat. She had the look of one who was beginning to look her recent gift horse in the mouth and wasn't sure that anything that came that easily from Mr. Devlin could be totally in her favor. Mr. Devlin set the hook a bit deeper.

"The district attorney says she's ready. In fact, she's on record before the court and about fifty newspeople bragging about it. The defense is ready, Your Honor. You have my word. I say let's get on with it."

Judge Posner looked to Ms. Lamb for reaction. She was stymied. If Lex Devlin wanted a trial date that close, it had to be for a reason that could only endanger her glorious victory. On the other hand, Mr. Devlin had boxed her in nicely with the reminder that she'd be quoted in every evening edition and news broadcast as champing at the bit for quick justice. Hard to go back on that one.

She took the least awkward path.

"Your Honor, I said the people are ready. I'll stand by that."

The judge played with the tips of his reading glasses at the edge of his mouth while the mental tumblers clicked into place. He finally called his docket clerk over with the court schedule.

"What about this, Peter? How does Tuesday look?"

"You have a light schedule, Judge. Remember you were going to leave next Tuesday for the Colorado conference. That takes out the rest of the week. You just have a pretrial conference on Tuesday morning."

The judge chewed a bit on his glasses before he looked up at his clerk.

"Set this down for Tuesday, Peter. Ten o'clock. Call Mary and have her move the pretrial back to four thirty Monday afternoon. And have her cancel my reservations for the conference. This is more important."

Judge Posner looked back at the two combatants.

"You have what apparently you both wanted, counsel. Let's go back out. I want this done publicly and on the record."

I CAUGHT A CAB BACK to my apartment by way of a brief stop at Mass General. Lanny was sitting up in bed, as bright and pretty as if she had not just been bombed out of a car. It was clearly the bright spot of my day to see her, and the feelings we had three nights before seemed to carry over in spite of the circumstances.

It was a briefer visit than I'd have liked, but I needed a shower, a change of clothes, and a few hours' sleep before a long night. It gave me the chance to think through the plan of attack Mr. Devlin outlined to me before we left the courtroom. I had to give the man credit for guts. Thank God he was lead counsel.

I had left him outside the courthouse, facing what looked like a porcupine of microphones in front of three rows of newspeople. The questions were coming six at a time, and I could see a bit of the old glory coming back in his eyes.

THE PHONE BROUGHT ME OUT of a sound sleep at six o'clock that evening. It had been dark for over an hour. Harry's voice lifted me somewhat out of the after-fog of a daytime nap.

"Mike, what time are you leaving?"

I checked my watch. "I'd better get rolling now, Harry."

"Good. You want to pick me up, or shall I meet you someplace?"

"You're not coming on this one, Harry. I can't repay you for what you've done already."

"I want to see it through to the finish, Mike. Can you pick me up?"

How could I refuse? Besides, the company would keep me awake.

"Half an hour. We'll eat on the road. Bring some coffee. And the dress code is definitely a business suit. Conservative tie."

THE RIDE TO CANADA WAS LONG, broken only by intermittent stops for food and changes of driver to keep alert. We crossed the Canadian border at six o'clock the next morning and drove the rest of the way to the motel where we'd left Mei-Li.

We picked her up and hit the road immediately. It was too close to Toronto to make it comfortable to spend excess time. Before we reached the U.S. border, we spread some blankets and made Mei-Li as comfortable as possible in the trunk of the car.

Whether it was the continual assault of the coffee on my nervous system, or the prospect of spending more years than I cared to think about in a federal penitentiary for alien smuggling, I couldn't tell. I only knew that my stomach was being eaten alive by hordes of rabid little cankerworms. Harry looked like he had the rest of the world's cankerworms in his stomach.

We passed the Canadian officials, who showed no great interest in our leaving their country. As we approached the U.S. customs officers, I gave thanks that Mei-Li was a light, petite size three. I remembered that back in the days when whiskey runs to Canada were practiced by Americans who otherwise wouldn't run a yellow light, customs troops always checked the trunks of cars that were riding too low on the rear springs.

As we approached the officer, I noticed that he was a walking mountain of starch. I could feel Harry tense up.

"This time I'll do the talking, Harry. Let me have your identification."

He gave a quick nod and handed it over. I drove up alongside the officer. He took the picture ids and gave Harry a good look. He checked them against our faces, but didn't hand them back right away. I could feel Harry's left leg begin to quiver.

"Do you have anything to declare?"

"No, nothing."

He took another look at Harry without handing back the passports. Harry looked straight ahead.

He looked back at me.

"What was your business in Canada?"

I gave him my best take-it-seriously look. "For the most part the usual, raping and pillaging the villagers."

Harry's leg shot straight out. I thought it was going to go through the fire wall. Fortunately the officer didn't notice. Everything in the sight line of the officer appeared calm as a duck on water.

The officer looked at me as if he might squash this impertinent bug. I said a devout prayer in the seconds that followed. When I looked back up at the officer, my entire body heaved a silent sigh. Inside all that starch, there lay a sense of humor. He was actually grinning when he handed back the id's and waved us on.

When we were driving safely on U.S. soil and at least ten miles out of sight of the starched guardian of the border, we let Mei-Li out of the trunk. We stopped at the next minor city to buy clothes for her—some jeans, shirts and sweaters, and a warm jacket—and food and coffee for us all. It took us another ten hours to hit the outskirts of Boston.

I pulled into a gas station. While Harry filled up the car, I got the number from information and called my secretary, Julie, at home. I knew she had an apartment with one other girl in Belmont.

Mei-Li, even considering *her* past life, had been through hell in the previous two days. I thought she needed some comforting female company in a safe environment.

"Julie, Michael Knight. I'm really sorry to bother you at home. I need a beaut of a favor. This is so far above and beyond the call."

She was the angel I'd anticipated. If it was an imposition, and I knew it was, she never let on. I knew Mei-Li would find some peace there.

I dropped Mei-Li at Julie's, Harry at Harry's, and I just plain dropped. When I hit the bed in my apartment, it was early Sunday morning, about the time I usually leave for church. I figured the Lord would rather have me alive in bed than stone dead of exhaustion in a pew at St. Basil's.

I woke up sometime Sunday evening, staggered to the kitchen for a glass of milk, and fell back on the bed in the deepest sleep of my life until early Monday morning.

27

MY FIRST STOP Monday morning was to pick up Mei-Li at Julie's. Julie had left for work. Her roommate, Liz, answered the door. Julie had apparently indoctrinated her, because she demanded identification before she'd produce Mei-Li.

The China doll looked even more radiant in American clothing. In jeans, sweater, and loafers, she looked like an American grad student.

Apparently Julie and Liz had fallen in love with her. They were sharing everything that Harry and I hadn't bought for her.

I was sorry to have to tell her about the morning's business.

"This is no way to begin your first week as a free American, Mei-Li."

Somewhere between Toronto and Belmont, I had made up my mind that she was never going back to the Chinese rat pack, if I had to adopt her.

"I need to have you come with me to the morgue."

I FOUND THE SAME ATTENDANT, who took us directly to the vault. Mei-Li was a soldier, until the attendant undid the covering and she saw the face of her friend, my little Red Shoes. I took her outside until she was able to face it.

"Which hand has the cut, Mei-Li?"

She indicated the left one.

I went back in and covered up the rest of the body, leaving only the left hand exposed. I brought her back into the room. She began weeping when she looked at the hand. That was all I needed to know.

The attendant asked if she could make an identification. I told him I couldn't be sure. I made a sympathetic gesture toward her obviously undone state and said that I'd be in touch with him.

After returning Mei-Li to Julie's apartment, I drove from Belmont to Cambridge. I called Tom Burns from Harvard Square.

"Tommy, it's Mike. This is the end of the trail. I need just one more favor. I need to locate Dolson, the arsonist that . . ."

He knew.

"That's the one. I need to find him *mucho pronto*. Like yesterday. Can you do it?"

"Shouldn't be hard, Mike. He's the type leaves a trail."

"Thanks, Tom. You might check the parole office. I don't see him staying out of trouble. If he's not in jail, he's probably on parole for something. Hey, why am I telling you your business?"

"Cause you can't help interfering, Mike. That's what got you into this in the first place."

"Guilty. I'm out of the office, Tom. I may be in a bad cell-phone position. If you come up with something, will you leave a message with Julie?"

It was ten o'clock when I knocked on the door of Barry Salmon's cocoon. I could see him through the opaque glass, weaving his way through the clutter. He opened the door and peered at me through red roadmaps of eyes. I don't have as much blood in my body as Barry had in his eyeballs.

"Barry, you gotta take better care of yourself."

"Mike! I don't see you for a decade. Now we're daily visitors. Come on in."

I waded through an aroma so sickly sweet that you could become a diabetic just breathing.

"A wee touch of the pipe, I detect here, Barry."

"Well, you know, Mike, it makes the sunrise that much more effective."

"There are no windows in this room, Barry."

"Ah. Yeah, that's true. But a couple of puffs and I can imagine it."

"As a matter of fact, that's what brings me here, Barry."

"You want a puff, Mike? I've got the best you ever smoked. Come over here. You're my guest."

"Barry, you're all heart. I need a different favor. You remember we were talking about Anthony Bradley. And maybe some of that group he belongs to that helps with tutoring students."

"Yeah, sure."

"Some of them are involved in another function, aren't they?"

Barry was not too far into the bag to recognize a thin-ice question.

"Mike, you're not with the feds or anything? You're not fuzz, are you? Cause if you say 'no,' and you are, that's entrapment."

Wrong, but this was no time for a law lecture.

"I'm just a lawyer, Barry. In fact, I'm a defense lawyer. I sometimes defend the people you're concerned about protecting."

"Oh, well, that's a horse of a different hue. What do you need?"

"I figure there's a clique within that club that's dealing drugs big-time. I think my client, Anthony Bradley, was the head of it. My intuition tells me that *numero dos* is a slick little dude named Abdul. How am I doing?"

"Um. I might have heard words to that effect. Nothing for the record."

"That's close enough, Barry. Could it be that you've dealt with Anthony or this Abdul on the odd occasion?"

"Without recalling anything specific, stranger things could have happened. Not with Bradley. Possibly with Abdul. Notice the use of the legal word, 'possibly.'"

"You're a paragon of caution, Barry. Could you give me a couple of other names you've 'possibly' dealt with in that little circle?"

He sucked in heavily what passed for air in that room and moaned, "Wow. I don't know."

"C'mon, Barry. We're just talking possibilities here. Nothing incriminating."

"Merely in the realm of possibility, could we say Tony Mazzarelli? We might consider the name of Rolf Samuelson."

"That'll do it, Barry. Here's the punch line. I need to know for sure about Anthony Bradley. It's an important piece. What I want you to do is call Abdul. Set up a meet someplace neutral. Make it that restaurant across from the T station in the square. Tell him someone from the Chinatown connection has some wonton soup they want to dispose of. Will you do it?"

He popped a cigarette between his lips—this time legitimate, Marlboro. He held the pack out to me. I shook my head.

"You don't even use these, Mike? Damn, what gets you through the day?"

"Willpower. What do you think, Barry? Will you do it?"

"See, I suspect that I'm cutting off a source here, Mike. You said I should take better care of myself. That's not taking care of myself."

"That's not exactly what I meant, Barry. Besides, you can't tell me that after all these years you don't know every source from here to Chelsea."

"You raise a legitimate point."

I detected a crumbling. "I really need this one, Barry."

He pulled over a phone and peered at the numbers he was hitting through a white cloud of Marlboro fumes rising from the stick between his lips. There was a pickup after three rings.

"Yeah, is Abdul there?"

There was a slight pause before even I could hear a voice crackling in rap rhythm from the other end.

"Hey, my man, Abdul. I'm just a conveyor here. I got a call from a dude says he's from Chinatown. Says he has some wonton soup to peddle. I don't know who he is. He wants to set up a meet."

There was another pause before Abdul spoke. Barry answered him.

"This dude says he wants you meet him in the restaurant across from the T station in the square. The sooner, the quicker."

Barry gave me the nod, *yes*. I flashed him the OK sign and mouthed the words "Booth in the back." On my way out, I could hear Barry relaying the message.

I reached the corridor and took a deep breath. It cleared the lightheadedness that was beginning to set in.

IN FOUR MINUTES, I was behind the sports section of the *Globe* in a booth halfway to the back of the restaurant. In another five minutes, I heard the bopping rhythm of Abdul's sneakers pass me on the way to a vacant booth at the very back. At ten thirty in the morning, there was no one else in that section.

I slid out of the booth and came around from behind Abdul. I slid in beside him before he could do anything but sputter jive. I turned off the flow and calmed him down by somehow getting enough words in to convince him I was there on business. He was trapped, but listening.

What I needed was to solidify a piece of the puzzle in my own mind. Were any members of the student organization into drug distribution at the university, and more to my purpose, was Anthony the point man dealing with Kip Liu and the tong for supplies? I was going on the Lex Devlin theory that you can best serve your client in a criminal case if you know the truth—the whole truth—and Anthony himself had perhaps not been a fund of that commodity.

"Abdul, you know whom I represent. Are we clear on that?"

His nervous brow was furrowed, but he gave me a slight, quizzical nod.

"Good. Then some business needs tending. There's a concern that you must be getting low on supplies. There's also a concern about interrupting the flow, losing customers. Not good for business."

He was soaking up every word, but there was no reaction. He was also not saying that he hadn't the foggiest idea of what I was talking about.

"My client had me make contact with the man where they sell the wonton soup. He's also concerned. My client may be out of service for a while, maybe permanently. Contacts would dry up unless someone takes the reins. My client says you're the man to take over the top spot. He thinks you're ready to go from Indian to chief."

Nothing. He was still looking. He was still not talking. I had to get a confirmation in my own mind about Anthony's connection.

"The question, Abdul, is are you up to it? Behind all that bopping jive, is there a businessman who can handle a serious operation? Needless to say, the position carries a higher cut."

The furrows grew deeper, but no words came out.

"Or do we look elsewhere? I'll tell you right now, you're not my choice, but my client insists on giving you a chance. Either way, I have to know immediately, because steps have to be taken."

He just looked from me to the table. I had to jar him loose.

"OK, Abdul. That answers it. The job interview is terminated. You'll be hearing from the new man."

I started to move out of the booth when he caught my sleeve.

"Hold on, man. Sit down. I don't know anything about you."

I settled back in.

"Well, I'll tell you, Abdul. You know the one I represent. You know I know about the Chinatown connection. You know I know about the operation here. You're smart enough to notice that I'm talking to you instead of to the U.S. Attorney. Maybe that tells you something. If it doesn't, so be it. You're out. I meet with a new contact, and you go on being a flunky. I'm happy either way. The only option I don't have is to waste time. There's a kettle of wonton soup waiting to be delivered."

The look on his face said the wall was cracking. One last thrust.

"Last chance, Abdul, I'm no dentist. I'm through pulling teeth here. We talk, or I walk. Call it. I have to get word to my client."

I gave a little move-out body language, and he grabbed my elbow again.

"All right. I'm in. Tell Anth . . . your client. I'm the man. I just gotta be careful."

That locked it shut. Now I knew. Whether or not Anthony pulled the trigger on Mr. Chen, he was no choirboy. While I was at it, I decided to work the mine a bit further.

"Careful is good. Careful is what keeps the operation going." I checked my watch. "Let's get this done, and I'm out of here."

I leaned in for the kill.

"How well do you know the operation?"

"I know it. I been around since right after . . . your client got in it."

"That doesn't tell me anything. Our friend wants me to be sure you can handle it. Who are the contacts on campus?"

He pulled back and looked around.

"I'm not gonna' say it out loud."

"There's no one here but us chickens, Abdul. In case you missed the point, this is a quiz. Before I put you in touch with Chinatown, you've got to convince me that you've got control of the operation. Point one, I want to hear the contacts. Not to make you nervous, but

198

I'm here to grade your paper. You miss one of them, and this inter-viewer finds another applicant."

He looked up at me and started slowly.

"Over at the gym, there's Matt Toner."

He paused. It could have been to see if it was what I wanted to hear. But there was something in the way he was looking in my eyes for a reaction that set off an alarm. I swung out of the booth.

"You're wasting my time, Abdul. You'll be hearing from whoever I pick. Have a nice life."

He jumped, "Whoa, man. I had to test you. I had to find out if you really knew them. Sit down. Gimme a chance."

I sat. Abdul was like a well that gives nothing until it's adequately primed, and then it gushes forth sweet water. He laid out the names and locations of every drug-dealing contact in the operation. As a check, I was glad to hear the two names Barry gave me. I was relieved to hear among the missing the names of Gail Warden and Rasheed Maslin, the two students I had first met in the office of The Point.

He even laid out the flow of the narcotics from the Chinatown con-nection through his organization's distribution to impress me with his grasp of the business. I was impressed.

I listened without emotion. When he finished, I nodded.

"You've got it, kid. Can you handle a shipment next week?"

"Yeah. Things're getting low."

"I'll be in touch. I'll leave a message at The Point when I want you to contact me. You better get out of here. I'll wait for a few minutes after you leave."

I let him out. He seemed to walk with less bop and more stature. Being an executive had apparently gone to his head.

When he cleared the door, I checked the recorder in my pocket to see that it was still running. I ran a rewind to check the quality of the recording. It sounded better than a Blue Note CD to me. I also noted that neither Anthony's nor my name was mentioned from the point where I had set it in motion in my pocket.

I popped out the cassette and put it in the envelope I brought in my pocket. I addressed the envelope to the president of Harvard University.

Before I sealed it and dropped it into a Harvard Square mailbox, I slipped a note into the envelope that just said,

Dear Mr. President:
Consider this my annual contribution to the Harvard alumni fund.

28

I USED MY CELL PHONE to call my number at Bilson, Dawes, which Julie picked up on the third ring. She was sweet as could be until she heard my voice. Then the whispered torrent started.

"What did you do to that poor girl? She was frightened out of her mind . . ."

"Julie . . ."

"She could barely eat. I don't know what you put her through, but if . . ."

There was no stopping her. I hung up and redialed. Before she could rev up again, I slipped in a couple of sentences.

"I didn't touch her. I saved her. I haven't got time to explain the whole thing. Someday I'll tell you. In the meantime, you're an angel to help her."

That got her back on earth.

"Julie, did Tom Burns call?"

"Yes. About ten minutes ago."

"And said what?"

"It was weird. He just said, 'Bingo. Walpole.' What does that mean?"

"It means I love you, Julie. I'll reimburse you for anything you spend on Mei-Li."

"Oh, no you won't."

"We'll talk later. Keep Mei-Li out of sight. Nobody sees her but me. I don't know if she told you, but there are those whose day would be made by her demise. They'd arrange it if they could find her. Do you understand, Julie?"

"As much as I understand anything you do lately."

"That's good for the moment. Someday I'll take a week and fill in the details. Right now understand this: you're on the side of the good guys. Bye, Julie."

I hung up and caught the T to Boston to pick up my car.

THE RIDE GAVE ME A CHANCE to organize some thoughts into what could only loosely be called a plan. With one exception, which I planned to handle that evening, things seemed to be in place for Mr. Devlin's game plan for Anthony's trial. I could have reported back to the firm for some scut work under Whitney Caster or I could take my best shot at something that seemed far more important. It was an easy choice.

I half walked, half ran from Park Street Station to the federal building. My acquaintances with the staff from my old days in the U.S. Attorney's office helped breeze me by the assistants to the ears of the man himself.

Peter Styles had been U.S. Attorney since before I worked in the office. He was straight as a line, and had precious little patience with those who weren't—particularly those in public office. He was truly the stuff of which prosecutors should be made.

When I arrived, he was on the fly out of his office to Judge Wyman's courtroom. I grabbed the arm that was not laden with files and walked him back into his office and closed the door. He looked as if he didn't know whether to smack me or have me committed.

Before word one escaped his practically foaming lips, I whispered the words that trumped even the fear of Judge Wyman—"Political corruption that could go as far as the Massachusetts Supreme Judicial Court."

He knew me well enough to freeze in midtemper. I gave him a rough sketch of what I thought I could deliver and got the commitment from him of a major weapon to carry into battle.

IT WAS A GOOD HOUR'S DRIVE out to the state maximum security prison in Walpole. From past cases, I was a familiar sight to the guards who handled lawyers' visits.

Within ten minutes I was sitting in the visiting room across from the infamous Frank Dolson. According to the guard, he was doing ten years on another arson. There was no denying that the man had carved out a specialty.

He was a gray-to-white–haired, late-fortyish type, with the kind of prison pallor that suggested that he didn't spend a lot of time in the yard. He had that slack ease with his surroundings that comes from a collection of years in an institution and a number of years yet to go.

He didn't know me from Mahatma Ghandi, but a chance for a trip to the visitors' room broke up a long afternoon for him. He was in no hurry.

"Mr. Dolson, my name's Michael Knight. I'm a lawyer. I work with Lex Devlin."

That brought a slow smile. "How's the old fox?"

"He could be better. That's what I want to talk to you about. I need some information."

"Doesn't everybody?"

202

"I suppose. I need to know about the jury on your first arson trial. I want to know about the fix, if there was one."

His eyebrows went up in controlled interest.

"Let me tell you how I see it, Mr. Dolson. I think someone bought a few years of your time. You agreed to plead guilty to an arson charge to prevent someone else from getting caught. The idea was to plea-bargain for a sentence of a few years, do the time, and come out to a bank account. When they found the bodies in the fire, it turned into a murder charge, which was more than you agreed to. The only way they could get you out of that before you started naming names was to fix the jury. My guess is that you had nothing to do with the actual fix. But you probably knew about it."

He leaned back in the chair. He was clearly on his home turf. The grin told me I was on target. The silence told me I was not even in sight of first base.

"I've got a proposition, Mr. Dolson. It could change your life from this minute on."

Nothing. Not a flicker. But he was listening.

"They hung that jury fix around Lex Devlin's neck. They never proved anything. The rumor was enough. He's worn it like a noose for ten years. It took the better part of his life. I think you're going to do the decent thing. You're going to give it back to him."

The self-amused grin broadened.

"What makes you think so?"

"Your own self-interest. I can make a phone call to the United States Attorney. He can have you out of here and into the federal witness protection program by tomorrow. It all depends on you."

Dolson kept the grin for show, but his eyes got curious.

"No free lunch, Knight. Never has been, never will be. What's the price?"

"Information. Later, testimony. You give the U.S. Attorney the names of the big shots who pulled the strings to fix the jury. It could start the dominoes falling. That's what the U.S. Attorney wants. Mine's more personal. I want it made clear that Lex Devlin had nothing to do with it."

The grin turned from time-killing amusement to contempt. He leaned across the table with a typical prison whisper.

"You said I'm going to do the right thing. Let me tell you what I'm gonna do, Mr. Lawyer. I'm gonna do another three years in this joint and go for parole. Then I'm clean. I walk out of here. I got no worries about my back from some big shot I ratted on. Nobody ever touched me with that jury fix. Devlin wants me to rat on someone? Tell him to go to hell."

I pushed back from the screen between us and stood up. I took my time buttoning up my topcoat to emphasize the fact that I was leaving and he wasn't.

"I don't think I'll give Mr. Devlin that message. I hope you're getting a big kick out of your smug little act, because in a couple of days you may find yourself indicted as an accessory to murder. That jury fix that you agreed to is all part of the arson that turned into homicide. By then I won't need your testimony. Don't count on being out of here in three years. I was willing to help you. Let's see how you make out with the U.S. Attorney when the fan gets a hit."

IT FELT LIKE A GOOD exit speech, but I knew I had hit a brick wall. Dolson was still not in a frame of mind to move. He knew a bluff when he heard one.

When you hit a wall, you've got three choices. You can back up and ram the wall, go around the wall, or quit. The last was not an option, so I decided on a combination of the other two.

I realized that I had tried to move Dolson with a carrot but no stick. It was a new league for me, but the lessons were coming fast. It finally dawned that I needed some serious leverage to get anyone involved in the jury-fix conspiracy to tumble.

MY NEXT STOP was the court clerk's office for another look at the transcript of Dolson's first trial. I remembered the day we had lunch with Mr. Munsey. He said that Dolson had an alibi witness by the name of Gallagher. I ran through the transcript until I found Gallagher's home address. He lived in a row-house section of Revere. Given the fact that Mr. Munsey pegged him as a low-grade boozer, the chances were good that he was still there.

I found the house in a neighborhood seven blocks back from the shoreline. From the looks of the peeling paint and overgrown patch of dandelion lawn, he was not on any twelve-step recovery.

The frazzled, life-worn woman who answered the bell confirmed the fact that it was the residence of her son, Frank Gallagher. She didn't say it as if she was bragging. It took only two questions to learn that my best bet for finding him would be the Clamshell Bar two blocks toward the ocean. It being somewhat after noon, he was probably there drinking his lunch.

I hustled the two blocks to get there before he got so deeply into the bottle that he'd deprive me of the pleasure and honor of treating him to his first or fifth drink of the day.

The bar was dark and long from front to back. The stench of ages of spilled beer and rotgut whiskey stung the nostrils. The ambience was also colored by the fact that it was unaffected by any regard for a smoke-free ordinance.

Frank Gallagher was easy to spot among the five or six bodies clustered at the bar. He was alone at the far end, perched over two elbows on the bar, contemplating the froth of a half-downed glass of beer. The cutoff T-shirt displayed two arms' lengths of cheap, mostly faded tattoos.

I took the stool next to him and tried to judge the degree of glaze in the eyes he turned in my direction. He seemed still to have enough brain cells in focus to have made the trip worthwhile.

"Hi, Frank. How's it going?"

He leaned away from me to get his eyes to focus on this unfamiliar face.

"Do I know you?"

"Well, maybe not. We've got a mutual friend. Same first name. Frank Dolson."

"Hey, you know Frank?"

He said the name with such admiration that I instantly became an old pal of Dolson's.

"That's right. I just saw him a little while ago. He said to come by and say hello. Told me to buy you a drink on him."

The first statement brought a smile, but the part about the drink opened his mouth in a full grin of anticipation.

"Yeah? Good old Frank."

"Yep. But not this stuff." I pushed back the beer in disgust. "I mean a real drink. Let's take a bottle over to the table."

The grin turned to absolute ecstasy. Life was truly good. It got even better when I said, "Frank, you like good Scotch?"

His eyes lit up like they were beholding the real Santa Claus. There was sincere enthusiasm in his voice when he said, "Yeah!"

I would probably have gotten the same reaction with bourbon, vodka, or belly-burner rum. But this was no time to turn cheap. I called the bartender and bought a bottle of Famous Grouse Scotch. I took the bottle and two glasses in one hand and Frank in the other to a table in the back corner.

Frank was salivating by the time I opened the bottle and poured the first shot. It disappeared in a flash over tonsils that must have thought they were dreaming. He laid the empty shot glass in front of me for more of the same.

I put the lid on the bottle and said, "Frank, let's talk."

The grin disappeared as he watched the unhappy closing. It was replaced by a look of shock and dismay bordering on anger. Before this caused the end of a budding friendship, I said, "There's more where that came from, Frank. First I need some information. The faster I get it, the faster the top comes off that bottle. What do you say?"

He leaned back in the chair. I could see that the Scotch on top of the beer or beers was beginning to take hold.

"What do you want to know?"

"Let's go back to the time when you were the alibi witness for Frank Dolson. Frank was charged with burning a building in the South End. You remember that?"

He looked a little hesitant. I uncapped the bottle and poured half a shot in his glass. It was gone by the time I recapped the bottle.

"You remember that, Frank?"

He reached for the bottle. I pulled it away.

"Not yet, Frank. Time to talk. When we finish, if I get all the information I need, this bottle is yours. Agreed?"

He looked at me with deep fear of not passing the test and losing the prize.

"What do you want?"

"The truth, Frank. You only get the bottle if you tell me the truth."

He nodded.

"You testified that Frank Dolson was with you the night he was supposed to have lit the fire. Was that true?"

His head rolled a little while he thought.

"Yeah. That was true. We were in a bar all night."

"OK, Frank. Here's where you earn the bottle. If he was innocent, why did he confess to the burning?"

Frank put his head down in his hands on the table. I was beginning to think I'd lost him with that last half shot. I tapped his elbow with the bottle. His head came back up. It turned out he'd been thinking, not sleeping.

"Frank told me he was gonna make a bundle. Things hadn't been going so good for him. Then this came along. He was gonna get sixty thousand dollars to take the rap for an arson. He'd get maybe three years and do the time. It was like insurance for the guy that really did the job. The guy was gonna blow the whistle if he got caught."

"That's good, Frank. But Dolson took back his confession when they found bodies, and it became a murder charge. You remember that?"

"Yeah. That's why that lawyer wanted me to testify at his trial."

"That's right. But Frank got scared, didn't he? He threatened the ones who hired him. He said he'd blow the whistle on the whole scheme if they didn't get him out of the murder charge. Is that right?"

"Yeah. That's right. Frank told me he scared them good. They came up with another way to get him out of it."

"And that way was?"

"Frank made them promise to fix the jury."

Pay dirt. That was why I'd come to Revere.

"Now listen, Frank. We're on the homestretch. You're this close to that bottle. I want the truth. Did Frank's lawyer, Lex Devlin, know about the fix?"

"His lawyer?"

"That's right, Frank. Lex Devlin."

I held my breath while he rubbed his head and massaged his brain cells. I couldn't tell if he was looking for a recollection or just the answer that would uncork the bottle.

"Frank, you only get the bottle if you tell the truth. I'll know."

He looked at me with the most pathetic look I'd ever seen.

"I need a drink."

"I need an answer. You go first."

He shook his head and nearly cried.

"I don't know. Frank never said one way or the other about the lawyer."

Frank's head was in his hands. For me, it was like I'd gotten a two-base hit when I was inches from putting the ball over the fence for a home run. I thought maybe I could stretch it to a three-bagger.

"Listen to me, Frank. Last question. Was the district attorney who prosecuted the case in on the jury fix? Did Frank say anything about that?"

Frank looked up. There was still hope.

"Yeah. Frank told me the DA was in a bind. He couldn't call the case off when it turned into murder. He had to go through with prosecuting it. But he's the one who told Frank not to worry. The jury was fixed."

I had that great feeling of capping off a stand-up triple. I took out the pad of legal paper I had in my briefcase and wrote out in easy English the major points of what Frank Gallagher had just told me. I had him read it and sign it under a line that said he was under pain of perjury.

I came out of that bar into the brisk, fresh air off the ocean and took my first full breath since I'd entered it. To my surprise, Frank came out right behind me, clutching that vessel of amber gold. He headed down the block toward the ocean for what must have looked to him like a promising day at the beach.

29

WHAT I HAD IN MY HAND at this point was a signed statement that was worth exactly its weight in scrap paper. As an offering in evidence, it arguably violated the hearsay rule, the best evidence rule, and probably twenty others. As a witness, Frank Gallagher himself could have been destroyed on cross-examination by any law student in the first week of law school. However, it felt like pure platinum in my hand. With the right bluff, it could be just the leverage necessary to tumble the next domino.

I called the office of the clerk of the Supreme Judicial Court and reached Conrad Munsey. He sounded surprised, but not hostile.

"What's up, kid?"

"You remember the conversation between you and me about a mutual acquaintance, Mr. Munsey?"

There was a tentative, "I do."

"I could use some information."

There was a pause. I heard his office door close, and he was back on the line.

"I hope you're not stirring up trouble nobody needs. Especially you-know-who."

"I hope the same thing. Isn't anything better than the status quo?"

"I don't know. What do you need?"

"The name of the district attorney who tried the Dolson case. It was before my time."

"Yeah, I guess it was. The DA of Suffolk County was a well-connected gentleman by the name of Martin Shortbridge. He tried the case himself."

"Do you have any idea where he is now?"

"Sure. As I say, he was well connected. He went into private practice with the Dunlevy firm. They handle a lot of private banks. He found his niche. Right now he's the president of the American Fidelity Mutual Fund. What about it?"

"I need to see him."

"Kid, you've got spunk. I hope you've got the brains to match. This is major-league wealth and power."

"Well, you remember the old saying, Mr. Munsey. 'The bigger they are, the harder they fall.'"

"You're a piece of work, kid. Just be sure nothing falls on Lex."

I CALLED INFORMATION for the number of the American Fidelity Mutual Fund. It occupied a building on State Street, the top floor of which was the office of Martin Shortbridge.

After a number of transferred connections, I reached his secretary. I knew that would be the end of the line for Michael Knight. On the other hand, as Oliver Shortbridge, nephew of the aforesaid Martin Shortbridge, calling with urgent news of the health of the latter's sister, Letitia Shortbridge, I got the word that Mr. Shortbridge was "at luncheon" at the Parker House. I wouldn't ordinarily play games with the health of any of these people; but since they were all fictitious, I took the liberty.

The maitre d' at the Parker House was kind enough to point out Mr. Shortbridge. He was, in fact, a short and portly soul. He'd been well rounded over the years, no doubt, on such dishes as the lobster thermidor that was currently before him.

He was seated with three other pin-striped suits of the same cut and price tag. Painful though it was to disturb his probably profitable repast, I had him paged.

When he arrived at the maitre d's desk, his expression was somewhere between curiosity and aggravation. He looked around, ignoring me, for someone who looked important enough to page him. I presented myself and spoke civilly.

"Mr. Shortbridge, my name is Michael Knight. Please forgive the intrusion. I need to see you on a matter that is seriously overdue. Approximately ten years."

He looked at me and seemed to have difficulty believing what was standing in front of him interrupting his "luncheon."

"This shouldn't take long. They'll reheat your lobster."

The curiosity was gone. It was pure aggravation.

"I don't think so, young man."

He signaled the maitre d' to come at once, presumably to bounce this paragon of impertinence on his posterior.

I leaned over and whispered, "Perhaps I should join you at your table. I came to discuss the Dolson case. Your friends might enjoy a good story about jury fixing."

The blood drained from his rosy English complexion. When the maitre d' arrived, he waived him off. He took me by the arm and escorted me around the corner to a quiet spot. When we stopped, his mouth was at my ear. I could feel a hissing stream of moisture with each word.

"Who are you? Who sent you?"

I slowly pried the grip of his fingers off of my arm. I was delighted to have his undivided attention. Now the trick was to gain control. I remembered Mr. Devlin's advice about not facing Angela Lamb on her own turf.

"My name's Michael Knight, Mr. Shortbridge. And nobody sends me. Including you."

He lost some of the bravado, but control was still in his court on his turf.

"We have business to do, you and I. It's been a long time coming, but I assure you it's here. You know exactly what I'm talking about. In five minutes I'll be alone at a table at the McDonald's on Washington Street. If you're not there within ten minutes, I'll presume you have no interest in righting an old wrong. Then we'll see what surprises lie in store."

I'll admit it was a touch dramatic and the phrasing was a bit stilted. I did, however, relish the symbolism of the transfer from the Parker House to McDonald's. That nuance came to me at the last minute.

The pleasure, however, was fleeting. After my exit line, I rushed to McDonald's and found an open table. I had five minutes to grow butterflies the size of armadillos.

Shortbridge had not only gained back his color, he had redness to spare when he came through the door of McDonald's, probably for the first time in his life. He found me, and I waved him to a chair. He sat. I took no small delight in the fact that he was responding to my hand signals. Then he put things back in perspective.

"Young man, I don't know who you are, but I'll find out. You will be broken in every way possible. You won't be able to shine shoes in this state. Who do you think you're dealing with?"

"'Whom,' Mr. Shortbridge. You mean, 'Whom do I think I'm dealing with?' Please, there are children here."

He bolted to his feet.

"Enjoy it now, young man. It will be a very long time before you'll enjoy anything again."

I remained seated, calm, and as quiet as Clint Eastwood.

"To answer your improperly phrased question, Mr. Shortbridge, I'm the person who can haul your larcenous, jury-fixing ass out of that tower on State Street and put it in Walpole State Prison where it belongs."

He stopped everything, including breathing, for a moment. He made an instant check to see if anyone was within earshot and scuttled back into the chair. I slid a photocopy of the paper signed by Frank Gallagher across the table. He scanned it, and then went back over it to read every word. When he finished he threw it back across the table.

"That's what you've got? That's what you dare to threaten me with? There isn't a court in the state that would admit that in evidence. And that drunken bum, Gallagher? You think you can put his word against mine? You don't have a shred of evidence."

He was back in control of his life when he stood up to his full five feet six inches. I retained the Clint Eastwood calm.

"You couldn't be more correct, Mr. Shortbridge."

He was nodding vigorously and on the verge of launching into another self-redeeming threat of financial annihilation.

"On the other hand, I never intended to take it to court. I never threatened you with prosecution. That would be a crime, as you know. It does, however, have news value. Imagine the smoke and fury the news media in this small town of Boston will raise when they see this. I can think of two tabloids and at least three radio talk shows that'll be delighted to put you in center stage. You'll be wishing I had taken you to court. At least there you'd have a chance to prove your innocence. No, you're going to find yourself skewered in the forum of the media, gossip, public opinion. I wonder if an operation that calls itself the American Fidelity Mutual Fund can afford a president that everybody knows got away with jury fixing in an arson case that resulted in homicide. Here, you keep this copy for a souvenir. I have plenty of others."

I flipped it back to him. It landed in front of him, but he didn't see it. He was just staring at the edge of the table. No one knew better than he did how the liberal powers behind certain media would celebrate the destruction of his conservative reputation. His mind went through several seconds of deflating computation before he muttered, "What do you want?"

I let it hang there for a few seconds to let him anticipate the worst.

"I'll tell you what I don't want. I don't want you. I don't give a damn if you eat lobster thermidor for the rest of your self-pampering life. I want information, and I want a signed statement. If I get it, I may never need to make it public. I can't promise that, but it's your only option."

He lifted his head to meet my eyes. His breathing had become labored. I wanted to finish this thing before he expired at McDonald's, giving the restaurant a bad name.

"If I don't get the truth, and I know most of it, I'm on my way. You get one shot at it. You understand?"

He nodded.

"Let's start with a simple one. The first trial of Dolson. Was the jury fixed?"

It took a second, but he nodded.

"I'd like to hear it out loud."

"Yes." It sounded as if a frog had taken residence in his throat. He cleared it and repeated the answer.

"That's right. That was a test. Were you in on the fix?"

He looked in both directions. There was a mother with three small children just sitting down two tables away. He leaned over and whispered.

"Do we have to do this here?"

"Yes. Were you in on the fix?"

He both nodded and whispered, "Yes."

It was time to go for the gold.

"Lex Devlin represented Dolson. Did Lex Devlin know anything about the fix?"

He thought for a long moment while everything inside of me stopped.

"I don't know."

"I want the truth or you're a dead duck."

"I swear I honestly don't know. I never talked to Devlin about it. I don't know if anyone else did."

I could feel the pit of my stomach drop three inches. One more domino had dropped, and I was still chasing pay dirt. I didn't know how many more of these I could survive. Anthony's trial was coming up the following day. Time was short, but I needed to push it to one more level before putting it on the shelf. I regrouped and tried to sustain the bravado, which was at this point running low.

"One more question. And you'd better find an answer for this one. This is the deal-breaker. Who put the pieces together to fix that juror? The money, the contact, all of it. Who actually did it?"

The sheet of moisture that covered his forehead beaded into drops that began coursing down his cheeks. I could see his hands clutch the edge of the table to stop the shaking. He took a deep breath and shook his head.

"I can't."

"Can't what?"

"He could . . . destroy me."

He was stymied with fear. The only thing that could drive him through it was a smack in the rear with a greater fear. I blocked out the overwhelming urge to cave in out of pity by focusing on the ten years of pain he had caused Mr. Devlin without a thought.

I leaned over the table.

"Look in my eyes, Mr. Shortbridge, and read the truth. He *could* destroy you. I *will* destroy you."

He shook until even the table couldn't steady him. It came out of him in a whisper.

I leaned closer. "What?"

"Loring. Robert Loring. He put it together. We all agreed to the plan, but he put it together."

It was like releasing a pressure valve. His whole body sank back in the chair as if it had been deflated. I recognized the name. Loring was the general partner of the limited partnership that owned the buildings that burned with the one that had been torched.

I let him catch his breath while I took out a legal pad and pen. I put it in front of him and told him to write it in detail. He took the pen and looked up.

"You said . . ."

"I said I *may* not have to make it public. I have just one interest in this business. Where it goes from there is out of my hands."

He nodded and started to write.

30

IT WAS TWO THIRTY in the afternoon when Shortbridge and I parted company under a giant grinning cutout of Ronald McDonald. I had one more part to play before I could get my mind fully back to the Bradley case.

Information gave me the number for Robert Loring's office on Federal Street. I had gotten the address earlier from Gene Martino.

Loring's secretary had an upscale coolness in her voice.

"Mr. Loring's office."

"Hello. May I speak to Mr. Loring?"

"I'm afraid not. Mr. Loring is out of the office for the afternoon. May I inquire what this is in reference to?"

I overlooked the fact that she was unashamed of ending a sentence with a preposition.

"It's in reference to his meeting with me in the Public Garden tomorrow morning."

"That's not possible. Mr. Loring has appointments in-house through tomorrow afternoon. Who is this speaking?"

"This is a man who wants Mr. Loring to know that he'll meet him tomorrow morning at nine o'clock at the bench in the Public Garden where they start the swan boats."

There was a little condescending laugh that sent my Latino blood well above 98.6. I nonetheless cooled it and let her finish.

"I'm afraid you'll be waiting there alone, whoever you are. Mr. Loring has no intention . . ."

"I'm not in the habit of giving legal advice freely, miss, so consider yourself among the elect. My very best advice to you is that you treat this as a 911 call and reach Mr. Loring as if his life depended on it. Tell him about the appointment at the swan boats tomorrow morning at nine o'clock. And in the course of the conversation, mention the name of Frank Dolson to him. When you do, have a chair behind him and two aspirin in your hot little hand. Have you got all that?"

There was nothing but pause on the other end. I figured I got her attention. I wished her a delightful afternoon and hung up.

THERE WAS ONE LAST BASE that I wanted to touch before Anthony's trial began. I drove over to Harvard and found Terry Blocher just coming back to Dunster House from class. It seemed like the first time all day I'd talked to another human being without trying to trick or coerce him into saying something he'd rather keep deeply buried.

Terry seemed open and anxious to help any way he could. His first words were a sincere inquiry about Anthony. It struck me that he

217

really cared as a friend, but then, my experience so far with this case had forced me to reevaluate my intuitive judgment of character.

He invited me in, and we settled down behind a couple of Cokes.

"Terry, I'm trying to piece together exactly what happened on that Sunday. Could you give it to me again? Give me all the details."

I appreciated the fact that he thought about it before beginning.

"I went down to Anthony's room here at Dunster about two in the afternoon. I think I asked what he wanted to do. He said he wanted to go into Chinatown for the New Year's celebration and have dinner. I said OK, so we went."

"And Anthony picked the Ming Tree restaurant?"

"That's right. It was new to me."

"Think back, Terry. Did anyone join you at the dinner?"

"No. Well, actually what happened was during the dinner Anthony excused himself and went into the back room. It looked like he was going into the kitchen."

"Could it have been the men's room?"

"No. That was off to the side. He was there for a few minutes. Then he came back to the table. There was a Chinese man with him. He introduced him, but I can't remember his name."

"Tall, thin fellow? Well dressed? Speaks excellent English?"

"Right. Exactly. Anyway, he asked if I was staying in Chinatown for the celebration. I had to tell him I was probably going back to Cambridge right after dinner. The noise when we came in was too much for my ears."

"So then?"

"That was it. We finished. We split the bill. Anthony and I walked downstairs. I left Anthony on the sidewalk. He wanted to see the dragon or lion or whatever it was coming up the street."

"What about the Chinese man?"

He thought for a minute.

"He walked downstairs with us. They were together on the sidewalk when I left."

I had a better picture of that afternoon. Unfortunately, it could have suited either Anthony's or the witnesses' version of the killing that followed.

"One last question, Terry. Are you a member of that group called 'The Point'"?

He shook his head. "No. I have trouble enough getting myself through the courses."

TUESDAY MORNING WAS a little milder than it had been, but the chill and the clouds let you know that it was clearly still February.

It was also the day Anthony Bradley's trial was to begin, at Mr. Devlin's request. I knew I should have been meeting Mr. Devlin at the courthouse, but I had to do this one other thing while momentum was overcoming the fact that I was petrified. They'd use the morning to pick a jury, and then Angela Lamb would come to bat for the prosecution. Heaven knows Mr. Devlin didn't need my help for that.

AT NINE O'CLOCK, I was standing by the swan-boat pond in the Public Garden. It was frozen over with the exception of a few circles of moisture that reminded me that someday this long winter would end.

The walking Boston office workers had passed earlier along the paths that led to the office buildings that ring the garden. I was alone, except for a woman on a bench a distance along the pond.

At exactly two minutes past nine, I saw an older man walking a little faster than what I imagined his usual gate might be. From the gray hair and the way the flesh hung on the bones of his face I figured that he looked a good bit older than he was. It made me wonder what had aged him. The Chesterfield coat over a gray, pin-striped suit of the finest wool said it certainly wasn't poverty.

He looked at me uneasily and took a seat on the bench. I walked over. No need prolonging his purgatory.

"Mr. Loring, you're right on time."

"I don't have time for this. Who are you?"

He would have sounded dominating and self-assured but for two things—the quiver in his voice, and the fact that he was there. That told me he was more frightened than I was.

I walked slowly over to the bench and sat down beside him.

"I'm the man who's going to relieve you of ten years' weight on your conscience, if you have one. My name's Michael Knight. I work with Lex Devlin."

Either a chill was setting in, or the fear was beginning to affect him physically. His hands were beginning to shake, but he looked me dead in the eyes.

"What do you want?"

"I want you to know that as of this moment, the life you know is over. Beginning now, it all crumbles to pieces. You'd better have your wits about you in the next ten minutes to come through it with as much as you can possibly hold together."

I let that sink in for a second while he just looked at me.

"Ten years ago, Mr. Loring, you did a despicable thing. You and that gang of respectable thieves that hide behind Adams Leasing hired a man to burn a couple of your rat-traps in the South End. You hired a man by the name of Frank Dolson to take the fall on the arson. It went sour when it turned to a felony-murder charge. Are you following me here?"

"That's absolutely absurd."

"We'll see. Now we get to the part that's going to bring you people to justice. You fixed the Dolson jury. And you hung it on Lex Devlin. You took the life out of a man whose boots you're not good enough to lick."

"I don't have to listen to this."

He started to get up.

"If you leave that seat, I send the evidence directly to the district attorney, and you lose the chance I'm offering you to buy leniency."

It was as if I had reached out and pulled him back to the bench.

"What evidence are you talking about?"

I reached into my suit-coat pocket and took out Martin Short-bridge's signed statement. I handed it to him. His hands were quivering when he took it; but when he read it, his whole body started to shake. He said nothing. I thought he was going to cry.

"Let me tell you where we're at, Mr. Loring. What you're looking at is evidence to convict you of jury fixing. That could be good for at least a five-year sentence. Believe it or not, that's the good news. The bad news is that it ties you in as an accessory to the felony murder of the men who died in that fire. That means that this could be the last time you'll see this beautiful Public Garden for the rest of your life."

That did it. Now he was weeping. I looked at him in his nine-hundred-dollar suit and thought of his life of posh clubs and lobster dinners and summer home on the North Shore. Then I thought of the last ten years of Mr. Devlin's life that paid for it, and I felt anger. At the same time, I couldn't help being stung with a degree of pity for him. But neither emotion mattered. I had to do what I came to do.

"There's a way of softening the fall, Mr. Loring."

He looked up at me with a face that was wet and almost pleading.

"What way?"

"Right now, you're the fall guy. You're the only general partner of the limited partnership that owns Adams Leasing. The rest of the thieves are hiding behind you in the hopes that you'll take all the heat. I know there are much bigger fish than you in this mess. Right at this passing moment, you have a chance to offer evidence and bargain for leniency."

It sank in for a second before he asked it.

"What will happen to me?"

"I can promise you this. If you pass up this chance, you'll go to prison for the rest of your life. If you make a statement now, before it breaks, it'll go lighter with you. How much lighter, no one can promise. I think you can topple some heads that will put the prosecutor in a generous mood."

He just sat there with his head submerged in his hands.

"It's your decision. I'm on my way to the prosecuting attorney right now. I can do it with or without your cooperation. What'll it be?"

The tears wouldn't stop. I heard a sob catch in his throat like a gasp. Then I heard it in a muffled voice, and my heart nearly sprang out of my chest.

"What do you want me to do?"

I stood up and waved to the woman who was sitting on the bench down by the pond. I had asked Julie to meet me at the Public Garden, but stay a distance away. She came at a run with a briefcase.

I gave her my seat. She took a laptop computer out of the case and brought it to life to take dictation.

"Mr. Loring, this is my secretary. I want you to dictate a statement. Miss Benson will take it down. She has the equipment to print it out, and you'll sign it. I'll see that you get full credit with the prosecutor for giving evidence. Are you ready to begin?"

He seemed unaware of Julie's presence, but he was focused enough to know that his neck could only be saved by seizing the moment. *Carpe diem.* And he did.

It flowed like honey from his lips, and Julie caught every word on the word processor. It was like tapping a gusher. He had no idea how much would satisfy me, so he spilled it all. He laid bare an association of some of the most powerful people in the commonwealth of Massachusetts that went back twenty years. He outlined dealings in real estate all over the city that would make Dillinger look like Billy Graham.

The shenanigans were made possible by the most foolproof protection I could conceive. They had a stranglehold on the laws affecting zoning, eminent domain, and private legislation through their own membership. It had taken years to develop, but they had placed members of the association in every branch of government from the governor's cabinet to the key committees of the state legislature to the Supreme Judicial Court.

I could feel my legs turning to rubber as I listened to the names of the people Loring implicated. I looked out over the pond where my parents had taken me on the swan boats as a child to feed the ducks. I was staggered as I remembered that time of innocence and trust, and listened as too many of the pillars of the state that was my home crumbled in a bone-heap of greed.

There were times when I thought I was going to be physically ill. I could easily have wept.

When he stopped speaking, I asked my own questions while Julie kept up on the laptop.

"How many members of the Supreme Judicial Court, Mr. Loring?"

"Only three. They're ordinary, impartial judges on most cases. They only serve the association's interests on rare cases where it matters to the business."

There were so many questions, but I had to focus on the reason I was there.

"Was this association behind the arson that Dolson pleaded guilty to?"

"Yes. We hired another man to do it, but he bungled it. When it became obvious that it was arson, and he could be prosecuted, he threatened to take us with him. We hired Dolson to take the prison sentence."

"But then it turned to murder, and you had to get Dolson off the hook for the murder. How did you do it?"

"We bribed a juror to produce a hung jury."

I held my breath. We were so close to touchdown. I looked to see that Julie was getting it all. I spoke slowly.

"Did Mr. Alexis Devlin have anything to do with the bribery of the juror?"

"No."

"Did he have any knowledge of the fixing of the juror at any time?"

"No. We planted the rumors that he was behind it to take suspicion off the association. We even set the procedure in motion for a bar disciplinary proceeding. Then we had it called off after Dolson entered a plea bargain for the arson."

I looked at Julie to see if she had it. She looked up at me, and I could see moisture swelling in her eyes. She just nodded.

"One more thing. Mr. Loring, is this association involved in the Anthony Bradley case?"

He looked at me. "What do you mean?"

"Let's break it down. Did the association have anything to do with the murder of the Chinese man?"

"No. We had nothing to do with that."

That was a disappointment. That still left Anthony as the most likely killer.

"Did the association have anything to do with the prosecution of Bradley?"

He thought for a second.

"Only indirectly. When young Bradley got into serious trouble it served our purposes. The balance on the Supreme Judicial Court is delicate. Right now, our three members are able to convince enough of the other conservatives to vote our way on land issues without them knowing what's behind it. That balance would be upset if Bradley joins the court. A scandal in his family is the best thing that could have happened for us.

"When Lex Devlin joined the defense, we were afraid he might get a defendant's verdict. We had Angela Lamb offer a plea bargain on a lesser charge. That would have been enough to taint Judge Bradley."

"Is Angela Lamb a member of this association?"

"No. Not a member. She's been under our control, though, since we financed her campaign to become district attorney. She follows orders whenever we need it. After Lex Devlin got involved in the Bradley case, we had her reduce the charge to something we thought Bradley might plead to rather than risk Devlin's getting him off. Even the lesser charge would have been an embarrassment to Judge Bradley. We could have used it to keep him off the court."

I checked my watch. It was nine thirty, and I had things to do before I could get to the courthouse. There was so much more to unravel, but I'd leave that to the prosecutors.

"One last question. Judge Posner, the judge who's trying the Bradley case, is he one of yours?"

He looked up.

"No."

I kneeled down beside Julie. "Let's wrap it up. Save it on a couple of discs and print it out. Three times."

I took a walk down to the pond while Julie worked with the laptop and the miniprinter she had in the case. I wondered when the swan boats would be launched in the spring. I resolved to come back and try to recapture those beautiful, innocent days of feeding the ducks.

Julie called me back when she had three verbatim copies of Loring's statement printed out. I checked them out. It was all there.

I took a highlighter pen out of Julie's case and marked in screaming yellow the section about Mr. Devlin's innocence of the jury fixing.

I gave one copy to Loring and told him to read it. It took him about five minutes. I was surprised there were no more tears.

He took out a gold-plated Mont Blanc pen and signed all three copies. As I took each one from him, I said a prayer of thanksgiving to God, who cares about old trial lawyers.

31

WHEN I LEFT THE PUBLIC GARDEN just after ten, I literally ran into a stationery store on Boylston Street. I bought three large manila envelopes, and I made two more copies of the signed statements of Frank

Gallagher and Martin Shortbridge. I put a copy of Loring's, Gallagher's, and Shortbridge's statements in each of the envelopes and sealed them.

I carried the first set to the United States Attorney's office in the federal building. I handed it personally to Pete Styles, the United States Attorney. I wanted him to know whom it came from in case he had any questions. I knew that he'd make the most of it under the federal corruption in public office statutes and that old beloved gangbuster, RICO—the Racketeering Influenced and Corrupt Organizations statute. Pete was as good a person as ever sat in that office. If the case carried him to the Senate or beyond, the people would be the winners.

My second stop was the Suffolk County district attorney's office. I handed the envelope to the deputy DA, Alice Wright, since Ms. Lamb, the DA, was at the moment in courtroom 809, selecting a jury to convict Anthony Bradley. Our soon-to-be-former DA was also implicated in Loring's statement.

That was all in the line of duty. My third stop was a labor of love. I removed the statement of Shortbridge from the third envelope because of my agreement to keep it out of the public eye "if possible." The chances were that it was an empty gesture, since he would undoubtedly be smeared by the exposure of corruption that was about to cut loose.

I hand-carried that golden third envelope with the statements of Gallagher and Loring and laid it in the hands of my buddy, Mike Loftus, the best columnist to whom the *Globe* ever gave the power of the pen.

He was surprised at my presence.

"Michael, aren't you supposed to be at trial in the Bradley case?"

"I am. I'm out of here. I just wanted you to know for sure where that envelope came from. It's exactly what it purports to be. I'm giving you an exclusive with my blessings. Just one request. The whole business is going to blow your socks off. You'll have material for columns through Labor Day. What I'm asking is this. For your first column, will you focus on the stuff about Lex Devlin? It's just a request. There're no strings."

He looked at me with a funny look. "What the hell's in here, Mike?"

There were no smiles when I said it. "It's what every reporter dreams about. Read it and weep."

32

I HIT THE STREET in front of the *Globe* building running. It was past noon. I figured that in the noon traffic I could get to the courthouse in better time on foot than in a cab.

I darted between cars on Franklin Street, collecting an interesting array of shouts and hand signals from drivers, for one of whom I nearly became a hood ornament. I took the steps of the courthouse in threes. I passed through security and pushed my way through the crowd in the lobby to the elevator.

I caught sight of Tommy Flaherty, one of the court officers, running toward the elevator. He was yelling something. I told him I couldn't hear. When he got to the door of the elevator, I could make out the words.

"You better get the hell up there, Mike! Lex Devlin!"

I yelled past the front line of people.

"What about him?"

The door closed. Tommy had time to get in just one word.

"Heart!"

When the door opened, I squeezed my way out of the elevator. A crowd of reporters and spectators had spilled into the corridor. They filled it with a nervous buzz.

I ran into the courtroom. There was a circle of people in front of defense counsel's table. I pushed close enough to see Mr. Devlin lying on the floor. There were three men in white uniforms working over him. His face was the color of ashes.

Anthony Bradley was standing closest to me.

"What happened, Anthony?"

"I think he took a heart attack. He put his hand up here on his chest, and he just went down. They called the ambulance. They've been working on him for fifteen minutes."

I worked my way through to kneel down beside him. He looked up at me. His eyes brightened a little.

"You picked a hell of a day to go on strike, sonny. Where've you been?"

"You'll know soon enough. How're you doing?"

"I'll be ready to play the Celtics tomorrow. Today I think I'll sit on the bench. We got the jury picked. Angela's about to fire her first salvo."

I looked around as Judge Posner kneeled down beside me.

"How is it, Lex?"

"Not so bad, Judge."

The judge said quietly to me, "They gave him a shot. I think he's settling down."

Judge Posner said to Lex, "They'll get you to the hospital in no time, Lex. You're looking better. I'll grant your motion for a continuance."

Lex's head came off the floor, and his eyes burned.

"No. No motion for a continuance."

"What do you mean, Lex?"

Mr. Devlin looked up at me. He said it quietly and deliberately. "I mean my cocounsel will handle the defense."

The judge looked at the two of us. I couldn't believe what I was hearing. I thought he might be delirious, but he never looked cooler. I was taking strength from what I saw in his eyes.

Judge Posner looked at me. "You'd better consult with your client, to see if that's what he wants, Mr. Knight. And perhaps Judge Bradley."

I looked around at Anthony. He was standing behind me. He nodded his head. "If that's what Mr. Devlin wants, that's OK with me."

Judge Bradley was standing at the rail behind the defense table. I looked at Mr. Devlin. He gave me a nod in the direction of Judge Bradley, and I called him over. He bent down over Mr. Devlin and put his ear close to Mr. Devlin's lips.

Mr. Devlin whispered something that brought a stunned, if not angry, look to Judge Bradley's face. He started to stand, but Mr. Devlin grabbed his shoulder and pulled him back. I couldn't tell what he was whispering, but I think he was disclosing his tactics to the only human being other than me to whom he could tip his hand.

When Judge Bradley stood up, he still had deep furrows across his brow. He looked at me for several seconds before going back to take his seat.

The judge called Ms. Lamb over from the prosecution table and whispered the situation to her. Needless to say, she approved of the substitution of counsel.

The men in white uniforms were lifting Mr. Devlin onto a stretcher. He waved me over, and told the others to stand back. I leaned down so he could whisper.

"You can handle it, sonny. Do you understand the game plan?"

I told him I did. We'd gone over it a number of times at our last meeting.

"Good. If it's going to work, it has to be now. We can't put it off. Go to it, sonny."

THEY LIFTED THE STRETCHER so that the wheels snapped down under it. They cleared a path through the crowd and moved him out of the courtroom fast. They had him at the door, when I remembered the news I'd forgotten to tell him.

I couldn't get through the crowd, so I yelled, "I'll see you later! I've got news! You're cleared!"

The crowd folded in behind him. I didn't think he heard. I prayed to God to give him time to hear.

By the time the judge got the courtroom reassembled, it was nearly one. He ordered a break for lunch. We were to reconvene at two. I had too much to go over with Anthony before the afternoon session to be able to follow Lex in the ambulance, so I tried to settle down to business.

AT TWO, THE JUDGE'S GAVEL brought silence to the arena, and the combat began.

Angela led off with an opening statement to the jury that was a masterpiece. She laid the blame for the bereavement of a persecuted people at the loss of Chinatown's grandfather squarely at the feet of the defendant. She did it so convincingly that I wanted to smack him myself.

The key at this point was to keep the cards close to the chest. I waived the right to make an opening statement.

The prosecution's first witness was the medical examiner who testified to the time and cause of death of Mr. Chen. There were no surprises. The time of death was midafternoon of the Sunday of Chinese New Year's. The cause of death was a thirty-eight-caliber bullet to the brain of the deceased. The gun itself had not been recovered.

The evidence went in smoothly and without objection from my side of the room. Judge Posner nodded to me for cross-examination after Angela finished.

I was brief. "No questions."

The judge looked at me a bit quizzically, but pressed on.

Angela's second witness was from the police lab. He discussed the trajectory of the bullet. He concluded that the assailant was standing in front of Mr. Chen when the bullet was fired. He was either in the area of the street or the sidewalk across from Mr. Chen's window.

I had no objections to the questions and no cross-examination. That brought another look from Judge Posner, and a smile to the lips of Ms. Lamb.

Then she got down to the heart of the business. The next witness was Mrs. Lee, the "owner" of the Ming Tree Restaurant.

She looked terribly worn as she crossed to the witness stand. She never looked at the prosecutor, the defendant, or me.

Walt Dougherty, the court clerk, swore her in. She appeared to understand his words, and she answered with a quiet "I do."

I found that interesting. She did speak English. Mr. Liu was no fool. The night I went to interview her, he said she spoke no English, which meant he had to interpret. Which meant he had total control over the interview.

Angela walked her through the opening questions—name, address, occupation—which last she gave as "restaurant owner."

"Mrs. Lee, do you see the defendant?"

I nudged Anthony to stand up. He did, and Mrs. Lee nodded.

Angela coached, "You have to say it out loud, Mrs. Lee, for the court stenographer."

She said a muffled "yes."

She had been merely tense up to this point. But now I noticed that her hands began kneading a small handkerchief.

"And did you see the defendant, Anthony Bradley, come into your restaurant at about three in the afternoon a week ago Sunday?"

"Yes." Quieter than before.

"Could you speak more loudly, Mrs. Lee?"

She moved closer to the microphone. "I said, 'Yes.'"

"And did he ask for a particular table?"

"Yes."

"And was it the table at the front of the restaurant toward the street?"

"Yes."

"And did the table look directly across the street to where Mr. Chen was watching the activity below?"

Judge Posner held up a hand to stop the answer. He was getting visibly concerned. He gave me the look of a law professor when a student seems out to lunch. He was worried about the defendant's getting a fair trial at the hands of substitute counsel who didn't have brains enough to recognize a series of leading questions.

I rose. "I have no problem with the question, Your Honor."

I hadn't set his mind at rest, but he motioned Mrs. Lee to answer the question.

"Yes."

Angela was on a roll. She strode to the far end of the jury box to draw Mrs. Lee's eyes to the jury and force her to speak up to be heard.

"And at the conclusion of his dinner, did you see a gun on the defendant's person?"

I was on my feet, partly to keep Judge Posner from having a stroke.

"Objection now, Your Honor. I'd like to hear the story in Mrs. Lee's words, not Ms. Lamb's. Leading question."

"Sustained."

Angela came at it again the right way, realizing that the mannequin at defense table had come to life.

"When the defendant finished eating, did you notice anything unusual?"

Mrs. Lee leaned into the microphone. She seemed rigid as a pole.

"I saw a gun tucked inside of his belt."

"And what kind of a gun was it?"

Mrs. Lee was out of her area of expertise.

"Was it a gun that could be held in the hand?"

"Yes. A gun for the hand. About this big."

"Thank you. And when you saw the gun, what did you do?"

"I watched. I saw him go down the stairs from the restaurant toward the street. I went to the window to see."

"And could you see him go out of the restaurant to the street?"

"Yes."

"Was there someone else with him?"

"Yes. Another boy had dinner with him. When they got to the street, the other boy left. He walked away up the street."

"Please describe what happened then."

"I saw that boy, Mr. Bradley, standing in the street. The drummers and the lion were coming up the street. He watched."

"Could you see the gun in his hand as he watched?"

Judge Posner looked at me. I shook my head.

"Yes."

"Please go on."

Mrs. Lee never took her eyes off of Angela.

"The lion approached the door of the grocery shop below Mr. Chen. Everyone was watching the dragon."

"Except you."

"Yes."

"And what were you watching?"

"Mr. Bradley."

"And what did you see him do?"

"He raised the gun."

"Please show us how."

Mrs. Lee brought her right hand up in front of her face as if sighting a pistol. Angela described it for the record.

"And then?"

She dropped her eyes. "He shot Mr. Chen."

"Did he aim deliberately at Mr. Chen?"

Judge Posner was not amused by my failure to object to the fact that the question called for a conclusion by the witness regarding the state of mind of the defendant. It was not my desire to annoy His Honor, but His Honor had no idea of what I was up to. I prayed that I did.

"Yes."

"Did Mr. Chen fall backwards?"

"Yes."

"And what did the defendant do then?"

"He walked up Tyler Street."

"Toward Beach Street?"

"Yes. He turned to the left."

"And what did you do, Mrs. Lee?"

"I ran down to where three policemen were standing in the street. I described Mr. Bradley and told the officers what happened. Two officers went after Mr. Bradley. The other officer went up the stairs to Mr. Chen."

"And once more, can you clearly identify the man you saw shoot Mr. Chen?"

She took a breath and brought her head up, "Yes." She pointed to Anthony Bradley.

Angela added the final nail. "May the record reflect that the witness is indicating Mr. Bradley, the defendant?"

Angela favored the jury with a knowing look, and the judge with a humble-servant-of-the-court smile.

"No further questions, Your Honor."

The judge nodded and signaled me to begin a rigorous cross-examination.

I rose respectfully.

"No questions, Your Honor."

He was on his feet and striding like Simba to the side of the bench away from the jury.

"I'll see counsel!"

I crossed paths with Angela halfway to the bench. She packed as much condescension as she could cram into one little smile and whispered, "A bit out of our league, are we, Mr. Knight?"

I smiled back. "I'm honored to learn at your feet, Ms. Lamb."

Smoke was rising around the collar of the judge's robe when we assembled at the side of the bench. He called the court reporter over to capture each word that hissed from between his teeth.

"I'm ready to call a mistrial, Knight. This is the most inept performance I've ever witnessed. Are you aware that a man's life in prison is at stake here?"

I leaned closer to be able to whisper.

"I know this is a bit unorthodox, Your Honor. I ask the court's indulgence. I didn't have a chance to finish before you called this sidebar. I'd like to request that Mrs. Lee be held for recall as a defense witness."

That snapped Angela's head around. The judge looked somewhat relieved that defense counsel had anything in mind.

"Yes. Granted."

"One more thing, Your Honor. I'd like to request that during the presentation of the defense, Mrs. Lee be permitted to remain in the courtroom. I'd like to have a seat reserved for her in the front row of the spectators."

Angela came out fighting.

"Your Honor, the prosecution objects. All of the witnesses are sequestered so that they won't hear each others' testimony and adapt their stories. There's no reason for an exception here. This is a key prosecution witness."

I stepped in.

"Your Honor, this witness has already testified. If the witness hears anything that could induce her to commit perjury in the future, the prosecution can renew the objection. It's an important request for the defense, Your Honor."

"For reasons that you're not at liberty to disclose at this time, Mr. Knight?"

"That's correct, Your Honor."

"I'm going to grant your request, Mr. Knight. But if I have to retry this case because of incompetence of defense counsel, it won't rest here. Am I understood?"

"Yes, Your Honor."

Ms. Lamb and I crossed paths again on the way back to counsel table. I winked and whispered, "Your play, Angela."

The prosecution had one more witness. Angela called Mr. Qian An-Yong, the Chinese herbal medicine man.

He took the stand and testified in corroboration of Mrs. Lee's testimony. He said that he saw Anthony Bradley come out of the Ming Tree restaurant and take a gun out of his belt. He said that while everyone was watching the lion in front of the grocery shop below Mr. Chen's window, the defendant was in the street. He raised the gun to aiming level and fired at Mr. Chen. Mr. Chen fell backwards into the room. The defendant walked up Tyler Street and turned left.

He said that Mrs. Lee came running out of the restaurant and went to speak to three officers. He went over to join them. He confirmed what she told them.

Angela took him through a description of the gun, which appeared to be a thirty-eight caliber, and the testimony that Mr. Qian was standing in the street close to the defendant at the time of the shooting. He was so stunned that there was nothing he could do at the time. She capped it off by having him formally identify Anthony Bradley.

This time the judge took it more in stride when I announced that I had no questions of the witness at this time. I made the same request in regard to Mr. Qian as I had made in regard to Mrs. Lee.

Angela made her objection for the record, and the judge granted my request.

With that, Angela declared that the prosecution rested.

IT WAS NEARLY FOUR. The judge adjourned until ten o'clock the following morning, with the usual instructions to the jurors not to discuss the case with anyone.

I went out to the corridor and called the cardiac unit of the Mass General Hospital. I got through to a nurse on the ward. She told me that Mr. Devlin had suffered a mild heart attack. They had worked on him that afternoon with tests and whatnot. He was sedated and sleeping at that point. He'd probably sleep through the night. She said it would not be a good idea to visit until the following afternoon.

I agreed. I had plenty of preparation to do for the next session anyway. The home team was coming to bat.

33

I WAS IN THE COURTROOM at quarter of ten the next morning. The press was jockeying for seats as fast as they could get through the security checkpoint. I noticed with pleasure that the bailiff was shooing away everyone who tried to take the two seats in the center of the front row of the spectator section.

At five minutes of ten, Mrs. Lee came in, escorted by Mr. Qian. The bailiff led them to the two front seats.

I was sitting beside Anthony Bradley, rechecking notes, when I could feel him turn around. When I looked up, his father had a hand on his shoulder. They both looked like they'd been drawn through a sieve.

They said a few words. Judge Bradley gave him a hug. Anthony put his head onto his father's shoulder. The judge held it there. It was a long time coming, and they seemed never to want it to end.

The bailiff came out of the judge's chambers, and Judge Bradley took his seat behind the defense section, but not before taking my arm and whispering, "Are you sure you know what you're doing, Mr. Knight?"

I looked him in the eye and said the only word that seemed right, if not completely truthful.

"Yes."

JUST BEFORE THE BAILIFF sounded the "All rise!" I caught a glimpse of Mr. Kip Liu slipping into the end seat of the last row. It was the same seat he had occupied the day before. I had asked the bailiff to keep that seat empty in the hope that he'd be there. The ducks were now properly in line. It was show time.

I was jotting a quick note, when Judge Posner mounted the bench and rapped for order. I waived the bailiff over and handed him the note.

Judge Posner looked at me like the proctor of a final examination.

"Are you ready, Mr. Knight?"

"I am, Your Honor."

"Then call your first witness."

I looked to the door of the courtroom and there, God bless her, standing just inside the door, was Julie.

"Your Honor, the defense calls as its first witness Miss Ku Mei-Li."

My eyes were riveted on Kip Liu. His eyes swung to the back door of the courtroom. He sprang up in his seat to see who'd come through the door.

When precious, bright Mei-Li walked into that courtroom, I saw fear, panic, and rage erupting in one expression. He looked as if he didn't know whether to stay or bolt. He sat tentatively.

Anthony was on his feet. His eyes locked with Mei-Li's as soon as she came into the courtroom. It was as if neither could believe they were seeing each other. The expression on her face told me why she had risked her life to be there. I was gratified and relieved to see the same expression in Anthony's eyes when he looked at her.

I took Mei-Li by the hand and led her to the witness stand. She was a radiant princess in a jade-green wool suit. Julie and Liz had taken her shopping. They had also done her hair and subtle makeup to perfection.

The court clerk swore her in. I looked at the faces of the jurors. They were captivated by her.

It was time. It all came down to this. I stood at defense-counsel table and asked her name.

"Ku Mei-Li." Her voice was strong.

"And how old are you, Mei-Li?"

"I am eighteen."

"And where do you live?"

Her head was up. "Until this week, I lived in a Chinese brothel on Beach Street."

The jury almost gasped. I had to move fast before the bottom fell out of their initial impression.

"And did you live there of your own free will?"

"No, I did not. I was sold to the people who brought me here from Hong Kong. I was in slavery. They compelled me to be a prostitute. I would never have my freedom."

"And how did you come to be in this courtroom this morning?"

While she answered I turned around and looked directly into the burning eyes of Kip Liu.

"I was rescued from my captors by a very brave act by you, Mr. Knight."

I wasn't looking for the "brave" part. I just wanted the jury to know how she got from there to here. I also wanted to give Kip Liu a crumbling sensation.

"Thank you. And do you understand that you're free, that you'll never be in their hands again? I promise you that."

That wasn't really a question. I'd just never had a chance to tell her. She never lowered her head, but a tear escaped and took some mascara with it.

"Do you know the defendant, Mei-Li?"

"Yes."

"How did you meet?"

"We were introduced by Mr. Liu."

I followed her eyes and realized that someone was moving toward the door of the courtroom. I turned around in time to see the bailiff and two officers intercepting Kip Liu as he reached the door. The bailiff had picked up on my note and had the officers ready. The last thing I wanted was Kip Liu roaming free.

"Your Honor, I'd like to request that the man with the officers be held as a material witness. I want him here in the courtroom while this witness testifies. There'll be further reason to hold him as the testimony goes on."

The judge gave the order to the bailiff and the officers, and Kip Liu was escorted to a seat. I turned back to the witness and pointed at Kip Liu.

"Mei-Li, was this the man responsible for bringing you into this country and holding you in slavery? For forcing you into prostitution?"

She looked him dead on. "Yes."

"Your Honor, there's material in this testimony for an indictment of Kip Liu. There'll be more. He represents an obvious danger to the life of this witness if he's not held in custody. I'm giving notice to the district attorney that she has full responsibility for Mr. Liu from this point on."

The judge gave the full effect of one of his looks to Ms. Lamb.

"I trust that the district attorney will carry out that responsibility. I'm assuming that she'll be requesting a bench warrant, which I shall issue immediately. Is that correct, Ms. Lamb?"

It was moving too fast for her to do anything but rise to say, "Yes, Your Honor."

"In the meantime, defense counsel's request will be honored. Mr. Liu will remain in custody in this courtroom for the balance of the proceedings."

I was beginning to feel the glow that brought me into this business.

The judge pounded for order. I waited for full silence. I wanted every word to be heard.

"Mei-Li, did you know the deceased, Mr. Chen?"

"Yes, I did."

"And how did you know him?"

"I saw him many times when I was sent to his grocery store to buy food. He was always very kind when he spoke. Then I saw him once at the Ming Tree restaurant."

That was a curve I hadn't expected. It did, however, resonate with a thought that had been tugging at my mental cuffs on and off. I decided to follow it for the moment.

"When did you see him at the Ming Tree?"

I was hustling through this line because it would be difficult at this point to explain the relevance to Anthony's case. I was not quite fast enough, however. Ms. Lamb was on her feet, drawling, "Objection, Your Honor. What's the relevance?"

The judge relayed the question to me with his quizzically raised eyebrows. I was determined to get it in.

"Your Honor, this could be terribly important. If I don't ultimately show the relevance, you have my offer to resign my bar membership. I'm that certain."

The judge peered at me over his half-glasses.

"I won't be requiring that, Mr. Knight. Nor will I require your suicide on the courthouse steps. I'd merely like a showing of relevance."

"Your Honor, I pray the indulgence of the court for no more than two more minutes. Literally. You'll agree that I haven't burdened the schedule of the court so far."

He nodded. "Two minutes, Mr. Knight."

"Thank you, Your Honor. Mei-Li, when did you see Mr. Chen at the Ming Tree restaurant?"

She seemed composed. She spoke softly, but every word was amplified through the microphone to the back of the courtroom.

"It was after Christmas. I was permitted to visit my friend, Lee Mei-Hua. It was four in the afternoon. There were no customers in the restaurant. I met Mei-Hua in the kitchen. Mr. Chen came in through the back door. I smiled, but he did not speak to me. He went quickly into Mr. Liu's office and closed the door."

"Was Mr. Liu there?"

"Yes."

"And is that Mr. Liu in the back of the courtroom?"

He was glaring terrifying daggers at her, but she never wavered.

"Yes."

"And could you hear what Mr. Chen and Mr. Liu said to each other?"

That brought Ms. Lamb vertical, whining, "Your Honor, relevance and now hearsay."

I preempted his response.

"Just one more question, Your Honor. I won't ask the substance of the conversation."

The judge clearly had me in his sights.

"That's a fine line, Mr. Knight. Be careful."

"Mei-Li, could you hear Mr. Chen and Mr. Liu speaking?"

"I could not hear much of the words."

I thought that particular well had run dry, when Mei-Li looked straight at Kip Liu and spoke directly into the microphone. I think she knew what she was doing.

"Mr. Chen was very angry. He yelled at Mr. Liu. It was about the *low faan*."

Ms. Lamb erupted, sputtering objections and motions to strike. The judge gaveled Mei-Li to silence, but I had the nugget I needed. I filed it away and got back to the business at hand.

"Mei-Li, did you go with me yesterday to the county morgue?"

She looked at me. "Yes."

"Did you see the body of a young girl there?"

"Yes."

"Could you describe her condition?"

She started to speak, but tears simply streamed from both eyes.

"Mei-Li, would it be fair to say that she was brutally beaten? Beaten beyond recognition?"

Angela was on her feet, but I sensed she was forcing herself. "Your Honor, how is this relevant? Objection."

I jumped in quickly to preserve the momentum. "Your Honor, I promise accountability for the relevance."

"Overruled. Please answer the question, miss."

Mei-Li's eyes dropped. "Yes, badly beaten."

I walked back past the defense table to the front row of spectators. I bent down and took Mrs. Lee's hand. I held it when I whispered, "I'm so sorry, Mrs. Lee. This will be a terrible shock. I want you to be ready for it."

I could see in her face that the shock had already set in. She didn't want to know, and I didn't want it said. But it had to be said.

"Who was the young lady, Mei-Li?"

"It was Lee Mei-Hua. Mrs. Lee's daughter."

I could feel Mrs. Lee's body shake as I put my arm around her shoulder. I could feel the sobs, as well as hear them.

I held her for a minute with the court's indulgence. I thought of my little Red Shoes, and the bravery in that little soul the night she gave me the message in the fortune cookie.

I left Mrs. Lee being comforted by Mr. Qian and came back to the bench.

"I have no further questions of this witness, Your Honor."

The judge looked at the prosecutor.

"Nothing just now, Your Honor."

I added, "I'd like permission to have this witness remain in the courtroom, Your Honor."

The judge nodded. Mei-Li left the witness stand. The bailiff brought a chair for her at the end of the spectator section. The judge looked back at me.

"Your Honor, I'd like to recall as a witness, Mrs. Lee."

I took her hand from Mr. Qian and walked with her to the witness stand. The clerk reminded her that she was under oath, but I'm not sure she ever heard his words. I went over to stand beside her.

"Mrs. Lee, I'm so sorry. She was a sweet, brave girl. They had no right to take her life. But they've taken all of your lives. Now they want to take Mr. Bradley's life. And they want you to be their instrument. There's got to be a time when it stops."

She was listening to my words, but her tears were still streaming. I wasn't sure she could speak.

I let go of her hand and stepped back. I asked her to look up at me. I pointed to Kip Liu.

"Look at him, Mrs. Lee. He's in custody. He'll stay there. He'll never force you to do anything again."

She looked, and she seemed to gain strength enough to let out her anger.

"When was the last time you saw your daughter?"

She spoke through sobs.

"A week ago Monday night."

"When she was working as a waitress at your restaurant?"

"Yes."

"And you haven't seen her since then?"

The sobs recurred when she realized she would never see her again. She could only shake her head.

"Before she disappeared, did Mr. Kip Liu, that man over there, make threats in regard to you or your daughter?"

"Yes."

"What threats?"

"He said we would be badly hurt if I did not do what he told me."

"And the night that I came to talk to you, the night after the murder, your daughter was there that night?"

"Yes."

"And did you know that she gave me a message that said that she'd help me if I'd help Mei-Li? Did you know that?"

Her hands ran to her eyes to try to stop the flow of tears.

"I was terrified when she told me. I was afraid Mr. Liu saw."

"I know. And did you daughter disappear that night?"

The "yes" was nearly choked off in the sobs. I stood back so that she could see Kip Liu beyond me.

"What did that man, Kip Liu, tell you about where your daughter was?"

She straightened up as if she wanted the world to hear her.

"He told me she was his prisoner. He said she would be returned unharmed if I continued to do what he told me."

"What did he tell you to do to save your daughter, Mrs. Lee?"

There was fire behind her tears now, and her voice was strong.

"He told me to swear that that boy, Anthony Bradley, killed Mr. Chen."

"And was that the truth?"

"No!" She nearly screamed it. "No! No!" Each word seemed to unburden a soul that was so full of pain it could burst.

For the first moment since that morning in Judge Bradley's chambers, my stomach began to truly unclench.

They say never ask a question when you're not sure of the witness's answer. In this case it was worth the gamble. I could never understand why Mr. Chen had been chosen as the victim. Piecing together what Harry had told me, I was beginning to see light through the clouds.

"And Mrs. Lee, did you see who actually shot Mr. Chen?"

She was standing on her feet and pointing.

"Mr. Kip Liu. I saw him shoot."

"Please tell us what happened."

She was still on her feet. Her voice filled the courtroom without the microphone. Through her tears she was practically shouting the words directly at Kip Liu.

"He was speaking to Mr. Bradley and his friend while they ate. Mr. Bradley and his friend got up to leave. Mr. Liu watched them go down the stairs. He came to the window of the restaurant. Mr. Liu had a gun. First, Mr. Bradley's friend left. Then when Mr. Bradley started walking up the street, Mr. Liu ran down the stairs to the sidewalk. I saw him from the window. He took the gun like this. He shot Mr. Chen. He shot Mr. Chen! Then he made me go down, tell the policemen it was that man, Mr. Bradley. The policemen went after Mr. Bradley. They arrest him. That was what I saw."

She was still standing, unable to stop sobbing, and looking directly into the burning eyes of Kip Liu.

The judge had to pound for silence.

When order was restored, I looked at Angela and said, "Your witness."

She just shook her head. I took Mrs. Lee back to her seat. I called Mr. Qian to the stand. The old man was shaking. I spoke from counsel table.

"Mr. Qian, you gave testimony here yesterday."

I looked back at Mrs. Lee. He looked at her, too. "Was it the truth?"

His eyes filled as he looked at her. It was not easy for this honorable man.

"No."

"When you said you saw Anthony Bradley kill Mr. Chen, was that the truth?"

"No." He shook his head as if to relieve himself of the lie.

"And why did you lie?"

It took him a moment.

"I'm an old man, but that's no excuse for weakness. They said they would kill me by a very painful death. I may still die at their hands. But I'll die after doing an honorable thing."

He looked up at me and pointed to Kip Liu. He spoke without being asked.

"He killed Mr. Chen. Your Mr. Bradley had left before the shot was fired. I heard a loud noise like a gunshot behind me. I looked back on the sidewalk. I saw Mr. Liu holding a gun."

He looked a hundred years old when he looked at me.

"May I go now? I'm very tired, and she needs me."

I looked to Angela Lamb for cross-examination. She just shook her head. The judge excused him. My heart ached for the two of them, Mr. Qian and Mrs. Lee, as he took her on his arm and escorted her through the door back to their world.

I walked to the prosecution table and spoke to Angela.

"Right now Mrs. Lee and Mr. Qian need protection more than anyone in this city. Those two could be the key to the biggest prosecution of organized crime your office ever saw. The man you have in custody over there, Kip Liu, is the head of Chinese organized crime in this city. You may have a couple of willing witnesses."

She whispered something to her assistant, who went running out after them.

I turned back to the judge. He was trying to pound away the roar that had set into the courtroom since Mr. Qian left the stand. When order was restored, he looked at me.

"Do you have a motion to make, Mr. Knight?"

"I do, Your Honor. Since the only two prosecution witnesses have recanted their testimony, I'm hoping that the district attorney will join me in a motion to dismiss this indictment."

He looked at her. She had little choice.

"The people assent to the motion, Your Honor."

"The indictment is dismissed. The jury is excused with the thanks of the court. The defendant is released from custody."

The gavel came down. The bailiff's "All rise" triggered a passage of the newsies through the narrow door that I hadn't experienced since my last trip to Filene's basement at the opening bell.

I turned around to find Anthony in the arms of his father. Mei-Li was standing beside him. I saw him take one arm and sweep her into the hug.

I walked over, and they included me in the hug. Handshakes are never enough at a time like that.

When the thanks and the congratulations subsided, I held father and son and said to Anthony, "You've got a lot to tell your father. Tell him everything. It's all going to break soon."

He was nodding a very sincere "yes."

"You were getting out of that business on your own anyway, Anthony. That'll count. You can also pay back a lot with your testimony, both about Chinatown and Harvard. It'll go a long way with the prosecution. Do you understand what I'm saying?"

"Yes, sir."

"Good."

I started to leave, but Anthony held me.

"When it comes to that, Mr. Knight, I'd like you to represent me, if you would."

I smiled.

"My future's a little uncertain. But we'll see."

34

THE CELEBRATION FELT GOOD, but I knew in my heart there was one raging loose end. If I left it untied, it could wipe out all of the good that had come out of a good morning.

I found Angela Lamb working her way through a cluster of reporters. I think she was relieved to be taken away, even by me.

"Angela, where have they got Kip Liu? Is he still in the building?"

"They have him in the interviewing room. They're waiting for transportation to take him to the lockup. Why?"

"I need five minutes alone with him."

She gave me one of her many looks. "Not a chance."

I took her off to the side of the room.

"Let's cut through the politically correct crap here, Angela. We haven't much time. You're looking for a one-way ticket to the state house."

"Listen, sonny boy. Just because you got lucky in there . . ."

"I can give it to you."

That cut off the flow and gave me an opening.

"I can give it to you. Are you listening?"

"What?"

"I can hand you the key witness to prosecute the most effective criminal organization in this state. You can get daily headlines from the *Globe* in the morning and the *Herald* in the evening. Maybe even the *New York Times*. It depends on how you play it."

"What are you talking about?"

"We're losing time. I need five minutes with Liu. Alone. You should know by now I deliver on my promises."

She was still leery—probably more leery of treating me like an equal than of believing what I promised. Still, the carrot on this particular stick was the stuff of which egos are made—particularly hers.

"All right. You have five minutes. There'll be officers just outside the door."

MR. KIP LIU LOOKED considerably less self-possessed in handcuffs seated in a metal straight-back chair.

"I'm going to make you an offer, Mr. Liu. It has a shelf life of five minutes."

He still had enough "face" to look at me with disgust.

"You can't threaten me. You have no proof of anything. I have witnesses who'll contradict everything those two say."

"Oh, I bet you do. I bet you could march half of Chinatown through here petrified enough to swear you're the Wizard of Oz. It doesn't matter. Whatever the DA does is up to her. You and I have unfinished business. You know what "business" is: I give you. You give me."

"One problem, Knight. You have nothing I want."

"How about that precious life of yours?"

He grinned. Still the upper dog.

"Are you threatening to kill me?"

"No. That's your line. I can just let it happen."

The grin was still there. He just shook his head in disgust.

"You still don't get it, do you, Liu? I'll lay it out for you. The way I see it, you met with old Mr. Chen in the back room of the Ming Tree.

He was yelling at you about the *low faan*. That would probably be Anthony and his non-Chinese drug operators. Breaks the old rule, doesn't it, about not dealing with people outside of the Chinese community? Sounds like Mr. Chen didn't like it. But the real question is how did Mr. Chen get the nerve to come down on you? That's the question that started the tumblers falling into place."

The smile was gone. If his eyes were hatchets, I'd have been in forty-two pieces. There was no sound. I came in close.

"I had it figured a long time ago that you're the tong's *fu shan chu*. The number two man. It always puzzled me that Mr. Chen was picked as the victim of the shooting. Could it be, Mr. Liu, that sweet old Mr. Chen was the *shan chu*, the number one? The Dragon Head? The one only you knew about? I think so. I think he was stepping on your operation with Anthony and the non-Chinese at Harvard. You were thinking maybe if he dies, you become the *shan chu*. You could operate to suit yourself."

He was frozen stiff. I think he saw where I was going.

"That means you committed the unforgivable. You actually killed the Dragon Head without the permission of the tong. You tried to lay it off on Anthony so nobody in the tong would know. It didn't work, did it? I saw at least fifteen Chinese in that courtroom. They heard what Mrs. Lee said. How long do you figure it will take for word to get to the top of the tong?"

I was next to his ear and whispering.

"Can you even imagine the death they'll dream up for you when the word gets back to Hong Kong? You could set new records for pain."

Not a muscle was moving.

"Where can you go to hide, Mr. Liu? Is there a hole on this earth where they won't find you? Actually, you'll be in prison for the foreseeable future. At least long enough to come to trial for the murder of Mr. Chen. You'll be waiting for them like a staked goat."

I moved back and sat against the table. I checked my watch in front of him.

"Well, that's five minutes. Nice chat, Mr. Liu."

I was moving toward the door, when I heard the words.

"What's the offer?"

I turned around and just looked at him for ten seconds. I don't know why. It just seemed to raise the tension.

"Witness protection program. The U.S. Attorney is ready to deal. You'll keep that expensive skin on those bones."

"In exchange for what?"

"Two things. The U.S. Attorney will want names, facts, and testimony about the tong. You'll be the star of the show."

He thought for a minute without saying a word. What I suggested ran counter to his thirty-six oaths and the whole code of tong existence. On the other hand, it was the tong that would be inflicting pain that even he couldn't imagine for committing the unpardonable.

When he spoke, the superior tone had lost its edge.

"And what is the second thing?"

I was directly in his face.

"This is the important part. If you go back on this, I'll personally find you and feed you to the tong. From this moment on, Anthony and Mei-Li are completely free of you and that gang of thugs you give orders to. No strings. Nothing. The same goes for Mrs. Lee and Mr. Qian. That's 100 percent nonnegotiable. It also includes me and anyone close to or connected with me. "

He was looking directly into my face, but he was saying nothing. I could read the struggle in his eyes. I gave it ten seconds. I shrugged and said, "Good luck with your playmates."

I was at the door when I heard a quiet, "All right."

From the door I said, "What?"

"All right."

I came back to stand in front of him.

"Not good enough."

He looked up at me.

"Swear it."

He did. I demanded it again. He did, and I demanded it a third time.

I figured a repetition of three would somehow resonate with the ritual code he lived by.

35

IT WAS WELL PAST NOON when I picked up a copy of the *Globe* at the newsstand in the lobby of the courthouse. I caught a cab on Tremont Street for the short hop to the Mass General Hospital.

The cab was moving before I had a chance to flip open the paper. There it was. Good old Mike Loftus. His column made the front page. I needed the old reading specs for this one. I didn't want to miss a word. It read like this:

> To Lex Devlin
>
> I. O. U.
>
> One name—untarnished
> (Signed)
> The City of Boston

Ten years ago, Lex Devlin was the brightest light that shone in the criminal trial bar. He had skill, wit, integrity—and he had a name. He had a name that brought hope to the prosecuted, pride to the trial bar, and a warning to prosecutors that they would pay dearly for the slightest lapse in ethics or preparation.

That name was his life, because it summed up what Lex Devlin stood for, and what he would not stand for.

He stood for the principles that drive young people with ideals into the law. He wouldn't stand for the kind of compromised ethics that drive disillusioned lawyers out of the law.

He had grit, and he had style—the kind of style that made people say regretfully, "There'll never be another Lex Devlin."

And he had that name that became shorthand at the bar for the best there is.

He had it until he stood in the way of a human machine so corrupt that it played without any rule but greed, so camouflaged by its outward face of public service that Lex Devlin never saw it coming or going.

When it was through with him, it had stripped Lex Devlin of the name that was the work of his lifetime. It left it tarnished with unfounded rumors of the cardinal sin against the law that he served flawlessly—the sin of jury fixing.

Lex Devlin has, for ten years, held a valid I.O.U. from this city for the redemption of that name.

So here's the payoff, Lex. Here's the best I can do for a start.

Thanks to the efforts of Lex's associate, Michael Knight, the District Attorney and the United States Attorney have received incontrovertible evidence that Lex Devlin was totally innocent of any complicity in the incident of jury fixing that occurred in the case of Commonwealth v. Dolson.

The tarring of those who were responsible will fill the pages of this newspaper in the weeks to come, as the greatest scandal in this Commonwealth's history unfolds.

But that's for another edition. The business of this day is belated justice. This column is the first brick in the pedestal that the City of Boston should build for a son who always did it proud.

This city has its heroes, and it has its villains. Sometimes, being human, we confuse the two.

This time we got it right.

God Speed, Lex.

I let the paper sit on my lap and just soaked up the truth Mike Loftus made public. I could visualize lawyers and judges all over the city, who had innocently fallen for the lie and perhaps even spread it, wondering what they could do to make up for ten years' shunning of one of their finest.

That thought carried me down Cambridge Street and up the elevator to the sixth floor of the cardiac unit of the Mass General Hospital.

The nurse pointed out his room. I asked how he was doing. She said, "He went to sleep last night like a hundred-year-old man. This morning, he was in his early thirties."

I walked into the room, and the first thought that hit me was that I was at his wake. There were enough flowers in that room to bury the president. In a quick check of the attached cards, I caught sight of names like the Boston Bar Association, the Mass. Trial Lawyers' Association, the mayor's office, and a who's who of the trial firms of the city.

He had a private room. He was in the bed, sleeping, with wires running to an assortment of machines.

Spread across his lap was the *Globe,* opened to the inside continuation of Mike Loftus's column.

I sat down in the chair to be there when he woke. The squeak of the chair made him look over. He seemed alert when he spoke. His voice had the old sand and gravel.

"Tell me about it. Tell me about all of it. Don't leave out one detail."

I talked for a long time. I told him about the business with Abdul and the drug ring at Harvard. I told him about my meeting with Loring and everything that went into his signed statement about the "association" and the jury fix in the Dolson case that was now in the hands of both the federal and state prosecutors.

Then I told him every detail that led up to the dismissal of the indictment against Anthony Bradley. The punch line was that his tactic had worked.

He had his head back on the pillow. He was Mount Rushmore with his eyes focused on something on the ceiling, but I could tell from the silence that he was drinking in every word. When I finished, there was more silence.

I let it lie for a minute, until it became awkward.

"That was one serious gamble, Mr. Devlin. That early trial date nearly blew me away."

"It was the only way. If we let them have time to pass around the word about that surprise witness, the boys in Chinatown could have come up with a dozen other trumped-up witnesses. If there was a chance Bradley was innocent, we had to ambush them."

"Did you believe Bradley was innocent?"

He shook his head. "I didn't care. If he was innocent, our best shot at getting Mrs. Lee to tell the truth was that young lady. If he was guilty, Mrs. Lee would have held up as a witness against him. Either way, justice would have been done."

I smiled. I was still on the side of playing hunches about the client's innocence. And he knew it. That's what makes horse racing.

"I'll give you this, Mr. Devlin. Your instincts about tactics were everything I've heard about."

There was no answer. I didn't understand why at the time. He took the free hand, the right one, the one with no tubes running into it, and he moved it slowly across his eyes. I could have sworn I heard the sound of an almost impenetrable wall crumbling. When he spoke, it was with a voice I had never heard before.

"Tactics are one thing. The talent to bring it off is what makes a lawyer."

He held out his hand, and I took it. I held it until I needed it back to get something wet out of my own eye.

He lifted up the paper open to Mike Loftus's column.

"Have you read it?"

I nodded. "Mike writes a good column. He had good material."

He laughed, and the paper rested on his chest. Then he stopped smiling.

"I don't think . . . I could ever put into words . . ."

"No need. I know."

He shook his head. "No, you don't. No one'll ever know what you did for this old man."

I looked up. "What old man? Who's the old man?"

His head came off the pillow.

"Damn! You're right. There's no old man around here. I've got to get out of here. I've got things to do."

"Whoa." I settled him back. "Soon enough. You'll be back soon enough terrorizing prosecutors and scaring the pants off the associates at Bilson, Dawes."

He rested back against the pillow.

"You're half-right. I'll be back. I can feel the years coming back to me. But not at Bilson, Dawes. I'm going to go back to doing what I should have been doing for the last ten years."

"Bravo! You're going to go it on your own?"

"Well, I suppose. Unless I can find some punk of a young attorney with enough salt and starch to run with me."

I caught his drift, and it sent my cranial cells racing. One on one for the rest of my foreseeable days with the crustiest, most cantankerous old battle-horse in any trial bar. If the Bradley case was any test, I'd probably never again have a pulse below a hundred or a stomach that didn't generate enough acid to melt diamonds. Was this what any sane human would want for a life? The answer was easy. Yes, more than any life I could imagine. Who ever said I was sane?

He looked over.

"What about you? What are you going to do? Are you back at the Bilson shop tomorrow morning?"

I shook my head. "No. After this I can't go back to running errands for Whitney Caster."

"What do you have in mind?"

"There's a tough old lion I hear is going to go into business stirring up trouble for prosecutors. I think he may be looking for an associate."

"Not me, sonny. No, I don't like associates. They're too damned in-

dependent. I have to nurse them along, and then they do what they damn well please anyway."

He looked over for a shocked reaction—which he didn't get. I was getting to know him; at least I thought I was.

"No, sonny, I'm thinking more along the lines of a junior partner."

This time he got the shocked reaction. I couldn't hold it in.

"I think you and I could make some trouble out there, son. What do you think?"

The grin on my face said it all.

"You know how partnerships are made, don't you, son?"

He held out his hand. I took it, and the firm of Devlin & Knight drew its first breath.

"You might be interested to know, Mr. Devlin, we have a client at the door before we have a door."

"Oh?"

"Anthony Bradley wants us to handle his case when they charge him with the drug dealing at Harvard. I think we've got a shot at a good plea bargain. He was getting out of that business on his own. As a matter of fact, Kip Liu called him in for a last meeting at the restaurant on Chinese New Year's. He told Anthony he was letting him out. It turned out he just wanted him in Chinatown to frame him for the murder. I talked to Anthony. He'll help the DA prosecute the heart out of the tong."

"Not a bad case for an opener."

I got up to go.

"Well, Mr. Devlin, the day's running out, and I've got three things to do."

"Such as?"

"The first thing I'm going to do is call a friend of mine in immigration. I'm going to start the process to get Mei-Li citizenship. Then I'm going to hand in my resignation at Bilson, Dawes."

"Sounds like a good start. What's three?"

"That's the best part. I'm going to pick up a certain gal who's been in this hospital for the last few days because she was crazy enough to go on a date with me. She's ready to go home. I'm going to see if I can make it up to her. Maybe for the rest of our lives. Who knows?"

His head was back on the pillow and he nodded. He had a sort of a smile that I don't think was for me. I think it was for someone who had filled his life and then left it ten years earlier.

I started to leave, and then turned around.

"Could I ask my new senior partner a favor?"

"Ask."

"Do you suppose you could call me 'Michael,' or maybe 'Mike'?"

He hunched up on his elbows.

"I'll never call you 'Mike.' It's too small. A name is something you earn. Nobody gives it to you. You've earned a proud name. You'll be 'Michael' to me from now on."

I started to say, "Thank you, Mr. Devlin," but something crawled up in my throat. I just held up a hand to him on the way out the door.

When I got to the corridor, I looked back. Some things you get to keep forever. I'll take to my grave the look on his face. He was rereading Mike Loftus's column.